Faron Goss

Faron Goss

A NOVEL

Diane Lechleitner

GREEN PLACE BOOKS *Brattleboro, Vermont*

Printed in the United States

10 9 8 7 6 5 4 3 2 1

Green Writers Press is a Vermont-based publisher whose mission is to spread a message of hope and renewal through the words and images we publish. Throughout we will adhere to our commitment to preserving and protecting the natural resources of the earth. To that end, a percentage of our proceeds will be donated to environmental activist groups and The Southern Poverty Law Foundation. Green Writers Press gratefully acknowledges support from individual donors, friends, and readers to help support the environment and our publishing initiative. Green Place Books curates books that tell literary and compelling stories with a focus on writing about place—these books are more personal stories, memoir, and biographies.

Giving Voice to Writers & Artists Who Will Make the World a Better Place
Green Writers Press | Brattleboro, Vermont
www.greenwriterspress.com

ISBN: 978-1-9505845-1-2
COVER PHOTO BY TIM FOSTER ON UNSPLASH

In loving memory of my father and mother,
George John Lechleitner and Dolores Edith Flood Lechleitner,
who gave so much and asked for nothing.

The desire of the moth for the star, of the night for the morrow, the devotion of something afar from the sphere of our sorrow.

—Percy Bysshe Shelley

Faron Goss

CHAPTER 1

TO THE MEN on the island Alison Goss was an intriguing, rawboned beauty. To the women she was a dark, willowy threat. So when she fell overboard and drowned on a calm, sunny afternoon in July, only some of the islanders cared. No one even knew she was missing until the next morning when Myron Sprague checked his lobster traps and found her dinghy tangled in one of his sets, held fast by an oar that was still mounted in its brass lock. Not long after, Alison herself drifted into Gallager's Boatyard and got wedged between the pilings at low tide.

Hodie Ebel, the harbormaster, found the body. It was all fouled in seaweed. Crabs and gulls had pulled and pecked at the bloated corpse—the eyes were gone—sockets cleaner than crow-picked roadkill. Hodie tugged at his scraggly beard—a nervous habit—and went inside the chandlery to find Jarry Gallager.

Jarry was bent over a case of snaps and shackles, cursing.

"What's wrong?" asked Hodie.

"Sent the wrong stuff. Again." Jarry's stringy blond hair always looked like it needed washing. He pushed it out of his face and glared at Hodie. "Need something?"

"Have to use your phone."

Jarry listened as Hodie called the sheriff to report the gruesome discovery.

"Come on," Hodie said when he hung up the phone. "It's a two-man job."

They went outside and snagged Alison with boat hooks, dragged her up the ramp into the parking lot, covered her with a blue vinyl tarp, and went for an early lunch at Scuppers.

Scuppers is one of two restaurants on the island. It's the first wind-blown building you come to when you get off the ferry on Sheepscot Road and turn left onto Harbor Street. Sixty-one-year-old Red Sedgewick bought the place when he gave up cod fishing twenty-three years ago—then a young man and already disgusted with fish politics.

An antique duckpin alley remains intact, along with the original lunch counter, which now doubles as a bar. Red's secret family recipe for hasty pudding, dating back to the 1800s, is still secret. His most recent concession to modern times was to make the restaurant one of the few nonsmoking areas on the island. After years of breathing cigarette smoke and grease fumes, something had to go, so it was the cigarettes. Red's no-smoking rule got people all riled up and caused an indignation meeting over at the school one evening, but he stuck to his guns—if you want to eat at Scuppers, you can't light up. In addition to the fourteen stools at the bar there are sixteen tables—seventeen if you count the small one under the dartboard. The place is always packed to the gills, and today was no different.

Jarry got the last stool at the bar and Hodie squeezed in next to him, standing sideways with his right elbow on the dark mahogany. After he ordered a beer and swallowed the first bite of a double cheeseburger, Hodie told everyone that Alison Goss floated into Gallager's yard and he and Jarry pulled her out of the water and left her lying on the gravel lot.

The lunch crowd looked at Hodie. Their mouths were open, but no words came out.

"What?" someone finally asked. Everyone had heard about Myron finding Alison's empty boat earlier that morning, but this latest news came as a shock.

Red Sedgewick poured both men another beer. "You sure it's her?" Red wiped his hands on his apron and leaned on the bar.

"Of course we're sure," Hodie said, between greasy bites. "I figure that rattletrap of hers must have broke down again so she was rowing across the cove, maybe for her weekly shopping, and stood up, for God knows what reason, and fell over the side. She couldn't swim a stroke and, like I've always said, she had no business being out alone in a boat in the first place—but try and tell her that. Hell, try and tell her anything."

Jarry and the other men at the bar agreed with Hodie's version of the gruesome event, but a brash bunch of fishermen's wives, sitting together in their usual lunchtime spot, assumed Alison had been going across the cove to meet Kate Sawyer's husband, Brad.

"She probably didn't want anyone to see her jalopy sitting out front, so she went by boat. The sneak," one of the green-eyed wives sneered.

"That whore was always fooling around with someone else's man. Whatever happened, it served her right," another woman concluded.

None of the men said too much more about it after that, certainly not that deep down they wished it had been them, not Brad Sawyer, that Alison had drowned over. More than a few of them would secretly miss the possibilities that only existed when Alison was around.

CHAPTER 2

MENHADEN ISLAND is named after a fish—a twelve-inch-long, algae-eating, shiny-blue baitfish, also known as a pogy. They aren't as plentiful as they used to be, but the old-timers remember when the Gulf of Maine teemed with them. On sunny, flat-water days, the shimmering fish could be seen rippling the surface of the ocean as they rose from the depths in huge dark-blue schools.

Menhaden's a tight-knit community of think-alikes—lobstermen, mostly, and the peevish women who marry them. There are barely enough children on the island to fill up the schoolhouse. Once they're grown, many of them leave for the mainland to work at desk jobs in the shadows of the now-defunct fish canneries where their grandmothers used to punch a clock and pack herring. Most who stay make their living from the sea.

At last count there were five hundred and ten individuals living on Menhaden Island, including the occasional transplant, but not counting tourists and summer residents. All told, the native islanders are a small bunch whose number keeps dwindling, just like the fish their island was named for. Heavy weather and an eight-mile stretch of water sets them apart from the rest and that suits everyone just fine.

Like generations before her, Alison Goss was born and raised on the island. Her mother hoped to marry the sweet-talking man who got her pregnant when she was still a teenager, but he was only passing through. The day he found out about the pregnancy, he took the next ferry to the mainland, and that was that.

The deserted mother-to-be lived with her father, Zediah F. Goss, in a small, brown-shingled house on Puddle Cove, facing the sea with nothing between it and the open water.

Zed was a tall, handsome ladies' man who drank too much, but after Alison was born, he looked after her as best he could whenever his own daughter was on a bender, which was more often than not. When he tumbled down a gangplank at low tide and broke his neck, everyone who was there swore he was stone-cold sober.

His daughter inherited the wind-battered house on Puddle Cove and scratched out a living housekeeping for well-off summer people and the few wealthy retirees who'd decided to spend their golden years in the middle of nowhere. Time passed bleakly for the unlucky young mother until she drank herself senseless one night and choked on her own vomit the day before Alison's eighteenth birthday.

After that, according to the local women, Alison got to know the island man by man, trying the only way she knew to fill the void where love should have been. Worn-out wives and husband-hunting single women all despised her, but the female contempt and long Maine winters only toughened her up.

Regardless of what people thought of Alison, they did pull together to give her a proper church burial after she drowned. She was, they reckoned, an islander, and deserved a decent funeral.

The service was brief and half the congregation came late—just in time for coffee and cake afterwards. As they milled around speaking in hushed voices, they did their best to keep ungracious words at bay. In the spirit of burying the bad with the bones, they tried to find something good to say about Alison Goss because, after all, she never had a chance, and somewhere in their weathered hearts her fellow islanders knew that. And, of course, there was the boy.

CHAPTER 3

FARON GOSS was a dark wisp of a boy, born in a winter storm when Alison was almost thirty-one and still unmarried. She went into labor on a bitterly cold night, but as she drove herself to the hospital her lightweight car spun out of control on the frozen road and lodged in a snowdrift.

After spinning the worn tires deeper into the snow, the car conked out and Alison climbed into the back seat, shivering in the ice-cold air. Her heavy breathing fogged up the windshield as she gasped for breath between contractions. A few hours later, numbed by pain and the below-freezing temperatures, she gave birth to Faron.

Exhausted and scared, Alison cut the umbilical cord with a chipped pocketknife that a one-night stand had dropped between the seats in his haste to get out of his pants. She tossed the knife aside and shook the tiny infant until he cried, wrapped him in her sweater and some old newspapers, and waited for help. Drops of milk oozed from her nipples, and the newborn wailed.

Around three o'clock in the morning, a road crew grazed Alison's snow-covered car with the edge of their plow and woke her from an uneasy sleep. She tried rolling down the windows, but ice sealed them shut. When she banged the glass with her fists and hollered for help, the two-man crew didn't hear and she slumped in the cold to wait for the next pass of the plow.

It was getting light when the truck finally came around again. This time the men saw the roof of Alison's car sticking out of a mound of frozen snow. They jumped down from the hulking steel truck into the flashing glow of its yellow emergency lights and chopped through the iced-over drift with axes and shovels, then smashed the car window and pulled Alison and the baby out.

Inside the cab of the truck, the men stripped down to their shirts and bundled the trembling mother and son in a thick assortment of their sweaters and jackets, then cranked up the dashboard heater and headed to town as fast as they could on the slippery road.

When Sheriff Alden Paisley got the call, he was over at Eileen's, a small café on the lower island near the public beach, where you can count on pie that's made fresh daily and a cup of coffee that's out of this world.

It used to be that Eileen's was only open from May through October, but after her husband ran off with a summer visitor, Eileen decided to stay open straight through winter. "Don't need the money. It's just less lonely," is what she told everyone.

Alden was happy about that, since he was a regular and couldn't get enough of Eileen's homemade pies. Overall, her food was better than Red's, and she let you smoke inside, although seating wise it's a tight squeeze—at least for Alden, who's a portly fellow. Being chief of public works, as well as sheriff—and a bachelor on top of that—he eats most of his meals out. Between Eileen's homemade desserts and Red's fried fish platters, Alden packs on the pounds.

This morning he was halfway through a bacon and scrambled egg sandwich when his handheld radio squawked the information about Alison and he had to leave. "Wrap this up for me, would you, Eileen?" He held out his plate. "Can't let something this good go to waste."

Eileen covered the sandwich in waxed paper and put it in a brown bag, with a complimentary slice of pumpkin pie—her winter specialty. "Here you go, and be careful out there—those lobstermen are a cranky bunch."

"Don't I know—I'm related to one." Alden took the bag and blew her a kiss. "So long, Eileen. With any luck I'll be back for dinner."

When Alison and the baby were wheeled into the emergency room on a gurney, Dr. Owen Batch was already at the hospital, tending to a man who had slipped on the ice and broken his wrist. He put the finishing touches on the man's plaster cast and turned his attention to Alison.

"You'll be fine," he reassured her, after giving her and the infant a thorough exam. "The baby, too." He ran a hand through his mop of graying hair and gazed at Faron. "He's a good-looking boy."

Alison gave Owen a slight smile, then fell asleep.

Owen was born on the island, one floor above the home office of his father, Dr. Harland Batch. The elder Batch was pleased that his son followed in his footsteps, hoping he would leave Menhaden for a more prestigious and lucrative career on the mainland, but in that sense, he was disappointed. Owen stayed on the island.

He was a humble man who everyone called Doc. He ran his practice from his father's old office and the modest twenty-bed Menhaden Hospital, which had been built through the generosity of a wealthy family on the Point.

He was married once, to a nurse he met in medical school, but it didn't last. After less than two years on Menhaden, she decided it didn't measure up to her dreams of being a doctor's wife. He's lived alone ever since, devoted to his patients and adored by all of them, including Alison.

Now, he patted her hand and sighed, watching her sleep.

"Everything all right, Doc?" Alden poked his head in the room.

"Couldn't be better. Alison's got herself a healthy baby boy."

Alden spoke in a whisper when he realized Alison was sleeping. "Got to fill out an accident report . . . but it can wait."

When the sun came out later in the day Alden instructed his deputy, Keith Cyr, to find some men to dig Alison's car out of the snowbank and see if they could start it up. "Might have to tow it," Alden guessed. "See what you can do."

Deputy Keith Cyr was a mechanic's son and, after fiddling with the engine a while, the old heap turned over. He rummaged through Alison's car for something to wipe the grease off his hands. "Tape some plastic over the broken window and drive it back to her place," he instructed his helpers. "Order new glass. Maybe the town will pay, since their guys broke it."

Two days later, Alison was ready for discharge. Deputy Cyr took her and the baby home to Puddle Cove and Doc Batch saw to it that the hospital didn't send her a bill because, despite the disdain of other women, there were those who felt sympathetic towards Alison Goss, and he was one of them.

CHAPTER 4

THE AFTERNOON coffee klatches were abuzz after Faron was born. Someone on Menhaden was his father, and if that someone was a married man, it meant his wife was cooking dinner every night for a cheating husband. But the wives knew better than to point fingers, since it might well be any one of them doing the cooking.

They had it all figured out mathematically. Faron was born at the end of January. That meant he was conceived in April or May, and there weren't any summer people on the island yet. There were a few strangers coming and going on the ferry that spring, sizing up Menhaden as a possible vacation spot, but none of them stayed long enough to get to know Alison.

Whoever fathered the child had to be a local, no doubt about it, and as Faron grew from an infant to a boy, the island wives kept him at a distance, worried that if they looked too closely they might see their husband's grin flash across his face.

Alison resented being a single mother and Faron learned early not to ask about his father.

"Who knows?" she snarled the few times he asked where his father was.

During winter she commuted by ferry to the mainland and waited on tables in a popular, gritty waterfront restaurant where the tips were good and after-work drinks were on the house.

Often, Faron returned home from school in the afternoons and Alison was nowhere to be found—still on the mainland sitting in a bar with a prowling man who smelled an evening's worth of opportunity.

Sometimes, women from church offered to stay with Faron, but Alison usually turned them down. "He knows what to do," she told them.

She raised him like he was another chore that needed doing. The sooner it was finished, the sooner she could go off and do what she wanted. She managed to keep him clothed, fed, and on time for school, but by his sixth birthday he'd learned to take care of himself and had more responsibility than any young child should.

On days he came home to an empty house, Faron sat quietly at the kitchen table doing his homework until suppertime, when he fixed himself a sandwich or can of soup.

In the summer the island population swelled to twice its size, and Alison didn't ride the ferry to her waitressing job. There was plenty of housekeeping work locally, in the refined enclave of summer people whose expensive homes overlooked the glittering sand beach on Preble Point.

Alison's own dreary house showed increased signs of wear each year. Paint cracked and peeled. Roof shingles blew off when fierce ocean storms thrashed the shore.

In fact, some folks thought it was the constant wind that caused generations of the Gosses to drink. "It's enough to drive anyone crazy," people said. "What, with that little house facing the ocean and not so much as a pine tree in front of it to block the wind."

But the cramped, dilapidated house stood its ground. Barely big enough for two people and cluttered with things that never seemed to get put away.

Alison had a good reputation with the families who owned the sprawling homes on Preble Point, many of them the same ones her mother had cleaned for. Word of mouth kept her busy, and she made good summer money every year.

Her generous employers were not only kind to her, they were curious about Faron as well.

"Where's your little boy?" they'd ask.

One in particular, a gracious silver-haired woman who caught glimpses of Faron in town, wondered where he was on fragrant summer days while Alison scrubbed other people's floors and squeezed fresh lemonade for their children. "Why not bring him along next time? I bet he'd like wandering around this big house. There are boxes of my children's old toys upstairs. Or he could play on the beach—right out the front door."

But Alison often refused their invitations and left Faron alone at Puddle Cove.

"Can't figure her out, depriving him of fun that way," the locals said, ignoring their own reluctance to have Faron play with their children. "The boy could be having a grand time out there on the Point, instead of sitting alone in that dump on Puddle Cove."

"I've got my reasons," Alison grumbled if she overheard the busybodies talking.

When she did occasionally let Faron tag along to swim and sail with the summer people, he charmed them all with his gentle, quiet demeanor, and got along well with their children.

"Bring him back anytime," their mothers told her. "He's no trouble at all." Although they couldn't help notice that he was a careful boy—too careful for a child so young—always fearful if he spilled something and made a mess, or if he dared to ask some boyish question about the distance of the stars or the shape of the moon.

Summer evenings after tidying up someone else's kitchen, Alison went straight home, although not always alone. Sometimes she was with a loud, drunken stranger, usually a summer visitor, but sometimes it was a man that Faron recognized as the father of a girl or boy he knew from school.

"Run off to bed," the liquored-up men said when they saw him. And if he didn't do as he was told, his mother smacked him solidly across the face with the back of her hand, cursing the frigid day he was born.

On those hot, sticky summer nights when his mother gave herself away in the next room and Faron couldn't sleep, he'd lie awake counting the insects that flew inside through the torn screens. He stretched out on his narrow bed waiting for the nighttime assortment of bugs, keeping the lights on to attract them.

The hum of mosquitos and the steady rhythm of moths and beetles banging against the windows distracted him from the grunts and groans coming from the other side of the wall that separated his mother and him, but he sensed that the odd noises coming from her room meant she was in a better mood.

Sometimes, after it all went quiet, he tiptoed through the dark into the kitchen, knowing she might be there, sitting on the man's lap, wearing his shirt, or maybe nothing at all. He pretended to want a drink of water, but really, all he wanted was to see his mother's face. It was the only time she had a smile for him—he wasn't sure why. Her eyes sparkled and she looked beautiful—pink cheeked and radiant. In those brief moments when she gazed at him, Faron felt the warmth of her afterglow. He lingered in the doorway sipping water, barefoot on the cool linoleum, basking in the presence of the closest thing he ever felt to maternal love, wishing for it to last. But even as he stood there, the good feeling faded quickly.

By morning, his mother's glow was gone.

"Where's the man?" Faron asked her, hoping her eyes would shine again.

"How the hell would I know? Shut up and leave me alone."

CHAPTER 5

SHEEPSCOT ROAD, East and West, makes a loop around the island from the ferry landing to the Preble Head Light and back again. The heart of the village is on the upper shore overlooking the harbor and facing the mainland. Brady's General Store, *The Island News* newspaper office, Scuppers, the church, a library, the hospital, Beaudry's Wharf, and the boatyard is all there is to it, except for a tiny U.S. Post Office tucked in the back of the store, and a small building behind that, which serves as the police station and Department of Public Works. Eileen's café is on the other side of the Puddle Cove Bridge on the lower island, next to the school, which doubles as the town hall.

Accommodations for tourists are scant—a rambling inn and a few rentals—although, to the disgruntlement of the locals, that's changing. Day visitors are on the increase and new rental cottages have sprung up.

The mailboat comes out several times a week and the ferry makes four round trips a day, fewer on Sundays and holidays and during winter. Even without ferry service, people get where they need to. Most have a skiff with an outboard, or they hitch a ride with one of the fishermen.

Father Quinn Gage is the island minister—Episcopalian, but since Good Shepherd by the Sea is the only church on the island, it's evolved into something more nondenominational. Father Gage's muscular arms and broad shoulders belie his occupation, although his eyes show the strain of managing other people's worries.

Everyone calls Quinn Gage by his first name, except on Sundays, or when things get serious—then he's Father Gage to all. Quinn likes to think the church is the center of the community, but deep down he knows it can't compete with Scuppers, and Red Sedgewick enjoys teasing him about it.

"Why don't you hold services over at my place? You'd get more of a crowd and half the congregation would still be there from the night before." Red said the same thing nearly every Sunday and always laughed at his own joke. So did Quinn, just to be polite.

Quinn's wife, Mary, lives with him in the drafty old rectory, made homey with Mary's quilts and embroideries. A childless marriage, they fill the empty time with church suppers, holiday parties, and Christian concern for other people's problems. They're often the first to be called during a crisis—like the day Myron Sprague found Alison's empty boat.

Faron was eight years old when his mother fell into Puddle Cove. Myron spotted her empty dinghy and untangled the painter and tied it to his stern. On his way back to shore he got on the radio and called Sheriff Alden Paisley.

Alden's first thought was Faron. He phoned Good Shepherd and asked Quinn to meet him over at the Goss house. "Maybe you could take the kid for a while," Alden suggested, "until we figure out something else."

Quinn drove his flashy, metallic-blue car too fast across the Puddle Cove Bridge.

His wife had been in the rectory when the sheriff's call came through and was in the car with him now. "Slow down!" she complained sharply. But he ignored her.

When they got to the Goss place, Sheriff Paisley was already there, giving Alison's rust-pocked car the once over. "Faron's inside," he motioned towards the house with his thumb. "Be right with you."

Quinn and Mary found the tousled boy sitting at the rickety kitchen table, spreading jam on a stale piece of bread with his fingers. There were dark circles under his eyes and his clothes looked as if he had slept in them.

"My mom's not home," he said.

"We know," Quinn assured the boy. "We've come to take you into town. You don't have to stay here alone today. Is there anything you'd like to bring?"

Faron bit his lower lip and twisted the lid back onto the jar of jam, licking his sticky fingers as he left the kitchen and walked towards his room.

Alden came inside and stood near the screen door, trying to take advantage of the slight breeze blowing off the cove. He watched Faron walk away and exchanged a puzzled look with Quinn. "Don't ask me," he said. "The kid hasn't uttered a word since I got here." He motioned for Quinn to step closer. "Just got a call on the radio," he whispered. "They found her under Gallager's dock."

Faron returned moments later, carrying a cigar box with air holes punched in the top. It was filled with moths. "I want this," he said, clutching the box.

Alden recognized the cigar box. He'd been in Alison's house before and he knew there was a colorful jumble of those old boxes scattered about. The boy's great-grandfather, Zed, had been a heavy smoker, expensive cigars being his favorite. Even now, a faint scent of Zed Goss's Cubans hung in the air. He used to order them from a fancy shop down in Portland and have them delivered.

"That's money that'd be better spent on his family," some folks grumbled whenever those fancy cigar boxes arrived on the mailboat.

Quinn knelt in front of Faron. "What's in the box?"

"Just bugs," Faron answered. "My mother doesn't care. They're mine."

"Well, then," Quinn stood up, "if it's okay with her, it's okay with me, too."

Faron didn't say anything else. He wrapped his jam sandwich in a paper napkin and followed everyone outside.

On the ride into town Faron closed his eyes and squeezed them tightly, holding the box up to his ear, listening to the moths flutter and hurl their fat fuzzy bodies into the sides of the tobacco-scented box, making a sound like the thrumming of tiny toy drums. As Quinn drove along the winding road into town, Faron barely heard Mary Gage explain he'd be staying with her and Quinn for a while.

CHAPTER 6

"WHAT'LL WE DO?" Mary asked her husband when they got home and settled Faron in the kitchen with a more substantial lunch.

Quinn watched the boy unwrap his bread and jam and put it on the plate next to the egg salad sandwich Mary made for him.

"I'm not sure," Quinn answered. "I guess the first thing we have to find out is whether Alison left her affairs in order. My guess is she didn't. I'll call Nye Standish, my lawyer friend on the mainland. He'll handle the legal end of things."

"Better do it right away. Avoid any complications."

"You're right." Quinn went into his office to find the lawyer's phone number and make the call. As far as he knew, Alison didn't have relatives anywhere else, but Nye would figure all that out. He assumed it should be fine if Faron stayed with him and Mary for the time being, but he'd ask Nye about that, too.

After Faron's mother washed ashore, the jealousies and imagined betrayals of the island women dimmed, and they treated Faron with a chary acceptance. After all, it wasn't his fault he came from a long line of bad seeds. And with Alison gone, it didn't seem to matter as much who his father was.

Some people from church volunteered to help Quinn close up Alison's ramshackle house on Puddle Cove. They shut off the plumbing and electricity and boarded up the windows with all of Alison's things still inside. When the dust settled at the end of the day's work, their curiosity got the best of them.

"You keeping the boy, Quinn?" a congregant asked.

"For now." Even as he said it, Quinn sensed something more permanent.

"He's so quiet," Mary commented one morning while Faron sprawled on their living room floor playing with some toys that the silver-haired woman from Preble Point had dropped off for him, "but very sweet."

"I know." Quinn looked at the boy intently, as though trying to place a face he couldn't quite remember.

Quinn and Mary had gone back to Puddle Cove to collect some more of Faron's things, including dozens of empty cigar boxes, which he had insisted on keeping. He kept them in his new room, stacked on a shelf by the bed, and often carried one around with him. He had one with him now, as he sat on the floor in a patch of sunlight, playing with miniature carved animals. Mary found Faron's attachment to the boxes worrisome.

Quinn didn't think much of it. "Guess they make him feel secure. No harm in it."

"I suppose not." Mary hesitated. "But what about the insects? The other night, when I went into his room, he was standing on a chair trying to catch another moth."

"So?"

Mary laughed at herself. "You're right. I guess it's nothing."

It wasn't long before Quinn and Mary knew they wanted him to stay. The lawyer started the paperwork to make them legal guardians and Mary came home with a kitten.

"What's that?" Quinn peered into the basket Mary set on the kitchen table.

"One of Clayton Jewett's barn cats had a litter." She lifted a tattered towel to show him a tiny orange-and-white ball of fur. "I thought it might help Faron feel at home."

Quinn rubbed the kitten's head and kissed his wife. "Good idea."

"Where is he?"

"Upstairs." Quinn picked up the basket. "Come on, let's go."

"What do you want to name it?" Mary asked, sitting on the floor with Faron and the mewing kitten.

Quinn knelt next to them, watching the tentative way the boy handled the scrawny cat.

"Mommy."

Mary's heart lurched. "What did you say?"

In the fleeting glance he exchanged with Mary, Quinn could see her hopes surge and recede all in an instant. He had the same reaction when, at first, he thought Faron was referring to Mary.

"I'm going to name her *Mommy*," Faron repeated, his face sparkling.

Quinn walked over to the window. The tide was coming in. Channel markers leaned toward shore. "I don't think that's a good idea, Faron. Can you think of another name?"

Faron's smile faded. He shook his head and watched the kitten wobble on its spindly legs. When he picked it up and tried jamming it into one of his cigar boxes, Mary took it from him.

"Well," she murmured, stroking the frightened kitten, "we'll think of another name."

A week later, when an envelope arrived from Nye Standish, Quinn had second thoughts. He went into the kitchen where Mary was fixing supper. "Maybe we should skip this legal guardian stuff and outright adopt him. What do you think?"

"Let's wait," Mary said, letting the oven door slam shut.

They knew about the bees, flies, moths, and anything else Faron could put in one of his boxes, but they didn't find out about the fans until their first winter with him.

"Faron!" Quinn hollered up the staircase. After calling twice and getting no answer, he climbed the stairs and knocked on Faron's closed door—still no answer. He turned the knob and peeked in. What he saw made him smile.

Faron was lying on the floor with a box fan on one side of him and a smaller, old metal fan on the other side. He had both appliances as close to his ears as possible, without shearing them off. His eyes were closed and he had a big grin on his face. He still didn't hear Quinn.

Quinn stepped into the room. "Faron?"

The boy startled and jumped up, tipping over the smaller fan in the process. The metal blade rotated in slow motion, making a dull knocking sound as it grazed the wood floor, lifting the base of the fan up and down with each rotation.

Assuming he was in trouble, Faron said, "I'm sorry."

Quinn bent over to unplug the fan and set it upright. Ancient dust clung to the oily wire. It was one that came from Alison Goss's house. Quinn was surprised it hadn't burned the place down. It, and the cigar boxes, had been all Faron wanted to keep.

"It's okay," Quinn reassured him. "You didn't do anything wrong."

Faron's face relaxed.

"Do you like listening to the fans?"

"Uh huh."

"Why?"

Faron smiled widely, revealing the blank space where one of his lower cuspids had fallen out. "I don't know, I just do. I can't hear anything except a windy sound in my ears. It makes my head feel good."

Quinn couldn't remember when he'd seen such a happy expression on the boy's face. He wound the cord around the old fan and set the fire hazard on a shelf next to the cigar boxes. "You know, if you want, I could get you a newer, bigger fan, like that." He pointed to the box fan. "You could still keep the old one."

"Will it be okay with Mary?" Faron sat on his bed fidgeting with the corner of a quilt Mary had made.

"Of course it will. Come on, let's go tell her."

"You don't think it's odd for him to surround himself with electric fans because he likes the noise?" Mary asked that night when she and Quinn were getting ready for bed.

Quinn watched Mary brush her brown hair, still as thick and wavy as the day they were married, though tinted now to a slightly lighter shade.

"No odder than any other imaginary games children play, I guess," Quinn said. "Remember that kid who used to drag a dog leash around town, with nothing on the end of it?"

"I'd forgotten about that. The Beaudrys's son."

"That's right. He's a banker now . . . down in Boston."

"Maybe you're right," Mary said, reaching to turn off the light. "There's probably nothing to worry about."

The next day, while Faron was in school and Quinn was writing a sermon for Sunday's service, Mary went into town to the general store and looked through the mail-order catalog for the biggest box fan she could find.

CHAPTER 7

Clayton Jewett and his beekeeper son, Stan, make their living from Ocean Meadows, an eclectic saltwater farm on the lower island. Their small herd of Holsteins produces enough milk and butter for the entire town, and their flock of high-strung leghorn hens keeps the locals in eggs. Jewett's Sugar and Gold Corn is worth waiting all winter for and Stan's red clover honey satisfies everyone's sweet tooth, sometimes as far south as Portland.

Clayton's wife divorced him early on, leaving him with a young child and a hankering for female home cooking. Fortunately, since he's the town mayor and past-president of the Historical Society, he's a frequent recipient of fresh-baked desserts, steaming casseroles, and other homemade offerings. In fact, he was walking through his property thinking about the last thick slice of Mary Gage's chocolate cake on the top shelf in his refrigerator when he spotted the boy.

Faron Goss was beautiful to look at, just like his mother—a lithe, winsome eyeful—but at a young age he began showing signs of being as troubled as she was. It was a year after his mother died when Clayton saw him running shirtless and barefoot through a field of bees.

"It was the craziest thing I ever saw," the farmer exclaimed later to Quinn. "I went out to my field to look at the hives and I saw this small boy running through my clover. Well, I knew the field was full of bees because the hives were empty. I shouted to him but he ran off into the trees with a swarm of bees chasing him, and, I'm not sure, but I swear I heard that boy laughing. *Why, that's the strangest thing,* I thought, but then, when I realized it was Alison Goss's kid . . . well . . . it didn't seem so strange anymore."

Faron ditched the bees by jumping into a shallow cow pond and holding his head underwater. When Clayton finally caught up with him, he dragged the dripping kid into his pickup truck and drove him to see Owen Batch.

Faron's feet and legs swelled up like ticks on a dog's ear. "Why did you do it?" Doc Batch asked the swollen boy.

"I wanted to see if the buzzing was louder than the stings," was all Faron said to the bewildered doctor.

"Louder than the stings? What do you mean? Stings aren't loud."

"They are to me." Faron put his hand over his mouth and wouldn't say another word.

That evening Mary fretted. "Maybe we shouldn't let him keep the cigar boxes."

Quinn disagreed. "We have to. They're the only things he seems attached to."

"I know. But he's still keeping insects in them . . . in the house. I don't like it. He'd rather be catching moths and beetles than playing with other children . . . and now, there's this thing with the bees."

They were in the kitchen. Quinn took a long look at his wife and knew he was blessed. Not only was she beautiful, with the smooth complexion and vibrancy of a much younger woman, she was smart, with a generous spirit—a good minister's wife. She went out of her way every day to help neighbors on the island, but when it came to Faron, she was different. She'd been thrilled to have him live with them in the beginning, but something had changed. The first year had been a challenge.

Quinn thought that maybe she felt left out. He and Faron had forged a nice relationship, but it was Mary who took on the added responsibilities that came with Faron . . . school, clothing, activities, meals . . . not to mention running the household and helping with church business. It was tiring.

"Mary, I know it's not the same as having our own child, but God has given Faron to us, and I wish . . ."

She cut him off, angrily. "Stop it. This has nothing to do with any of that." She started clearing the table, stacking the dishes together loudly. "I just think he's got problems and I'm worried for him, and for us."

Quinn watched her from behind as she put plates in the sink. She stood there quietly for a few moments, running hot water over her hands, then turned to say, "I wish you wouldn't let him bring those boxes of bugs to church on Sundays."

"Okay. I'll talk to him." But in his heart, Quinn knew he'd never discourage the boy in the way Mary wanted. Although he didn't know why, it was clear Faron found solace in the odd things he did, and Quinn wasn't going to take that away from him.

Months later, Faron started pulling out his hair. At night while he lay in bed, he plucked the dark strands until he fell asleep. In the morning, there were small specks of dried blood and loose hairs on Mary's embroidered pillowcases.

"Why are you doing this?" Quinn's worried wife asked, with waning patience.

Faron shrugged. "It feels good."

He kept at it. Night after night—pillowcase after pillowcase—until there was a perfectly round bald spot the size of a quarter on the crown of his head.

Quinn took him to see Owen.

"You know, young man," Doc Batch explained, after examining Faron's head, "sometimes when you feel hurt on the inside, it makes you want to hurt yourself on the outside. Is there anything you want to tell us?"

Faron's sad face brightened. "When I pull my hairs out it sounds so loud that I can't even feel it."

"Well," sighed the confounded doctor, after exchanging stunned glances with Quinn, "if you don't stop yanking out your hair, you might have to take some medicine."

The next day Faron went into the church, found the matches that were used to light candles for Sunday services, and set fire to his balding head. Fortunately, the choirmaster walked in for practice right at that very moment and smothered the flames with altar linens.

Except for gagging on the smell of singed hair and some minor burns, Faron was unharmed. He wore a cap to cover his charred head until his hair grew back, but it didn't hide his strangeness. His teacher called Mary to tell her the children at school were teasing Faron.

"He really needs to see someone," Mary suggested to Quinn.

Quinn dug in. "No. It hasn't been that long since his mother's death. He's still adjusting. I want him to come to us with his problems, not some stranger."

"But he set his head on fi—"

"No." Even as he interrupted her, Quinn wasn't really sure he was making the right decision. Unsoundness settles in early and the hurt that spawns it ran deep in Alison Goss's boy. He wondered if it was already too late to help Faron feel safe in the world.

CHAPTER 8

THERE WAS ONLY ONE SCHOOL on the island—kindergarten through high school, all in the same building. Faron was a good student, but shy, so Mary saw to it that he mingled with his classmates, making sure he was included in every school play, holiday party, and other special events. She encouraged him to socialize, hoping it might help overcome his tendency to be alone.

On his tenth birthday she and Quinn helped him plan a party.

"Is there anyone you want to invite, besides the children in your class?" they asked on the snowy evening the three of them were making the guest list.

Because the school was so small, there was an agreement among the parents that on birthdays their child would invite the entire class, so no one would feel left out, but they were allowed to invite others as well.

"Can Mrs. Ebel come?"

Connie Ebel, the harbormaster's wife, had a wide beam and sea-green eyes, and Faron had a crush on her.

Mary looked at Quinn, then back at Faron. "Leslie Ebel's mom? Don't you think Leslie might feel funny about that?"

"Okay." A cloud of melancholy passed across Faron's face but, as usual, he didn't argue. Just gave in. While other parents had to endure endless negotiations to get their children to comply, Faron rarely questioned anything he was asked to do.

He left the room for a glass of milk and Mary noticed Quinn stifle a smile. They were both aware of Faron's attraction to Connie.

"I don't think it's funny," Mary said.

"Oh, come on. Lots of boys his age have crushes on their friends' mothers."

Mary had to admit he was right. The truth was, she was jealous. She wished Faron didn't keep her at such a distance. She was annoyed at Quinn, too. He'd never done anything about Faron bringing the insects to church, and there were still cigar boxes all over the boy's room.

"I've got an idea," Mary said when Faron returned with a large glass of Clayton Jewett's milk and a handful of her oatmeal cookies. "We'll invite all the moms, including Mrs. Ebel. I can always use some extra help."

Faron's face brightened.

The day of his party, Faron sat down on the couch next to Mrs. Ebel and hardly budged.

Mary served a hot lunch and a three-layer lemon cake, Faron's favorite, and Quinn bought plenty of ice cream and soda to go with it. There was a steep hill out in back of the house where the kids were having fun sledding and throwing snowballs—rushing in through the kitchen door for hot chocolate when they got cold, then running back outside again—everyone except Faron. He was content to stay inside with the adults, only getting up from the couch to fetch Connie Ebel second helpings of everything.

When it was time to serve cake, Quinn called the children inside. "Come on, everyone, let's gather around and sing Happy Birthday to Faron!"

Just then Jeannie Ebel, Leslie's younger sister, came

running down the stairs from Faron's room, waving a cigar box and shrieking, "There a 'pider in here! There a 'pider in here!"

But it wasn't a spider. It was a moth, spending the winter in the warm house. When Faron caught it that morning, he put it in the box. He'd been delighted to find it on his birthday and was planning to let it go after the party.

Now he froze, watching the little girl dash around the room while everyone looked on. "Give it to me," he pleaded. But she didn't.

"Jeannie!" her mother yelled. "You come here right now!"

But before Mrs. Ebel, or anyone else, could stop the girl, the box flipped open and the moth fell to the floor, where Jeannie promptly stepped on it.

It was a terrible accident. The clumsy misstep of a four-year-old. In the seconds afterwards no one said a word, until Faron burst into tears and threw himself into Mrs. Ebel's arms . . . and then all the children erupted in laughter.

"What a baby!" Billy Gallager shouted. Billy, Jarry's eldest, was always giving Faron a hard time.

Mary didn't know what to do. She clapped her hands and raised her voice over the childish jeering. "Okay! Let's have cake!"

"Cry baby!" another boy taunted. "Run to Mommy!"

Where the mention of cake didn't quiet things down, the next remark did: "Faron doesn't have a mommy," Jeannie Ebel announced.

Silence. Even cruel children knew when enough was enough.

By the time Quinn managed to pry Faron off Connie Ebel, and the boy gave one long, tearful puff and blew out what was left of his half-melted birthday candles, the subdued voices of children filled the room and Mary wiped the squashed moth off the wide-plank floor.

School had been a safe place for Faron when he lived on Puddle Cove, a place with bright rooms and things to do, a place where he could raise his hand and ask questions without worry. But as he got older, it was different. Some of the boys, especially Billy Gallager, picked on him incessantly.

"Hey, box boy," Billy taunted when the teacher wasn't watching, "who do you like better, your real mother or the fake one?"

At times like those Faron felt his heart quicken and he struggled to hide the rage he felt. He put his nose deeper in a book, hoping Billy would stop.

"The Lord will fight for you; you have only to be still," is what Quinn quoted when Faron told him he wanted to punch Billy in the face.

"But I'm taller and stronger," Faron protested. "I'd knock him flat!"

Quinn was startled at Faron's uncharacteristic anger, worried it might be a glimpse of something deeper, but he was also pleased to see him speaking up for himself. "Maybe you should try out for a school team, like the other boys. You've got the build. It'd be a good way to let off steam. I bet the coach would love to have you."

But Faron was different from the other boys. He didn't like sports. He preferred being by himself. He loved taking long walks around the island, or sitting in one spot, watching turtles sun themselves on logs, or ants crawl from chore to chore.

His third Christmas with them, despite Mary's mixed feelings, they bought Faron a butterfly net. Even in cold weather, he hiked through the snow, alongside half-frozen creeks and streams, looking for stoneflies as they emerged in late February and March.

One afternoon Quinn spotted Faron sitting on the edge of Keeps Pond, sketching dragonflies. It wasn't the first time he'd seen Faron drawing. He'd recently noticed him doodling in the margins of his homework. "I think we should encourage it," he told Mary.

On their next trip to the mainland, they bought a sketchpad and charcoal pencils. The gift lay on Faron's desk, untouched for weeks, until they noticed it mixed in with a stack of his textbooks. He'd been taking it to school.

"These aren't bad," Quinn said to Mary as he leafed through Faron's sketch pad one evening. Some of the drawings were of people and animals but most of them were of insects.

"He say you could look at those?" Mary didn't look up from her knitting.

"No, but he left them right here in the living room. He's usually more private than that, so I figure it was no accident."

Mary got up and peeked over Quinn's shoulder. "You're right. These are quite good."

Quinn nodded in agreement. "Funny that he never showed an interest in art before now."

Mary sat back down on the couch and picked up the row of stitches where she'd left off. "He's funny about a lot of things, if you ask me." She didn't sound mean, just weary.

When Faron asked if he could get a part-time job, Quinn tried convincing him that it might be more fun spending time with friends.

"You're only fourteen," Quinn said. "There'll be plenty of time for work. Why don't you just enjoy yourself?"

"I'd enjoy working." Faron stood his ground. "Red says I can help out at Scuppers, cleaning tables and stuff, a couple of hours a day."

Quinn was surprised. "You already spoke with Red?"

"I talked to him yesterday." Faron bit his lower lip, waiting for an answer.

Mary sat quietly, listening.

"What do you think?" Quinn asked her.

"I think it's a good idea."

"Well," Quinn relented, looking at Faron, "I guess you've got a job."

Faron bussed tables, washed dishes, cleaned fish, and did whatever else Red needed. It may not have been the social life the Gages had in mind, but it was better than nothing. Got him around people, and he seemed to like it, so much so that he kept the job at Scuppers all through high school.

On weekends he got up early and worked the breakfast shift. During his break, he liked to sit with the same group of stout wives who came in for coffee and gossip every Saturday morning. They never actually invited him. He just eased his way to the end of their table and, since he had turned out to be the spitting image of Zed and Alison Goss and not any of their husbands, they let him stay.

As small as the island school was, students managed to create cliques, and Faron had a hard time fitting in, except with the girls. At sixteen he looked older than his age, and his dark eyes and long, lean limbs were the cause of many schoolgirl crushes.

When girls chased after Faron, the other boys were jealous. "You shouldn't talk to him," they said. "He's weird. All he does is catch butterflies and draw bugs. His whole family was crazy."

But the girls didn't listen to them. Although Faron was shy, his lovestruck admirers were bold. They passed him notes in class. In the hallways they clamored for a whiff of him. The braver ones arranged to meet him after school, hoping he'd fondle their breasts in the deep shadows of covering pines. Sometimes they sneaked away to their fathers' snugged-up boats after dark, wanting him to pin them down on fish-stained decks, longing to feel the weight of him on them.

But it was more than his dazzling good looks that attracted them. They were fascinated by the magical way he made insects come to life with a pencil—making them even more beautiful than they actually were, and, secretly, the girls wished he might do the same for them. They swarmed around him while he sketched, posing themselves in ways they hoped might catch his eye.

The summer after graduating high school, Faron kept a full-time job at Scuppers, where he traded bits of conversation with the shapely female summer residents who sought him out when they came into the restaurant under the pretense of ordering one of Red's fatty, fried meals, which clearly wasn't part of their usual diet.

They were well-tended women—*Preble Pretties*, the locals called them—on the island alone with their children and nannies during the week, while the husbands worked on the mainland. It wasn't unusual to see them saunter into Scuppers during Faron's shifts.

"Will you look at that?" Brad Sawyer complained to the sheriff one day while they were both sitting out a sun shower at Scuppers, eating lunch at the bar. He lifted his wrist an inch off his soup-stained placemat and flicked it toward two evenly tanned women who were vying for Faron's attention. "Don't they know they're old enough to be that kid's mother?" He did a double take. "Hell, maybe even grandmother," he scoffed. "Ain't that the limit?"

"Brad, if there's one thing I've learned after all these years, it's that a lot of folks on this island don't pay any attention to limits—not speed limits, not alcohol limits, and not age limits."

"Still, it ain't right."

Alden Paisley couldn't help himself. "Things have reversed."

"What's that supposed to mean?"

Alden slid backwards off the stool and stood up. He picked up his coffee cup and finished the sweet dregs at the bottom. "This time it's the husbands with a case of green-eyed envy, not the wives."

"Speak for yourself."

Alden laughed. "I'm not married." He slapped Brad on the back. "See you later."

The sheriff hiked up his wide leather gun belt and headed toward the door, tipping his hat to Red. "Thanks for lunch." He gave a sidelong glance toward Faron, who, in the rain-washed sunlight that streamed through the windows, looked just like his mother.

CHAPTER 9

SOMETHING GOT Mary Gage's cat. A neighbor's flop-eared gun dog found it under a bird-ravaged blueberry bush and dragged it out with its soft mouth, frantically wagging its tail as it dropped the stiff lump of fur on the back doorstep of the rectory, where Faron found it, partly pulled to pieces and covered with flies.

He went into the kitchen and took one of Mary's eight-ounce canning jars off the pantry shelf. It was easy to salvage small bits of the cat's carcass since it was already falling apart. He dropped the pieces into the jar and left the lid off, then carefully picked up the rest of the cat and headed to the garage to find a shovel.

He scouted the woods on either side of the hill behind their house and located a nice spot in a birch grove, then dug a hole about two feet deep and gently lowered the cat's mangled carcass into it.

By the time he'd thrown the last shovelful of dirt on the grave, said a prayer, and put the shovel back in the garage, the canning jar was buzzing with flies. He put the metal lid on the jar and poked air holes in it with an awl. He decided to hide the jar under his bed until he could figure out a better place for it, then got out of his clothes, tossed them in the washing machine, and took a long, cool shower.

"Quinn!" Mary shrieked several days later when she was vacuuming upstairs and knocked over the jar under Faron's bed. "Quinn!"

Quinn bounded up the steps two at time.

Mary was perched on the edge of a chair in Faron's room, her face as white as a sun-baked shell, the vacuum still going. Quinn bent to turn it off. "What's wrong?" he asked, gulping for breath.

She pointed to the overturned jar, prodded out of its hiding place when she poked the vacuum hose under the bed.

Quinn picked up the jar and turned it in his hands. There was no mistaking the orange-and-white tufts of fur stuck to the inside of the glass. He felt sick.

Later that night, after they'd spoken with Faron and gone to bed, Mary cried in her husband's arms. "He has to leave," she sobbed. "I've tried all these years to help that boy—to love him. When he was younger it was easier. But he scares me now. I mean . . . putting pieces of our cat in that jar. And not even telling us he found her . . . when he knew I've been sick with worry. Please, Quinn. He's old enough now to be on his own. Maybe he should move back to Puddle Cove. You always said the house was his when he was ready."

Quinn stroked his wife's arm, thinking. He didn't agree that Faron was 'ready,' but he was concerned about Mary. Maybe she had a point. Faron was finished with high school and had turned up his nose at college. He was spending too much time alone and seemed more interested in walking around with a cigar box than his sketchpad, which bothered Quinn. The boy had talent and Quinn hated to see it wasted. He was also spending more time on the drinking side of Red's bar than Quinn liked. And there were those rumors about the women who came into Scuppers. Maybe it was time to plant him somewhere else and see what sprouted.

Quinn sighed deeply and reached to switch off the bedside lamp. "You may be right, Mary. I'll take care of it. Let's try to get some sleep."

The more Quinn thought about his conversation with Mary, the more he realized it might be good for Faron to be on his own. There was just one problem. Faron had lost his job.

"I'm sorry, Quinn." Red Sedgewick opened a window to let out the smell of stale beer. White eyelet curtains embroidered with anchors blew in the breeze. "You know my sister's oldest, the girl? Well, she's waiting a year before going to college and she needs a job. I couldn't say no to my own sister. You know how it is."

"Sure, Red, I understand. But what about part-time? Is your niece going to be able to do all the heavy-lifting Faron did?"

Red set a glass of cold beer in front of Quinn. "Here, it's on me. Listen, Quinn, I can't pay the both of them. Maybe next year when the girl leaves Faron can come back. It's got nothing to do with him—he did a great job." Red grinned. "Even brought in new customers . . . if you get my drift."

"Yup." Quinn knew Red was referring to the women from Preble Point, and the inference made him uncomfortable. "You know, there's nothing going on with Faron and those women, they're just friends."

"Ayuh." Red busied himself with a bar towel, averting Quinn's eyes.

Quinn downed his beer in several long swallows, shook Red's freckled hand, and went home to make some phone calls. Before stopping by Scuppers to try and convince Red to take Faron back, he'd made the rounds and not one fisherman or carpenter or anyone else on the island had a job that wasn't already filled by a son or nephew or a cousin. But Quinn did have a few connections on the mainland.

"Captain Boyd," Rick Boyd answered on the first ring.

Still the same commanding voice Quinn remembered from college.

"Hello, Rick. This is Quinn Gage."

"Well I'll be damned. Oops, sorry Father. How the hell are you? Damn. There I go again."

Quinn laughed. "Don't worry about it. I hear worse language than that all day long on this island."

They made the small talk of two men who hadn't spoken in quite a while, then Quinn got to the point. "I've got this boy, Faron, who's been living with us. Got a few problems, but he's a good kid, and right now he needs a job. Any chance you can hire him?"

Captain Boyd didn't hesitate. "Sure can. I run two good size lobster boats out of Willisport and one of my sternmen just ditched me for something better, or so he thinks. When can your kid start?"

Quinn couldn't believe his luck. "Right away. He doesn't have much experience, but he learns fast."

"Oh, he'll learn fast all right. I'll put him on the boat with me and if he doesn't show promise, I'll throw him right back to you like he was undersized. Fair enough?"

"Fair enough." Quinn was relieved to find a new job for Faron but there was one other thing he wanted to do . . . something he'd thought about for a long time.

CHAPTER 10

QUINN GOT OUT OF HIS CAR and ambled through a thin cluster of pines along a meandering slate sidewalk that led to Owen Batch's house. Owen was standing outside, in front of the doorway, sipping hot coffee.

"I put a pot on right after you called," Owen said, waving the steaming cup in the air for emphasis. "Got something important on your mind?"

"Yes. And you're the only one I can talk to."

"Come on in." Owen pulled the screen door open and held it while Quinn walked through ahead of him.

Owen's living room was bright and airy, tastefully furnished with comfortable upholstered chairs and a couch that had belonged to his parents. A flattering portrait of the elder Doctor Batch hung above the hearth of a large stone fireplace. A row of wide windows looked out beyond the patio and into the woods. Several windows were propped open with thick leather-bound books, and a piney breeze wafted in, freshening the room.

Owen gestured toward two floral-patterned needlepoint chairs near the fireplace. "Have a seat," he offered. Both men sighed as they settled into their chairs, a low marble-topped table between them. "Would you like some?" Owen asked, pointing to his coffee. "Or a cold drink?"

Quinn declined. "I had a beer. Over at Scuppers."

"I hope that's all you had. Too much of Red's cooking will clog your arteries. Make your blood run slower than a toad in a tar bucket."

Quinn laughed and Owen took a sip of coffee, waiting to hear the reason his friend was here.

Quinn cleared his throat and rubbed the graying stubble on his chin. "I'd like a paternity test done on Faron."

Owen set his coffee cup down on the table. He wasn't sure what he'd expected Quinn to say, but this wasn't it. "Why?" he asked, trying not to sound too taken aback.

"I think I might be his father. His biological father."

Now Owen couldn't contain his surprise. "What?"

While Quinn told him everything—from sleeping with Alison Goss to finding pieces of Mary's cat in a jar—Owen listened quietly, his reaction subdued now after the initial shock.

"Has he ever asked about his father?" Owen inquired when Quinn finished talking.

"No. I brought it up a few times, in case he wanted to talk. The last time I mentioned it he said there was nothing to say about someone he never knew."

"Have you always thought it might be you?"

"From the day he was born. Just a feeling. Then as he got older and I saw him around town, I thought there was a resemblance."

"Why didn't you try to find out before now?"

Quinn shifted nervously in his chair. "I didn't have the courage," he admitted. "I'm a married man, an Episcopal priest. If Faron turned out to be my son, it could have cost me everything—my position in the church and community, maybe my marriage." He avoided the other man's eyes. "You know Mary and I were never able to have children of our own. It would have been very hard on her if Faron turned out to be mine. I don't know what she would have done. I still don't."

Owen got up and walked over to the windows and stared out. "But you're willing to find out now?"

"I am."

"Why? What's changed?"

"Only me," Quinn said. "I can't help thinking that if I'd done this sooner Faron might not be . . . so strange. Maybe it's not too late to fix things."

"Okay," Owen said, sitting back down. "If you're sure it's what you want."

Quinn stood up abruptly and paced back and forth. "Darn it, Owen," he blurted out. "That's the problem. I'm not sure. What's wrong with me? One minute I am and the next I'm not. I've been agonizing about this for years and I just keep going back and forth in my thinking. If I wait until he's eighteen I won't be able to do it without telling him and . . ."

Owen interrupted, trying to ease Quinn's turmoil. "I understand. There's no reason to tell him unless it turns out that you are the father. I'll tell you what, Quinn. You don't have to decide everything right now. I can help arrange for the test. In fact, I believe Faron's scheduled for his yearly visit next week, if I'm not mistaken."

Quinn nodded. "Yes, he is."

"Okay. I'll make the arrangements and work it into that visit. It takes a while for results to come back. I'll hold on to them and you can call me when . . . and *if* . . . you want to know the results. It's not unusual for people to change their minds on something like this. Sound good?

"Sounds good." Quinn felt himself relax.

"If it turns out you're not the father, no one ever needs to know about this except you and me. But if it turns out the way you think it might, then Faron may need all the support he can get and I can help you with that. Agreed?"

Quinn breathed a sigh of relief. "Thank you, Owen. I was worried what you might think of me." A burden lifted as he spoke. On Menhaden everyone always came to him with their problems. It felt good to be able to have someone listen to his for once.

"You should know better than that, Quinn. You and I have been friends for a long time." Owen paused. "Besides, I've been to enough of your sermons to know that none of us is in a position to judge another. That's up to Him," Owen said, gesturing with his thumb toward the ceiling.

CHAPTER 11

Quinn bought himself a new Chevrolet Suburban and gave Faron the metallic-blue Chevy so he could get around on his own.

"Thanks," was all Faron said when Quinn led him out to the driveway and handed him the keys.

Faron's glum mood was obvious. He'd been that way ever since they told him about moving back to Puddle Cove.

"You know," Quinn said, "we're not kicking you out. We just thought it might be time for you to be a little more independent. What do you think?"

Faron opened the car door and sat in the driver's seat. He ran his hands across the steering wheel. "Whose idea was it, yours or Mary's?"

"What? The Chevy?"

"No. The leaving."

"Both." Quinn hunched slightly, one hand on the car top and the other on the open door. "We thought—since you didn't want to go away to college—that the next best thing is living on your own and working on the mainland." Quinn waited for Faron's reaction, but there wasn't any. "A change of scenery might do you good."

The house on Puddle Cove needed weatherproofing, and much more. Quinn rounded up some willing neighbors to help with the work, and Alden and his brother, Emmett, went to Willisport for roofing materials. When everyone got to the Goss place at seven o'clock on the following Saturday morning, there were rolls of underlayment and bundles of new shingles stacked neatly in the gravel driveway alongside the house.

Myron Sprague, who worked construction when he wasn't catching lobsters, acted as foreman and was on the job before anyone else. "About time you got here!" he shouted to the men. "Hop up on the roof and let's get at it!" At forty-eight, Myron still moved as fast as he did at twenty-eight, and in one weekend they ripped off the leaking asphalt shingles and installed a new roof.

It was one of those clear, humidity-free Maine days when Quinn and his helpers returned to the site the following weekend. The bunch of them stood around for the first half hour, enjoying coffee and doughnuts, compliments of Myron.

"I like my crew well-fed and happy," Myron joked, taking a bite out of his second doughnut. "Eat fast, though, before the weather changes."

Quinn was climbing a ladder to admire the new roof but stopped halfway up when he heard what Myron said. "What are you talking about?" Quinn asked. "It's supposed to stay like this for the rest of the week." He thrust his face upward to the sunny sky for emphasis.

"Obviously, you don't have a drop of fisherman's blood in you, Quinn. I'm telling you that it'll be raining sometime after lunch. That's a fact."

One of the other guys piped up. "I got to agree with Myron on this one. Behind that blue sky is one heck of a wicked storm gathering."

Quinn stepped backwards down the ladder and sat on a stack of two-by-fours. He took off his cap and ran a hand through his hair. The morning sun was already warm and it felt good on his bare head. He wasn't sure if the guys were teasing him or not. "I don't know how you boys do it, but I have to admit you're usually right about the weather. What is it, telltale arthritis from all those years on the water?"

"Huh. Says you. Nope, we just got finely honed instincts, is all. Know when to go out and when to come in." Myron seemed confident in his opinions, enough so that he changed the subject. "Where's Faron today?"

"Fishing. Guess Captain Boyd isn't as good at predicting the weather as you."

Myron crushed his empty paper cup with one hand and tossed it at Quinn. "Oh, that's real funny. And if you weren't a preacher, I might tell you what I'm really thinking. C'mon, let's get to work."

Five hours later, they'd pried boards off the doors and windows, filled nail holes, caulked gaps, replaced rotting wood, hammered down loose cedar shakes, and rebuilt the back steps. Myron really knew how to organize his men.

Quinn had just finished scraping and painting a bit of white window trim when a carload of ladies from church showed up with a hot lunch. They served it to the men on the new back steps, where the sweet scent of freshly cut lumber was as pleasing as the aroma of the homemade meal.

After stuffing themselves, the men mowed and raked the overgrown grass in the small front yard. Some of the more spry ladies weeded around the brick foundation and planted flowers. The front porch still needed to be replaced, but otherwise, from the outside, the house had never looked so good.

Just when the fresh paint on the window trim was dry to the touch, a fast-moving cover of clouds rolled in. It rained like a son-of-a-bitch and everyone looked at Quinn.

"Told you so," one of the guys declared, fingers in his mouth, picking lunch from his teeth. He loosened a caraway seed and spit it out. "Ought to have fishermen doing the forecast, instead of those know-nothing meteorologists."

Myron agreed but he didn't have to say a word. The self-satisfied expression on his face said it all.

A mile north of Willisport, and at least that far out, Captain Boyd had no intention of coming in. He, too, had sensed the rain, but he also knew it wouldn't last long. He scanned the horizon in every direction and switched on the autopilot, with just enough power to keep the bow headed into the wind. His sternman was tidying up the deck, dripping wet.

"What do think, Faron, should we take a break?"

"Sounds good."

Rick poured them both a cup of hot tea from a grungy container. "A genuine Thermos," he boasted, screwing the top back on. "Still keeps things hot enough to burn the tongue." He saw Faron eyeing it. "Don't pay any mind to the greasy fingerprints—it's clean on the inside."

"I wasn't thinking that," Faron said, sounding apologetic. "Just that it looks like you've had it a long time."

"Fifteen years. As long as I've owned this boat."

The boat was large, with a roomy, enclosed pilothouse that extended well forward of the wheel. That's where they were huddled now, taking a breather and drying out until the worst of the rain passed.

Rick leaned back on an upturned plastic milk crate. "So, tell me, how come you haven't worked as a sternman before now? Seems like you're pretty good at it."

"Quinn doesn't have a boat."

"None of your friends do?"

"No."

"But you've been on a boat before, right?"

"Sure. And one summer at Beaudry's Wharf some fishermen took me out and showed me how to bait and set traps."

Rick sat upright and leaned toward Faron with a serious look on his face. "The reason I'm asking is, I've noticed you shut your eyes sometimes, when we're hauling . . . just about when the traps surface."

Faron got nervous, and it showed.

"No need to worry. I'm just telling you—keep your eyes open. Handling traps is dangerous work . . . even in good weather, but more so on a day like today. You need all your wits about you, so don't go closing your eyes. Okay?"

"Okay."

Quinn finished counseling an alcoholic congregant and was thinking how fortunate it was that Faron hadn't inherited the propensity for drink that the rest of the Goss clan had, when the phone rang.

It was Rick Boyd. "You know those 'problems' you said the boy has? What are they, exactly?"

Quinn's stomach clenched. He thought about lying but as a man of the cloth, he couldn't. So he just omitted a few things. "His mother died when he was eight. That's how we got him."

"No father in the picture?

"Nope."

"How'd she die?

"Drowned. Fell out of her skiff crossing a cove to town. Faron had nightmares when he was younger." He didn't tell the captain Faron still woke some nights drenched in sweat, or that he used buzzing insects as white noise. "Why?"

"Well, it's probably nothing, but when we're hauling traps, your boy shuts his eyes tighter than a clam at low tide. I mean, it's only for a few seconds when the traps break water, but he should really be watching what he's doing. It's dangerous."

Quinn had expected something much worse and slumped in his chair with relief. "I agree. Have you said anything to him?"

"Sure I have, but he still does it. Just wanted to let you know . . . in case . . . well, I thought it might be some kind of seizure or something. Maybe you'll talk to him about it?"

"Of course. I'll mention it to him tonight. How's he doing otherwise?"

"Great. On the quiet side . . . but that means I get to do most of the talking, which suits me just fine."

That night after Mary cleared the supper dishes from the table, Quinn told Faron about the call from Rick. "Any idea why you close your eyes?"

Faron knew damn well why but he wasn't going to admit it. "I don't know. I just do."

Mary dumped table scraps into the trash. "Maybe he's not cut out for fishing. I suppose we could try to find him something else."

Faron tensed. Sometimes Mary had a way of talking about him like he wasn't there. He looked at her. "I like working on the boat."

Maybe he didn't grow up with a father who fished, but he was born on this island and in that sense, fishing was in his blood. And he did his job well, eyes open or not. Why, just the other day, when they were steaming for port, full throttle in choppy seas, he'd clung to the foredeck, eyes shut, calmed by the deafening sounds of the wind and the diesel engine. He told the story to Quinn and Mary now, in his own defense, ". . . and even with my eyes closed, I knew we were getting close to shore because I could smell the pine trees."

Quinn and Mary passed a bemused glance between them and let the subject drop.

Not long after, Quinn made the mistake of repeating the story to one of his congregants and before he knew it, it had made the loop around Sheepscot Road and into Scuppers.

"He does *what*?" Hodie Ebel was incredulous.

"He closes his eyes and smells the pine trees!" someone shouted from the other end of the bar.

Hodie ordered another beer. "Wow! Imagine how good he must navigate in fog."

Quinn pushed aside his empty glass and got up to leave. "Very funny."

CHAPTER 12

THEY WERE MAKING steady progress on the Puddle Cove house. The work crew was ready to start on the inside of the house as soon as Myron figured out the schedule. The women had already scrubbed the kitchen and bathroom, but the rest of the place was still in disarray. Everything inside was coated with dust and cobwebs, and rodents had nested between the walls and eaten through the electrical wiring. But Faron was suddenly anxious to move in.

Quinn thought he should wait, at least until the contents of the house were sorted through—a task he worried might upset Faron. "Can't you hold off a while? Myron thinks we'll be done next weekend, or the one after."

"Quinn's right," Mary agreed. "There's no electricity. Why don't you stay here a little longer?"

"I'd rather go now. I'll be all right." They were sitting on the front porch having a beer and watching the last red sliver of sun disappear behind the trees. Faron looked at Quinn. "Would you help me bring some things over tomorrow?"

"I guess," Quinn answered reluctantly. "If that's what you want."

The next day he and Faron lugged a bed and a few other essentials over to Puddle Cove.

Many of Alison's belongings were still inside the house, strewn about by young vandals trying to get even for the times she lured their fathers away from family suppers and football games. Faron had seen the mess before. He'd sneaked in plenty of times over the years, although no one knew it. He'd shake the dust off the blanket on his old bed and lay there thinking, still longing for the things that hurt, trying to imagine his mother in the next room.

Now, Quinn stood in the doorway between the kitchen and living room, holding a stack of linens. "You sure about this?" he asked. "In the dark? Without electricity?"

"I'll be fine. Let's finish unloading the truck."

After they unloaded everything and Quinn said goodbye and left him alone in the grim, mouse-filled dampness, Faron went into his mother's room and gathered her clothes. He took them out to the backyard, doused them with gasoline and set them on fire. Flames flickered on the low, lichen-covered rock outcropping. Black smoke burned his eyes. Sparks and charred fabric rose and floated in the updraft while he wiped away tears and watched the remnants of his mother drift through the air.

That first sleepless night was relentless—fingers stuffed in his ears, thinking he heard the coarse laughter of one of his mother's drunken friends until, finally, he slept.

Alden and Quinn pulled into the driveway at seven thirty the next morning and stepped out of the car into an ocean-scented drizzle. A feisty flock of pine siskins sang loudly over the distant sputtering of someone's cantankerous two-stroke outboard motor.

Faron was already up, bleary-eyed and sifting through the damp ashes of last night's fire, suddenly wishing he had saved something. "Good morning, Quinn. Alden."

"Morning," they both answered.

Quinn kicked at the ashes with his foot. "Had a fire last night?"

"Yup."

"Trying to keep warm?"

"No. I burned some old stuff."

Quinn wondered what, but didn't ask. It must have been difficult sleeping among Alison's things. It looked like Faron had slept in his clothes, and his hair was uncombed. "That's good," Quinn replied. "The place could use some emptying out. Matter of fact, after we're done with the wiring, the three of us could start on some housekeeping."

"Not too much, I hope," Alden chimed in. "Cleaning house isn't my strong point. Besides, Zelly's coming over later with some of the gals to help straighten up."

Alden's secretary, Zelly Sprague, is Myron's wife, and she's as persnickety as her husband when it comes to getting a job done, which makes her a good person to have around when something needs doing.

Alden took the lead on the electrical wiring, and Faron seemed to pick it up fast. Quinn was good at following instructions and between the three of them, the work went quickly. When Zelly and her friends arrived with lunch, the men were ready for a break.

Zelly handed Faron a plate of cooked shrimp and butter beans.

"Looks delicious."

"Glad you think so." Zelly ducked the compliment. "Eat up. There's potato needhams for dessert."

While the men ate, Zelly and the girls marched inside with sponges and buckets and got to work. A short while later Myron showed up to finish off some carpentry repairs on the interior. By dusk the place was spotless and completely rewired.

That night, Faron sat with the lights on, watching hordes of insects bump into the taut new screens. The steady drone of mosquitoes and sounds of other night fliers calmed him, and just before midnight he fell asleep on his mossy patch of rocky land and aching memories.

Once Faron was settled in, he did little more than sweep mouse droppings off the cracked linoleum floor every few days, but Mary went over regularly to give the place a thorough cleaning and keep the kitchen cupboards stocked with food.

Her kindness didn't go unnoticed by Quinn. "It's nice—what you're doing for him."

"Same as I always have."

"I know, but you really don't have to now that he's on his own."

"Maybe. But cleaning and cooking for him was never the hard part."

Quinn knew what she meant, and didn't pursue it.

On a Sunday after church Mary said, "Lets go to Willisport tomorrow. See if we can get him some furniture. He's got nothing but the bed and kitchen chairs, and that teetering folding table."

They borrowed a truck from Alden's brother, Emmett, and caught the early morning ferry to the mainland where they got a good deal at a thrift shop—a proper kitchen table with matching chairs, a couch, and a comfortable chair for the living room. They tied everything down with rope for the ferry ride back, and that evening they hauled the furniture over the bumpy roads to Puddle Cove.

Quinn stopped by at least once a week after that to check on Faron. During his visits they sat in the kitchen talking and enjoying the scrumptious snacks Mary sent along. Sometimes they played cards.

"How's the job?" Quinn prodded one chilly September night, when Faron was even more quiet than usual.

"Fine." Faron bit into a piece of Mary's apple pie, savoring the thin buttery crust and tart apples. "Mmm. Tell Mary this pie is delicious."

"I'll will, although you could tell her yourself. Just pick up the phone."

Faron blushed. "I know. I'll call." He took another big bite of pie.

Quinn smiled. No matter what was troubling Faron he always had a good appetite for Mary's cooking.

They were playing gin rummy and Quinn showed his cards. "Sorry, beat you again." He used both hands to gather up all the cards and reshuffle them. "Guess Captain Boyd thinks you're doing okay, since I haven't heard from him lately." He dealt ten cards to each of them.

Faron studied his hand intently. "I guess."

Quinn gave up on the small talk and concentrated on the game. The light in the kitchen gradually changed from golden to blue-gray dusk and Quinn felt a disturbed sadness settle around them with the shadows.

The kitchen walls were still covered with the same flowered wallpaper that had been there when Alison was alive, and her mother before her. Quinn looked at Faron and, for a brief moment, saw the same forlorn boy with sticky fingers who—so many years ago—had taken nothing from this house but an electric fan and a box of moths. He had, it now seemed to Quinn, returned with even less.

Quinn started to reach for the jack of hearts Faron discarded but changed his mind. Maybe it was time to let him win.

CHAPTER 13

"HOW LONG you been a sternman now? About a year?" Billy Gallager didn't bother with a spoon, just poured sugar straight from the glass dispenser into his coffee.

It was a crummy morning and the gang couldn't go out, so they crammed into Scuppers, talking shop over a leisurely breakfast.

Billy was a lot nicer to Faron since graduating from high school. Now there were more important things to worry about than teasing or competing for girls. Billy was married and worked for his father part-time at the boatyard. He filled in the rest of the week on another man's boat.

"It'll be a year in August, I think," Faron answered. He didn't keep close track of time. All he knew was he didn't like living in his old house. The long nights alone on Puddle Cove seemed darker than anywhere else on the island.

He wasn't sure why, but he had always resisted the kindness the Gages showed him, especially from Mary. Now he missed living with them. There were times he was bursting to tell them that he wanted to come back. It may have only been a year, but it felt longer.

"Pass the cream, will you?" Billy took off the baseball cap he was wearing and put it on the window ledge. "You still drawing those butterflies—or whatever they are?" He didn't say it unkindly, but like he was really interested.

Faron appreciated Billy's good-natured question. "Not much. I don't have a lot of time, what with the ferry ride back and forth to the mainland and the long days on the boat."

"Boy, you can say that again. Out of the sack at four A.M.—what a bitch. At least we're in at a decent hour though."

"Yeah. That part's good." Faron liked commiserating this way. It made up for all the things Billy used to say about his mother when they were kids.

Quinn joined them just as Faron was saying, ". . . I like the ferry ride . . ." Quinn winced. Faron made the crossing the same way he did as a child—standing on the foredeck hanging onto the railing with his eyes closed, letting the full force of the wind muffle any other sound. But Billy probably already knew that. Word gets around.

"Hi, Quinn. What's the matter—church too quiet for you?" Billy asked when Quinn sat down.

"Something like that." Quinn knew Billy had been a bully in school, but if Faron could forgive him, so could he. Besides, these days, the guy was just plain likeable.

Quinn snuck a proud glance at Faron. The face he saw was not only handsome, but smiling. He had to hand it to him—in spite of some strange behavior, the boy had an engaging presence. No wonder all the girls liked him—that, and the drawing. They were always hovering around trying to get him to sketch their portraits. Sitting there watching the two young men laugh and talk, Quinn had a feeling the worst was over.

CHAPTER 14

EARLY ON a breezy summer morning, in the purple light before the sun came up over the sleepy island, Mabel Pinkham heard rabbits screaming. She shoved her arms into a sweater, grabbed her shotgun, and got outside just in time to see a fox ravaging a rabbit's nest that she knew was in the ankle-high grass on the other side of her compost pile, for all the world to see. Mabel always marveled at the logic of rabbits: hiding in plain sight. They didn't count on their enemies trotting out into the open. But a fox—that's another thing.

The bushy-tailed bandit snapped the neck of the last terrified baby rabbit and ran off into the woods before Mabel could lift the twelve-gauge to her shoulder and take aim.

"Tarnation!" Mable broke open her gun and left the shell in the chamber. Just before turning to amble back inside the house to phone Sheriff Paisley, she caught a glimpse of a man parting some thick weeds near the burrow, watching.

"Sheriff'll be there quick as he can, Mabel," Zelly Sprague said when she answered the desk phone at the station.

But Alden took his time. He was used to these calls from Mabel, an elderly widow who prayed for disaster so she could summon help, just for the company. In the old days he used to hightail it out to her place, concerned for the safety of someone so sweet and helpless. But he soon learned she wasn't all that helpless—or sweet—the day she lambasted him for getting there too late.

"Had to take care of it myself!" she'd admonished him, holding up the bloody remains of a large rat she'd whacked with the business end of a hoe. "Thanks for nothing."

Today, he finished his breakfast before getting into his patrol car and heading over to Mabel's to take a report and get a description of the intruder—something about rabbits and a man—Zelly had told him when she called him on his car radio.

"Guess it's just as well I didn't shoot," Mabel said when Alden showed up. She sat in a rocker on her porch, cradling the shotgun in the crook of her arm. Box of shells at her feet. "I think it was the boy. Old man Goss's great-grandson. Takes right after him, in the good looks department," she added wistfully.

Alden was confused. "Faron Goss? He killed the rabbits?"

"No," Mabel growled impatiently. "Of course not. The fox killed the rabbits. The boy was just standing there, ninny!"

Alden took a deep breath. To be sure, Mabel was the only person on the island who could get away with talking to him like that—well, except maybe for his brother's wife, Betsy, who wears the trousers in the family.

It was clear that he'd run over here on a wild goose chase. He spent a few more minutes listening politely as Mabel reminisced about Zed Goss, but when she began describing one particular summer night out on the Point, Alden cut her short. That was one image he didn't want to be stuck with. He tipped his hat and said goodbye. "I'll stop by later, Mabel, if need be."

Alden headed toward Puddle Cove driving faster than he ought to, but then caught himself and eased his foot off the accelerator. "I shouldn't be so hard on Mabel," he announced to no one, indulging in his habit of talking aloud to himself while driving. "Who knows? That could be me someday. Old and lonely."

Just before the Puddle Cove Bridge, he slowed the cruiser to make the turn down a dirt road leading to the Goss place. He didn't like involving Faron in this. The poor kid was probably just out on one of his long nature walks. Everyone knew about those. He didn't do it as much now that he had a job on the mainland, but when he was younger it wasn't unusual to see him walking along Sheepscot or one of the side roads—or through someone's backyard—carrying a cigar box and a net. But since Mabel had insisted on filing a formal trespassing complaint, Alden had to go through the motions of checking it out.

When he got to Faron's house, he parked the patrol car and laughed out loud, slapping his knee with one hand. "That Mabel's really something! I bet she's just trying to get a better look at Zed's great-grandson, by way of lodging a complaint against him."

Alden shook his head and snickered, then put on his hat and got out of the car, slamming the door behind him. The morning breeze had a tangy, piney scent that he never got tired of.

He didn't see Faron's Chevy, but he climbed the back steps to the house anyway and knocked on the screen door, cursing when several dead insects came loose and landed on his polished black shoes.

Just as he thought. There was no one home.

Alden looked at his watch. It was nearly seven. The annual July Fourth parade was due to start at ten. It was going to be a busy day. He and his deputy, Keith Cyr, would have their hands full with traffic, and illegal fireworks—not to mention the drinking. Beer would flow all day, and then some.

"Oh, what the hell," Alden said out loud, thumping the hood of his car with his palms. "It's only one day a year."

It was true. Thanks to Menhaden Island's northerly location in the Gulf of Maine, frequent foul weather, and a long ferry crossing, the island isn't usually overrun with tourists, except on the Fourth of July, when they came in droves. He wasn't looking forward to it, but by tomorrow it would be over.

Walking back to his car, Alden took off his hat and wiped his sweaty brow. It was already a hot one. He got in the cruiser and started it up. Mabel's complaint about Faron could wait. He wasn't driving all over the island because the kid trespassed and got a look at a brood of rabbits. He backed out of the driveway and headed over to Eileen's. He'd call Quinn from there to find out if he knew where Faron was, and after that he'd hook up with the deputy and make sure the parade route was squared away.

Eileen's was mobbed. There was no place to sit so Alden ordered a slice of raisin-apple pie and a large sweet and light coffee to go. He put in the call to Quinn while he waited for his order but there was no answer. It took him about two minutes to down the pie out in the parking lot, but he stayed another twenty, nursing the coffee and chitchatting with the other customers who were coming and going. Many of them had unfamiliar accents. There were more and more out-of-staters coming to the damn parade every year and he didn't much care for them, especially the New Yorkers, who seemed to think Manhattan was the only island inhabited by intelligent life.

At eight o'clock, Alden went to meet Keith Cyr at the sheriff's office. Zelly Sprague was there, too, dressed in her usual attire: a short-sleeved plaid shirt and a pair of tan, lightweight men's slacks. Her long bleached-blond hair was pulled back in a ponytail that stretched her facial skin taut, giving the appearance of an instant facelift. Zelly was Alden's secretary, confidant, dispatcher, adviser-of-all-things-female, and anything else you could think of. He didn't know what he'd do without her.

She was sitting behind her desk, grinding out a cigarette in an ashtray overflowing with lipstick-coated filter tips.

"Morning, Zelly. Morning, Keith," Alden said, heading straight for the bathroom.

"Good morning to you too," Zelly called out as Alden squeezed by her desk. "Wonder what his hurry is?" she said to Keith.

"Don't know." Keith licked an envelope and sealed it. "Too much of Eileen's pie, most likely."

Zelly laughed. "Too much pie? Who, him? Why, everyone on Menhaden knows the sheriff's got a cast-iron stomach."

"I heard that, Zelly!" Alden came out of the bathroom, drying his hands with a paper towel. He looked across the room at Keith. "And for your information, I only had one slice."

"Maybe sometime you'll bring back some for me," Zelly teased, shoving a folder into the file cabinet.

Alden chucked the wadded paper towel into the trash and patted Zelly's broad shoulders. "Maybe one day I will, Zelly. In the meantime, here's a report I just took from Mabel Pinkham. Type it up for me, will you? Me and Keith'll be down at Harbor Street monitoring the festivities."

Zelly spun her chair around, facing Alden. She took the slip of paper from him and dropped it in a tray to the left of the phone. "Sure, boss. I'll get right on this—later. Have fun!"

Harbor Street was crowded. Alden couldn't remember when he'd seen this many people in town. Gets worse every year. Tourists. All here for the July Fourth celebration. He remembered the rabbits and scanned the crowd for Quinn or Faron, but didn't see either of them.

"Keith, why don't you go down to the other end of town? No point in both of us standing in the same spot." Alden preferred patrolling alone, anyway, rather than with Keith, who tended to be a chatterbox.

"What about the thing with Faron? Want me to apprehend him?"

It was all Alden could do not to laugh. *Apprehend him?* Keith was a wonderful fellow. Loyal as all get out, and followed orders precisely, but he could also be the epitome of a small town cop: one hand on the holster, always on the lookout for the bad guys.

"No. Just let him be. Mabel's making a mountain out of a molehill."

"Don't you mean making a mountain out of a rabbit's nest?" Keith cracked up at his own bad joke before Alden even had a chance to scowl.

Alden rolled his eyes. That was another thing about Keith—his stupid sense of humor. Yeah, there was the occasional funny pun, but most of them were duds. "Go on, get out of here." Alden raised a foot to give Keith a kick in the behind but the deputy tucked in his rear end and scooted out of reach, doubling over with laughter.

When he was alone, Alden surveyed the crowd one more time. No sign of Faron. Minutes later he forgot all about it.

The parade got underway at eleven, an hour behind schedule. It was over by noon and at twelve twenty the photographer from the *Island News* was taking pictures of the newly crowned Lobster Queen for the newspaper's centerfold. She was sixteen—a long-legged, unblemished blonde who accepted the attention with a squealing giddiness not uncommon for girls of her age.

"Isn't she a pretty little thing?" her proud family and friends exclaimed. "The judges made the right choice!" they boasted.

The locals didn't agree. They looked on with tongues held between their teeth. The new Lobster Queen wasn't from here. She was a transplant.

"There's a first time for everything," someone muttered to Alden as he passed by.

Later, in the evening, people gathered at the Point for the annual fireworks display. They lounged in beach chairs and spread out blankets on the ground to watch the colorful bursts of fireworks shoot up over the water. Rockets whistled and exploded, lighting up the ocean and the faces of spectators. The Lobster Queen sat in a place of honor high atop one of the lifeguard chairs, shrieking with her girlfriends at each booming barrage.

The next morning, in her family's rambling oceanfront home out on the Point, the Lobster Queen didn't come down for the special celebratory breakfast her mother prepared. When her father went upstairs to his daughter's room to see if she was awake, she wasn't there. The window was wide open, chintz curtain fluttering softly in the balmy breeze. The floor was littered with flies, alive and buzzing around a putrid piece of decayed meat in a cracked glass jar that was labeled, 'Elderberry Jam.'

CHAPTER 15

THE TIRES on Faron's secondhand car hummed evenly and the old blue Chevy seemed to drive itself while he enjoyed the warmth of the morning sun beaming through the windshield.

If you looked to the east, you could see where the sky stretched out and paled, the way it does when it's headed for the ocean. The roadside was lined with tall, scraggly pine trees, set firmly in mossy soil between mica-studded rocks that glittered in the cloudless light. Loose stones flew up and clanged against the salt-corroded metal of the undercarriage as the car turned off the highway and cut a bumpy path through Clayton Jewett's sweet corn, toward a clover field and a short row of beekeeper's hives.

The Lobster Queen, bound and gagged in the trunk, let out a few muffled cries, which made Faron think of the rabbits squealing in the stalking shadow of the fox in Mabel Pinkham's yard.

Unseen from the road, he stopped the car and got out. He unlocked the trunk and hauled the dismayed, leggy girl to the ground, dragging her closer to the hives. He pulled off his shirt and unzipped his pants, letting them drop to his ankles, thinking of all the times he had run naked through these fields. Fields full of bees. He got caught once, when he was a little boy, but he had kept doing it and no one ever knew after that first time. He wasn't sure why, but each time he was stung it became easier to bear the pain, and the hum of the bees silenced everything else.

Foraging honeybees flew around Faron's head as he knelt towards the struggling girl. He ripped the tape off her mouth and let her scream. She nearly choked on an angry bee. She was saying something he couldn't understand, but it didn't matter anymore. Soon he wouldn't be able to hear her over the buzzing, and nothing would ever feel better than this, stingers and all.

The Ocean Meadows farmhouse sat on a hill overlooking the corn and clover fields. Clayton Jewett was just sitting down on his front porch with a tall glass of iced tea when he saw the rusty blue car cut through the corn and into the clover, on his land. It wasn't unusual for teenagers to drive into his fields at night to get drunk and swap spit, but not in broad daylight. Didn't seem right, so he called the sheriff.

"Oh, the sheriff's nearby to your place," Zelly said to Clayton, when she answered the phone at the police station. "Called in from Eileen's, not two minutes ago. Having his breakfast."

When Alden Paisley got the radio call, he was in Eileen's parking lot. He had just downed two aspirin, still trying to clear his head from last night's festivities—he'd stopped off at Scuppers after his shift and had a few.

He was picking his teeth with a peppermint-flavored toothpick and reaching for the glinting chrome handle on the door of his patrol car when he heard Zelly's garbled voice coming over the radio.

"Clayton Jewett just called. Seen someone drive into his fields. Going like stink."

"I'm on my way," Alden said into the radio.

The field wasn't too far from Eileen's, a straight run along East Sheepscot. When Alden got there, the sunburned farmer was standing on the shoulder of the road, pointing to the freshly made gash in the tall corn, flattened by the blue car.

"It's the Goss boy, I think. His car, anyway . . . in my field!" Clayton shouted toward the cruiser as it turned off the road, spewing a cloud of dust and gravel into his face.

Alden followed the broken corn, rolling up his windows to keep out the airborne dirt, bugs, and bits of stalk. He hadn't driven too far when he came out of the corn and into an open, sunny clover field. About one hundred yards in front of him he saw a screaming girl, running and waving her hands wildly through the air. He drove over to her and stopped the car.

He recognized her right away. It was the girl from the parade—the Lobster Queen. He'd seen her yesterday while he was directing traffic and she was riding atop a gaudy float, waving to the crowd, and again later, on the beach, where she was gawking at the fireworks with her girlfriends.

Now here was the same girl, hysterical, and with strips of duct tape dangling from her wrists, swatting at a sparse halo of angry bees. Alden immediately felt a pang of regret when he thought back to the widow Pinkham and her rabbits—if only he had kept looking for Faron, this might not have happened.

"What the hell am I talking about?" he exclaimed aloud, smacking the steering wheel with his hands. "Whatever's happening here has nothing to do with Mabel's rabbits."

Alden jumped out of the patrol car, grabbed an emergency blanket from the trunk, and wrapped the girl in it. He helped her into the backseat so she could lie down. As far as he could tell, she wasn't in bad shape. He didn't see any blood, only red lumps—bee stings. He rummaged through the glove compartment for an EpiPen and jabbed her in the thigh, just in case, then got on the radio and called Zelly for an ambulance, and his deputy.

"Just about to call you," Zelly said through the squelch. "The parents phoned it in. They went up to their daughter's bedroom and she wasn't there. Is it her?"

"It's her all right, and Faron Goss. See if you can find Father Gage. Have him get over to the station and wait for me."

Sheriff Paisley signed off and hung the microphone back on its hook.

He didn't bother asking the girl what happened, he'd write his report later. He left her whimpering in the backseat and walked toward the blue car. It was Faron's, all right. Used to be Quinn's until he gave it to the boy and got himself the big Suburban.

The hives were set out side by side. Stan, the farmer's son, had also seen what was happening and rushed across the field in his pickup to get control of the agitated bees. He wore a netted helmet and was gently prying open the top of one of the wooden boxes with his hive tool, the other hand puffing smoke from a metal can. The smoke made the bees gorge on honey, and that calmed them. It also prevented them from releasing pheromones as an alarm signal. The last thing Stan needed was reinforcements. Usually, the smoked ones didn't sting. It's the ones outside the hive you had to worry about.

"Faron's in the car," Stan said when he saw Alden approach. "Move slow. You'll be fine. There're just a few mad ones. If one lands on you, let it alone."

"Okay." But Alden didn't listen. A bee landed on the underside of his hat brim and hung upside down. He couldn't help it—he lifted the hat and knocked the bee off, frantically waving it away with both hands when it doubled back toward his face.

"Stop doing that!" Stan yelled. "You'll get them all pissed off if you jump around like that!"

Alden froze. Embarrassed. Sure enough, the bee lost interest in him once he was still. He turned his attention back to Faron, much less afraid of him than the bees. He actually felt sorry for the boy. He had known him a long time—since the snowy day the kid was born. Had known his mother, Alison, too—the same way a lot of other men had. She really wasn't as bad as the women around here would have you believe—just lonely. She was on the quiet side, even when she was drinking. Drunk or sober, she was gorgeous, which Alden figured was the real reason the island wives hadn't liked her. They would have preferred if she'd taken after her mother, who was uncomely in every way.

"The good-looks gene must have skipped a generation," women used to say about Alison's mother. "What a sorry sight."

But Alison took after her grandfather, who had every female on the island chasing after him. Faron was the same way, handsome and sought after, although he didn't seem aware of it.

Alden remembered the day Faron was born. It was during one of the worst snow storms they'd ever seen on the island. He'd been on duty when the road crew brought Alison and her newborn son to the hospital.

He had to file a report and sat in the hospital lobby with the men who found her, jotting down details of the rescue. Afterwards, when Alison was well rested and awake, he went down the corridor to her room to see her and the baby. Asked a few questions.

Weeks later, after another heavy snow, Alison moseyed by the sheriff's office, giving him a long sultry stare through the condensation on the plate glass window.

"Thanks," was all she said when she opened the door and stood there with her loosely bundled infant in her arms.

In spite of the frigid air blowing in through the open door, Alden had broken into a sweat. "I'm not the one who rescued you," he'd said, wondering if a baby that young should be out in such cold weather. "It was the guys from Public Works."

She gave him a look that went right through him, under his skin, deep to the bones. "I'm not interested in them."

Near the end of his shift that night he drove over to her place, carefully following the icy road from town. He pulled into her driveway and turned off the cruiser's headlights and radioed Keith, who was working late at the station, trying to catch up on all the paperwork he'd let slide.

"I'm on Shore Road. All's quiet so I'm heading home a little early," Alden lied.

He sat for a moment, deciphering Keith's reply through the radio static, then got out of the warm car and made his way across the unshoveled path that led to Alison's back porch.

"Can't come in through the front," she'd said when he called earlier. "Snow's drifted. Blocking the way."

She answered the backdoor on the second knock. The wind was up and her hand-me-down house rattled as they stood in the small, unlit kitchen.

"Take off your coat. Want a beer? Wine?"

"Beer. Please." He rubbed his cold hands together.

Alison opened the refrigerator and the interior light illuminated her. She was thin, even after giving birth. Her cheap clothes were too large, but she was beautiful.

They sat in the dark, drinking, not talking, radiators clanking in the well-heated silence. Halfway through his beer Alden's eyes adjusted to the dark. On his second bottle he said, "I'm not the marrying kind. Just want you to know that."

Alison took a long swig of beer and wiped her upper lip. "Neither am I," she said. "But since there's no secrets on this island, we already know that about each other, don't we?" She got up with her drink and walked away. "Are you coming?" she called, minutes later, from her bedroom.

He found her sitting on the edge of the bed, already undressed. A wedge of moonlight blazed in through a dirty window and he could see her breasts, swollen with milk. She motioned him toward the bed.

He stripped quickly.

From the next room, Faron cried softly, then louder.

"Shouldn't you go feed him or something?"

"He can wait."

But the baby kept crying until she finally gave in and went to him. He was already nursing when she carried him back into her bedroom and sat down on the bed next to Alden.

"Here," Alison said, shifting the infant in such a way that she could put her other breast against Alden's lips.

He'd been surprised by the sweet, creamy taste of breast milk. Never forgotten it.

They made love quickly, with Faron at the foot of the bed.

Alden snuck away before sunrise, feeling guilty. Not for what he did, but for doing it with the baby a leg's length away.

He confided in his brother days later.

"Betsy says Alison's not fit to be a mother—just gives the kid the tit so she can save on milk money and spend it on booze," Emmett said.

Alden never slept with Alison again, but he remained friendly. Sometimes he gave her a lift in his patrol car, or carried groceries to her skiff when she rowed across the cove from her house to the general store. And he always had a special feeling for the boy.

Each year at Christmastime he bought presents for Faron and delivered them to Alison's house, along with a tree. She watched him decorate it with bulbs and tinsel, a beer in her hand, embarrassed by the charity, but with a faint look of childlike wonder in her eyes.

Now, here was the same boy, nearly twenty years later, a young man. Alden wasn't nervous as he approached Faron's car—nothing to be afraid of. As far as he was concerned, Faron was still a helpless boy at the end of the bed. In fact Alden was having a hard time believing the kid would be capable of harming anyone, but that's sure what it looked like.

Faron sat in his car with the windows rolled up. There were still a few bees walking across the glass. He was only partially dressed—in shoes, socks, underwear, and unzipped trousers. His shirt lay in a heap near the sheriff's feet, covered with sluggish, smoke-calmed bees. The trunk of the car was open.

When Alden tapped on the window to get Faron's attention, the bees scattered, and one went straight for his hand and stung him before he could brush it off. A bright red welt rose on one of his knuckles. He stayed as still as possible, like Stan said. He could hear the blare of the ambulance siren getting closer.

Faron seemed dazed.

"Follow me," Alden mouthed through the glass.

Alden walked slowly back to his car, sucking on his bee-stung hand.

Deputy Cyr was already on the scene, checking on the girl. He didn't look up when Alden approached but asked, "What's going on?"

Alden looked at the girl, wondering the same thing. "Wouldn't I like to know?" He reconsidered asking her right then and there, but when he saw the flashing red lights of the ambulance making its way through the cornfield, he decided to wait.

Faron shook the bees out of his shirt and watched the smoky insects drop to the ground in a straight line, like heavy, fuzzy pellets. He finished dressing and drove over to the other vehicles, idling alongside them. There were still some disoriented bees staggering across the inside of his windshield. This time he rolled the window down when the sheriff spoke to him.

"Faron, follow Keith into town," Alden said sternly, "I'm going to the hospital with the ambulance. You wait at the station. We'll talk later."

Faron looked scared.

Alden's voice took on a gentler tone. "Quinn should be there soon. Don't worry."

CHAPTER 16

Jarry Gallager's redheaded wife, Brenda, was pulling ambulance duty. She applied cold compresses to the girl's bee stings to make her more comfortable.

"Clyde! Can't you make this thing go any faster?" Brenda shouted to the driver.

"I'd like to see you do any better, Brenda!"

Anyone who's available drives the ambulance, and today it was Clyde Beaudry's turn. He was doing his best, clutching the wheel as he drove through Jewett's bumpy cornfield, trying to follow the same rut he drove in on. Once he hit the paved road he sped up to twenty miles over the speed limit, lights flashing and siren blasting.

Alden followed them, scraping the underside of his rear fender as he drove onto the shoulder of East Sheepscot and turned towards town. He looked in his rearview mirror and saw Keith driving up onto the pavement, with Faron following closely behind.

Doc Batch was waiting for them at the hospital, already assured by the girl's parents that she didn't have an allergy to bees. He examined her all over and shot her up with antihistamines to ease any discomfort from the stings. Told her parents she might have a headache and flu-like symptoms later, from the stings to the head.

"Nothing to worry about. You can take her home whenever the sheriff says it's okay." He didn't mention their daughter's high blood alcohol level.

Her mother and father weren't happy. They wanted to leave right away. "What's the point of questions, Sheriff?" they asked Alden when he introduced himself. "We all know what happened. Can't we do this another time?"

Alden didn't particularly like these people but he tried not to show it. "Let's do it now," he said patiently, "that way I won't have to bother you later."

They sat in a small alcove near the emergency room. The girl was calmer than before. Drowsy from the antihistamines. "Mom," she said, sleepily, "it's not a big deal." She stretched her arms over her head. "He let me go."

Alden looked surprised. "What do you mean? You seemed pretty scared when I found you."

"Don't say anything else." Her father took her gently by the elbow and tried lifting her out of her seat, but her knees buckled.

"I wasn't scared of him—just the bees." She could barely keep her eyes open.

Alden took a pad out of his chest pocket and leaned on a small table to take notes. His interest piqued.

The girl's father watched him write. "Come on, Sheriff," he groaned. "She doesn't know what she's saying. She's all drugged up. You're not going to let him go, are you? He took her. He climbed through her bedroom window and took her!"

The Lobster Queen yawned, sending a spray of spittle into her mother's face. Her eyelids drooped. Her face and arms were speckled with bee bites. She scratched at a spot on her neck. "He didn't take me, Dad," she whined.

The three adults looked at each other.

The stunned father flashed an angry look at his daughter. "What?" he asked, through clenched teeth.

She yawned again and dropped her head so her chin rested on her chest, then slouched in the chair. "I'm tired, Mom. It was the bees that made me run, not Faron."

Her mother pulled her close, kissed her forehead. "What do you mean . . . he didn't take you?"

Her daughter shrugged, not seeming to understand the trouble she and Faron were in. "We planned it. Wanted to make it look like he kidnapped me. We drank some beers first. It was my idea." Her voice was husky. She giggled. "He's so cute."

Alden was getting it all down, secretly relieved to hear this strange stunt was the girl's idea and not Faron's. His heart raced. This was getting interesting. "Why?" he asked the sleepy girl, trying to keep his voice even.

"Huh?"

"Why did you and Faron do this?"

The girl yawned widely, showing a mouthful of white teeth. She slumped lower in the chair. "I did it so Mom and Dad would worry about me." Her speech was slurred but Alden understood every word. She looked at her parents with a coy smile. "I wanted you to feel sorry for me so you'd buy me that car . . . you know . . . the red one?"

The mix of antihistamines and alcohol were acting like a truth serum. Alden couldn't believe what he was hearing. But then again, these folks weren't islanders. Moved up here from a toney New York suburb only two years ago. Thought it was "quaint," he overheard the wife say one day while he was standing behind her in line at the Post Office. She was some kind of consultant—didn't matter what kind, they all made too much money for doing nothing, in his opinion. The husband was on early retirement from a large financial firm. Lots of dough between the two of them. Bought the biggest house on Menhaden and spent a fortune making it even bigger. Kept the island carpenters busy for a year.

Alden heard a rumor that the girl was trouble and the parents figured this would be a better place for her to attend high school. He stared at the groggy girl. Seems it might have been true—the trouble part.

But he couldn't help wondering who was more at fault, her or the parents. From everything he knew, they gave her a free rein—only sixteen and allowed to hang out in town all hours of the night, or ride the ferry to Willisport whenever she felt like it.

Come to think of it, Alden had seen her talking with Faron one day last week: the both of them standing outside Scuppers. She was holding a cigarette—an exaggerated gesture like a movie star. He had thought it odd to see them together since Faron was older than she was, although you wouldn't know that looking at her. The little lady was quite filled out, and flaunted it.

Alden asked the woozy girl another question, more out of curiosity than anything: "Is Faron your boyfriend?"

Her mother was aghast. "What? She's just a ch-ch-ild," she stammered. "She couldn't possibly . . ."

Her daughter interrupted, wide-awake for a brief moment. "No!" She seemed horrified by the sheriff's question. "He's not my boyfriend. It's just that he's always friendly when I see him in town and he has a car . . . even if it is a wreck. He's nice, and good-looking. All the girls at school think so too. Once, he drew my picture. He buys me cigarettes and beer, so I figured he'd help me out."

Her old man looked like he was going to retch. Alden guessed the 'cigarettes and beer' came as a surprise. "How did you plan it?" Alden asked, "Did you know Faron would lock you in the trunk?"

The worn-out girl shook her head. "No. Not really. I guess he just did that to make it look good."

Alden's free hand went to his chin, and then dropped to

his lap. Drummed his fingers on his knee. "Did you climb in yourself?"

"No. He picked me up and put me in . . . after he taped up my mouth and hands." She smirked at her father. "I knew he was going to do that—the taping part. I gave him the duct tape." She tried to focus on Alden but her eyes kept closing. "I took it from Daddy's workshop. But I didn't know about the trunk or the bees."

"I see." Alden kept writing.

The girl's father sat quietly with his head in his hands, rocking slowly back and forth.

"Were you frightened in the trunk?" Alden asked.

"Yeah. A little. It was dark and hard to breathe. But then . . . it seemed like we didn't drive very far and he took me out. Besides, I knew it wasn't for real."

"Then what?" Alden's bee stung hand was throbbing.

"He pushed me down on the ground and took off his shirt. Then he took some of the tape off my hands and mouth and I started screaming, because a bee stung me—I almost swallowed one—and I yelled at him that I changed my mind. That's when he let me go . . . not at first, but the second time I said I changed my mind, he did."

"Changed your mind about what? Being kidnapped?"

"No." The girl yawned again, rubbing her watery eyes, then said, matter-of-factly, "About having sex. I told him we could have sex if he fake-kidnapped me."

"Okay, that's it!" The father stood and stormed out of the room, his face red with rage.

Her mother cringed and sobbed.

In spite of not liking them, Alden felt sorry for them. Even though he didn't have a kid of his own, he knew something like this must be tough on a parent.

He looked at the sting-covered girl. She was about to fall over so he held her shoulders to steady her. When she was vertical he let go, keeping his hands cupped at her elbows, just in case. Then her head flopped backwards over the top of the chair and she fell sound asleep, snoring lightly, mouth open. Her mother stopped crying and stared at her grass-stained daughter as though she were a stranger.

Alden closed his notepad and put it and the stubby pencil back in his shirt pocket. He stood up slowly, scratching the welt on his hand, looking at the disheveled girl and thinking—*Who would have ever thought there'd be a Lobster Queen from away?*

On the way over to the police station Faron thought about what it would be like to escape—to board the ferry to the mainland and keep going. Except for Willisport and Portland, and an occasional trip with Quinn and Mary to visit their relatives, he'd never been anywhere other than the island. Maybe now was a good time to go somewhere new. But he didn't. He drove dutifully behind the deputy, following him into the dirt parking lot behind the station.

He stopped alongside the police car and turned off the Chevy's engine, leaving all the windows down so any remaining bees could find their way out.

Deputy Cyr yanked the handle on Faron's car door and held it open. "Come on, let's go."

Quinn was already inside waiting for them. He grabbed Faron by the arm and forced him into a creaky wooden chair near the front desk.

"Why, Faron?" he asked. "What in the world were you thinking?"

Faron said nothing. Just sat in the chair, hands folded in his lap, eyes cast downward.

Quinn inched closer, thought he smelled liquor on Faron's breath. "First I get a call that you were snooping around Mabel Pinkham's place yesterday, and now this. Zelly said you were running off with a sixteen-year-old girl. Is that true?"

Faron lowered his head further, rubbed a bee sting on his arm.

"Faron, look at me!" Quinn was angrier than he'd ever been—at least angrier than Zelly Sprague had ever seen him, and she was taking it all in, shuffling papers at her desk and pretending not to listen.

"No," Faron whispered. "It's not true."

Quinn stopped talking and peered at the young man sitting next to him, wondering if any of the kindness he and Mary had shown him over the years would ever make a difference. It didn't look that way. "Okay. I guess when Alden gets here the three of us can talk it through." He rested his hand on Faron's for a moment. "Whatever it is, I'll do anything I can to help you."

Quinn inhaled some deep breaths to calm himself. He noticed a slow-moving bee, hung over from the smoke, crawling through Faron's mussed hair. When he tried knocking it away it stung him. The nerve endings in his fingertip felt like they were on fire. He shook his hand until the bee fell onto the floor. It couldn't fly, just buzzed helplessly on its side, turning in frantic circles at their feet while Quinn and Faron looked on.

That's how Alden Paisley found them when he came through the door—hunched over watching the bee. Quinn had the tip of his stung finger in his mouth. A bead of sweat rolled off his face and left a dark wet spot on the dusty wooden floor.

Alden hung his hat on the coatrack and walked over to them. He stood there quietly for a moment, looking down at the bee, then let out an exaggerated sigh and said, "Go home, Quinn. Take Faron with you—not to Puddle Cove, to your place. We'll do this tomorrow."

CHAPTER 17

IN THE MORNING a thick mist wrapped the island and fishermen tinkered in their sheds, waiting for the fog to lift. It had rained all night, and when Mary Gage walked around the side of the rectory, stooping to pick blueberries for breakfast, rainwater rolled under her cuffs and over the loose edges of her rubber boots.

She was at the kitchen sink emptying the berries into a strainer when Faron came downstairs. He looked like he hadn't slept much.

She forced a sunny greeting. "Good morning. Hungry?"

"A little."

Mary spooned some berries into a bowl of cereal and set it down in front of him. "Try eating something. It'll make you feel better. There're biscuits in the oven."

"Smells great in here," Quinn said, also trying to sound cheerful as he barreled in through the back door from his morning walk and got a whiff of the biscuits. He'd been up for several hours, unable to sleep.

A pot of coffee percolated on the stove. When it was done, he helped himself to a cup and sat down next to Faron. Mary brought over the hot biscuits and two more bowls of cereal and joined them. After an awkward attempt at conversation, the three of them ate in silence, listening to rain drip off the gutters.

When Quinn and Faron arrived at the police station, Alden was sitting at his desk, slumped over a grease-stained paper bag, his cheeks full of cheese danish.

"Morning," he mumbled through a mouthful, motioning for them both to sit.

He stuffed the last of his breakfast into his mouth, crumpled up the bag, and tossed it into the trash can. He brushed stray crumbs off his desk with the palm of his hand.

"Listen," he said, sucking bits of pastry from his teeth, "I talked to the girl and her parents yesterday." He looked at Quinn. "Did Faron tell you everything?"

"He said the girl planned it. Wanted her parents to buy her a car."

"That's about it." Alden swiveled in his chair and poured himself a cup of steaming coffee from the pot behind his desk. Added cream and heaped in sugar. Took a short noisy sip and turned to face Faron. "Why'd you do such a stupid thing?"

Faron shrugged. "I don't know. I just did. And the bees . . ."

Alden put his hand up as if he was stopping traffic. "Enough with the bees—you need a lawyer." He looked at Quinn. "You know someone, right?"

Quinn nodded. "My old college friend on the mainland. The same one who helped us after Faron's mother died."

Alden furrowed his brow, thinking hard. "I vaguely remember. What was his name?"

"Standish. Nye Standish."

"That's right. That's the guy. I hear he's good. Quite a character, as I recall. Get ahold of him. I've got to keep Faron here, for now. I'll take fingerprints, start things rolling. Don't worry, that lawyer friend of yours will straighten this out."

There wasn't a jail cell in the police station, just a small room that locked from the outside. There were two single beds in it, where Alden let the occasional drunk and disorderly sleep it off. The Overnight Room, they called it.

Alden shuffled some papers and tilted back in his chair. He burped pastry up his gullet and cleared his throat. "We'll keep you comfortable here, Faron, and I'll do what I can to keep you out of the county lockup, but I'm not making any promises. It ain't what it used to be, if you know what I mean.

"I got people from the outside looking over my shoulder these days, especially since the girl's family isn't from here. Good news is, the parents don't want things to get out of hand. They're embarrassed about this nonsense. Asked me to keep it quiet. That'll work in your favor."

Quinn stood and offered the sheriff his hand. "Thanks, Alden. I'll call the lawyer. Is it okay for Mary to drop by later and bring some things for Faron?"

Alden nodded. "No problem. She can come anytime. Someone'll be here. Let me know if that lawyer can see you today and I'll get Hodie to give you a ride over on his boat, since this is official business, more or less."

It was drizzling steadily when Quinn got home. Except for a foghorn sounding its warning, and a light patter of rain on the roof, he thought it seemed unusually quiet. Maybe because the birds were still hiding from the weather, he thought. He ran up the back steps into the mudroom and took off his wet jacket and shoes and walked across the tiled floor in his damp socks.

Mary was at the kitchen counter picking stems off the remaining berries. "How did it go?"

Quinn pulled out a chair and sat. He was tired. Beyond tired—exhausted. "Alden had no choice but to keep him at the station. A formality. No way around it. The parents were insistent, even though the girl was complicit. Alden says it'll work out later. For now, he's trying to hush things up."

Mary's expression indicated that made sense. "Good. I would think the parents don't want things getting around either, especially since their daughter instigated everything."

"You're right. They said as much to Alden." Quinn shivered.

"Cold?"

"A little."

"You should get out of those wet clothes."

"I will. First I have to call Nye Standish. You remember him—the lawyer in Willisport?"

Mary sat at the table. "Of course I remember. He's the one who did all the legal work when Alison died."

"I'm hoping he can get us out of this mess," Quinn said.

"I hope so too." Mary watched a whippoorwill shake water off its wings below the eave outside their kitchen window. She tried picturing Faron as a small boy, but she couldn't get past the day she found pieces of her cat in a jar under his bed.

Quinn took Mary's hand in his. "Thank you. I know it hasn't always been easy on you—and now this. I hope you know how much I appreciate all you've done, and I know Faron does, too, even if he doesn't always show it."

There was a time when the touch of her husband's hand made everything all right, but this morning, for the first time in their married life, it didn't.

As if sensing that, Quinn pulled away and went to call Nye.

"Be here at one o'clock," Nye said. "We'll talk over a late lunch. And Quinn? What's the sheriff's number? I'd like to speak with him."

As soon as Quinn hung up, the phone rang again. It was Alden. "Did you talk to the lawyer?"

"I just did. I got an appointment for today, at one o'clock, and he's going to give you a call later."

"Good. I'll go ahead and arrange your ride with Hodie. It'll be better if he can take you early. How soon can you get down to the dock?"

Quinn checked his watch. "I can leave here in about fifteen minutes."

Quinn changed into dry clothes, said goodbye to Mary, and walked out to his car. It had stopped raining and the sun was peeking through the clouds. He was relieved. He hadn't been looking forward to a pounding boat ride in the rain. It'd be more comfortable now, and they'd make better time with the flatter seas.

Nye Standish was a large man whose tight pinstriped suit barely contained his wide girth. A fast talker who ran one sentence into the next.

They had lunch at the same dingy restaurant that Alison Goss used to work at, near the ferry dock. Waitresses as old as grandmothers barked out orders to the kitchen staff and wedged their wide hips between crowded tables, balancing trays loaded with beer and clam chowder without spilling a drop.

"You've eaten here before, right?" Nye scanned the menu with bifocals that sat on the tip of his bulbous, veined nose.

"Believe it or not—no." Whenever he and Mary came to town they always bypassed this restaurant for a fancier one a few blocks farther in.

"Really?" Nye pushed up his glasses with an index finger. "Well, wait until you taste the food. It's much better than the tourist traps in the center of town."

They reminisced about college days until their meal came, then got down to business. Quinn started telling him what happened, but Nye waved him off. "No need. I already spoke with the sheriff. Just fill me in on the kid—what's he been like since living with you? Sheriff said something about him being a little odd?"

"That's true." Quinn told Nye about the cigar boxes, the field of bees, and Faron setting his head on fire. "And he closes his eyes whenever he hauls a lobster trap." Quinn could see from Nye's facial expressions that he was giving good examples of Faron's quirkiness.

Nye interrupted now and then, for clarification. He talked with his mouth full. Bits of food clung to his lips and chin and Quinn had to resist the urge to wipe away the debris that was piling up on the lawyer's face.

"Here's the plan," Nye said, finally taking a swipe at his mouth with a napkin. "We want to keep this thing out of court—not have it go to trial—not that I think it would from what you told me, but anything's possible. Oh, by the way, the parents called the sheriff today while you were on your way over here. Apparently, the girl's changed her story. Says she had nothing to do with it. Says it's all your kid's fault."

"But that's not true."

Nye held up his hand with an outward palm to show Quinn he shouldn't be concerned. "I know. That's what the sheriff said. Don't worry. I may eat in dumps like this, but I've got friends in high places." He took a noisy swig of beer. "I'm certain I can get the charges reduced, and that means no jail time—record expunged. Hell. It's a kid's prank. The girl talked him into it and now she's lying. Besides, I know the judge and I'm pretty sure he'll be sympathetic." Nye winked and shoved fried clams into his mouth. "The clincher is, because it's on the record that your boy was drinking at the time of the offense, and because there's alcoholic history in the family, I'm recommending he goes away for therapy."

Quinn balked. "You mean a hospital? No way!"

"Calm down. It's not a hospital. Besides, whatever it is, it's better than prison. And may I be blunt? Your kid did a dumb thing here, and with someone under twenty-one. Things could be a lot worse." He nibbled at his salad. "Good thing you called me."

Quinn poked at a French fry. Nye was right, it could be worse.

"The place I have in mind is a fancy drunk tank. How long anyone stays is up to the folks who run it, not the judge." Nye drank some more beer and continued. "It's about one hundred miles inland from here." He could see the skeptical look on Quinn's face. "Trust me, it's not what you think. It's like one of those country clubs where all the movie stars go to get sober."

"You mean rehab?"

"Yeah, that's it, rehab." Nye chewed the last of his clams. "You say your kid's an artist?"

"Yes. He likes to draw."

"Good, good. This place is perfect for him. Real artsy. They've got a . . . whatchamacallit . . . a place where artists paint . . ."

"A studio?"

"Right. A studio." Nye let out a loud belch and rinsed his mouth with beer. Pushed his chair away from the table and patted his bulging stomach with two hands. "They've got great coconut custard pie here. How about it?"

CHAPTER 18

WHEN CAPTAIN RICK BOYD called looking for Faron, Quinn was half asleep. He grabbed the phone on the first ring, but it took him several sleepy seconds to collect his thoughts. He spoke softly, trying not to wake Mary. "I'm so sorry, Rick. I meant to call you."

Quinn related the events from recent days, deeply embarrassed. "I feel badly letting you down this way. I know Faron does too. He'll tell you himself, when he can." Quinn stifled a yawn and sat fully upright in the bed. "I'm really sorry. I hope you can find another sternman on such short notice."

Rick had been listening patiently. "You've got enough on your mind, don't worry about that. Besides, business has taken a real downturn the last month, so there are plenty of guys out of work looking for a job," Rick chuckled, "including the one who left me for something better a year ago."

"Well, I'm glad for that. I'll tell Faron you called."

"Sounds good. I hope it all works out. Oh, he's got some of his stuff on board—a dufflebag—I'll see that he gets it."

After they said goodbye and hung up, Quinn sat quietly, listening to his wife's breathing, trying to determine if she was awake. He thought about snuggling next to her and getting some more sleep but he knew it was useless. He was wide-awake now. He eased himself off the bed and crept out of the room, clutching his clothes so he could dress downstairs without disturbing Mary.

Things moved quickly after the first meeting with the lawyer. The presiding judge, the Honorable Riley P. Talcott, turned out to be more than a casual acquaintance of Nye's—he was an old hunting pal, which didn't hurt Faron's case. That, and an agreement the girl wouldn't be charged for her part in the scheme, made for the quick outcome Nye had predicted, in spite of protests by the girl's family.

"Lets not forget who orchestrated this thing," Nye reminded them. "Sexual favors in return for a staged kidnapping—that was your daughter's idea."

"It's not true!" the girl's father blurted out, backing up his daughter's new version of events.

"That's what you say, but not what Sheriff Alden Paisley, the investigating officer says in his report. And you were present when he interviewed your daughter." Nye let that sink in for a moment. "Sure, we could go to trial—your word against ours—but everything will be aired."

The parents and their lawyer put their heads together for the inevitable.

"Why did we ever move here?" The Lobster Queen's mother whined as they agreed to the deal. "You're all inbred!"

"Quiet," ordered Judge Talcott. "We're done here. Mr. Goss will go to Gannon Mill for rehabilitation." Talcott leaned forward and spoke directly to Faron. "Your counsel will give you the details. You're to arrive there August sixteenth. That gives you plenty of time to say your goodbyes. Don't do anything stupid between now and then."

A few days later, Quinn and Faron drove to the mainland for a morning meeting with Nye. They had a nine o'clock appointment but Menhaden was clogged with people seeing off a fleet of tall-masted Canadian schooners that were getting an early start south, by way of the island. Quinn and Faron missed the ferry and had to beg another ride from Hodie, which meant waiting for him to get through his morning routine, and they ended up being late for their appointment.

"It's okay," Nye assured Quinn when he called to explain the delay, "it'll give me time to run a few errands."

When they finally got to Nye's office, he led them to a light-filled room with a distant view of the bustling waterfront. There were several comfortable chairs, a small kitchen counter, and a half-eaten box of doughnuts in the center of a highly polished oblong table.

"Have a seat. Would you like anything? Coffee?" Nye poured himself some.

"Not me," Quinn said, hand on his stomach. "I'm still full from breakfast."

Faron eyed the doughnuts. "I'll have one of those."

"Help yourself." Nye blew on his hot coffee, took a sloppy sip, and sat at the table. "Okay. The guy who runs the alcohol treatment center is Sander Gaines. Nice fellow, from what I could tell. Says you can bring Faron down yourself." Nye took another slurp from his cup. "Of course, I'll ride along, Quinn, if you want. Gaines says you can spend the day, then no visits for a few weeks, until Faron gets the routine down."

"But I'm not an alcoholic," Faron protested.

"Maybe not. But you were legally intoxicated when you took the girl. Good thing, too, because your high blood alcohol level made it possible for me to get you into rehab and keep you out of jail. Capeesh?"

Faron hung his head sheepishly.

Nye grabbed a sugarcoated doughnut from the box and took a big bite. Grape jelly oozed out the other end onto the table. He chewed thoughtfully for a moment then began going over all the details of the arrangement, explaining how, after spending time in rehab, Faron would have a clean slate. "No police record to follow you around. It's a good deal." He scooped up the spilled jelly, licked it off his finger, and started on a second doughnut. "Any questions?"

Quinn and Faron looked at one another. Neither could think of any. Quinn had poked around and done a little research about Gannon Mill and liked what he found. If Faron had to spend time somewhere, it sounded like the right place.

Quinn pushed his chair back from the table. "I think you've covered everything, Nye. We really appreciate your help."

When he and Faron got up to leave Nye stood, too, brushing powdered sugar off his dark-blue suit jacket. He held out a sticky hand. "Good seeing you again, Quinn. Let me know if there's anything else I can do." He clapped Faron on the shoulder. "Keep your nose clean, kid."

CHAPTER 19

THE MORNING of August sixteenth was bright blue. Already warm at seven A.M. The smell of balsam floated through the open kitchen window of the rectory. The lobster fleet had headed out hours ago but you could still hear gulls squabbling over bait drippings down at the harbor.

Mary made banana pancakes for breakfast, using the last of the maple syrup from her uncle's sugarhouse on the New York side of Lake Champlain.

She had gone over to Faron's place a few days earlier and helped him pack two suitcases, which were now on the floor by the front door.

"Sure you won't come?" Quinn asked while she served him a stack of flapjacks.

"Can't. It's my turn to set up for the monthly potluck. Remember? It's tomorrow night."

"Oh, that's right." He'd forgotten all about it. This one would be the first that Faron wouldn't be attending since he'd come to live with them.

Mary sensed his disappointment. "You'll be there, won't you?"

He put on a smile. "Of course I will. Just like always."

They left soon after breakfast—Mary waving from the back porch. Faron drove while Quinn pretended to relax in the passenger's seat, looking out the window at the unbroken morning light. The ferry was at the dock when they got there and they were boarded immediately. After hitting some traffic in Willisport. they made good time the remainder of the trip and arrived at Gannon Mill just in time for lunch.

Nye was right, it was a nice place. There were quaint buildings and several hundred acres of woodland, fields, ponds, and apple orchards. It had been a commercial cider mill previously, owned by a man named Tom Gannon, who also kept some milking cows, goats, sheep, ponies, dogs, chickens, and any other critters that needed a home.

There'd always been a small facility next to his property—a popular drying out place for alcoholics, big business in rural Maine—and Tom Gannon considered them good neighbors. They were quiet and didn't complain about noisy farm equipment or the stench of manure.

In time, Tom became quite friendly with the director, Sander Gaines, and he let the residents wander his farm whenever they liked. When he died at age ninety-four, he left the entire estate to the rehab center, which Sander Gaines renamed 'Gannon Mill' in honor of his friend's generosity.

The approach was a long, winding dirt driveway, cut through an apple orchard. At the top, Faron parked the car in front of the main building. He and Quinn went inside and were greeted warmly by a young woman who asked them to have a seat on a cushioned bench near a large brick fireplace.

They only waited a few minutes before a heavyset man in shirtsleeves and a loosened tie walked briskly through the front door and came over to them, offering his hand and a sparkling blue-eyed smile. "Father Gage? I'm Sander Gaines."

"Nice to meet you," Quinn said. When he stood to shake the man's hand, he had to look up. Gaines was nearly a foot taller than he was. He was quite a bit older, too, and there was something about him that put Quinn immediately at ease. "And this is Faron."

Gaines clasped Faron's hand. "Welcome. Come on, let's get something to eat. You two must be hungry. Leave your bags here. We'll get them on the way back."

The hallway leading to the dining area was wide and the trio of men walked side by side. Gaines made small talk, asking them about the drive over—weather and traffic. Faron was silent but Quinn did his best to keep the conversation going.

When they got to the dining room, Gaines led them to one of the smaller round tables near a window overlooking the orchard. He pulled out a chair for himself and gestured for them to have a seat.

The room was lovely. Knotted pine floors creaked underfoot. A wall of windows revealed a magnificent view. The comfortable assortment of wooden tables and chairs made the room cozy.

"Feels just like home in here," Quinn said.

"That's because this was once a farmhouse. We tried our best to keep the original ambiance of the place, although we had to make some renovations to suit our purposes. This room was opened up. We knocked down walls to make it one large space and bumped out the original kitchen . . . over there." The director pointed to a set of double doors inside an alcove, near a window opening in the wall, where dirty dishes were stacked. "We normally have between fifteen and twenty guests here, and at least as many staff, so this space is perfect."

He looked at Faron. "You'll get your meals at the serving table and bring your empty tray up to the window when you're finished eating. Colleen's usually there—great gal—she runs the kitchen and just about anything else you let her," Gaines said with a chuckle. "Ready to eat?"

Throughout the meal he filled them in on life at Gannon Mill. "All our residents have to work. There's an old cider mill behind this building. We operate it and sell the apple products locally. We also tend the grounds and the gardens, and everyone takes turns working here in the dining room. You'll have a full schedule.

"There are no milk cows here anymore, but we've still got a hungry herd of goats to keep the weeds down, and some sheep in the lower pasture."

The atmosphere was friendly and casual, he assured them. He described Faron's room and said he'd take them upstairs to see it after lunch.

"Are you warm?" he asked when he noticed Faron wiping his brow with a napkin. He turned in his chair and slid open a window, letting in some cooler air and the zesty smell of rotting apples. "There. That better?"

"Yes, thanks." Faron gazed out at the view. It was much different than the island. He'd had an immediate sense of strangeness being this far from the ocean and the familiar sound of buoy bells and gulls, but as he looked out at the orchards and heard cicadas singing whole songs on one long breath, he began to relax.

After lunch, they returned to the lobby and picked up Faron's luggage, then followed Gaines up one flight of stairs to the residence where Faron was to have his own room. It was small, but comfortable.

There was a single bed, a nightstand, and a large closet. A small window looked out across a garden to the barn and orchards. There were two shared bathrooms in the hallway, several doors down.

Sander Gaines looked at his watch. "I've got a meeting in fifteen minutes. Someone'll be up here shortly to show you the sights. Dinner's at five thirty." He turned to Quinn. "You're welcome to stay as long as you want, until lights out at ten o'clock."

Quinn sat on the edge of the bed. He was heartbroken about leaving Faron here, but he tried to sound optimistic. "It seems like a nice place. What do you think?"

Faron stood in the middle of the room. "It's okay."

"I know it's strange, but you'll get used to it. It won't be for long." Quinn stood up to work a kink out of his hip. "Even though I won't be allowed to visit for a while, I'll call everyday."

While they were talking, a woman tapped on the door and walked in. "Want to see the rest of the place?"

An hour into the tour Quinn decided not to stay for dinner. He was tired, and feeling a little guilty about Mary having to plan the church potluck on her own. "I'll call you tomorrow," he promised, embracing Faron in an awkward hug.

CHAPTER 20

SUNLIGHT AND BIRDSONG pulled Faron from sleep. When he woke in the small room, he wasn't sure where he was. He rubbed his eyes and looked at the clock, then he remembered. It was ten past seven. Late. He should have been up and dressed. They told him yesterday that someone would be here at seven thirty to take him to breakfast.

He jumped out of bed, still in his clothes from the day before, and went into the bathroom. He was rinsing toothpaste out of his mouth when he heard a knock on the door.

"Name's Dean," a short, skinny man said when Faron opened the door. "Ready?" His bushy eyebrows went upwards with the question.

Dean jabbered all the way to the dining room. "Been here five months," he said. "Second time around. Here we are." He pointed to a table where three other men were already seated. "We'll sit there after we get our food."

Faron helped himself to a generous serving of eggs. The other men greeted him enthusiastically when he sat down with them. They were a noisy bunch and didn't hesitate to talk about themselves. Within minutes he knew that they were all alcoholics, hit bottom, and ended up here, one of them for the fourth time.

Faron ate quickly while the men talked. He'd fallen asleep after his tour of the grounds yesterday and had slept soundly through the night, without anyone waking him for dinner. Now he was starving.

"What about you?" one of the men asked when there was a lull in conversation. "Why're you here?"

In spite of the unfamiliar setting, it was a beautiful morning and Faron didn't want to ruin it with the truth. He soaked up the last bit of egg yoke with a piece of bread and was about to tell a whopper when Dean suddenly looked at his watch and said, "Hold that thought, Faron. I'm supposed to take you over to the medical building." He scooped up his tray. "Let's go."

Faron followed him to the window in the alcove. "You'll bring your dishes here after each meal," Dean told him.

"Good morning!" A smiling, chubby, freckle-faced woman spoke loudly over the noisy dishwasher and clanging silverware. She took Faron's tray. "I'm Colleen," she said, tossing silverware into a large plastic container. "You'll see a lot of me around here. Just holler if you want anything!"

Faron smiled back. He liked her. He was about to say something, but Dean tugged at his shirtsleeve. "No time for small talk. Gaines won't like it if you're late."

He took Faron to the edge of a birch grove, then said, "Follow the path through the trees. Someone'll be there. See you later."

When Faron got to the building, he was greeted by an efficient-looking woman dressed in scrubs who led him to an examining room on the second floor and told him to take off his shirt.

The exam went quickly, just a brief listen to the heart and lungs and two vials of blood. The nurse labeled the specimens and left them on the counter. "Okay. You can get dressed.

When you're ready, I'll walk you downstairs to Gaines's office. He's not in yet, but you can wait there for him."

Faron liked the office. It was dimly lit, with wide glass doors that opened to a patio and garden. There were two leather club chairs and an earth-toned upholstered couch. He especially liked the paintings. There must have been twenty of them—maybe more—covering most of the walls.

He hadn't seen much art before. There were some religious paintings and landscapes at home, in the rectory, and a painting of a schooner in the church annex that he had always admired. And there was a large painting of some kind of duck hanging over the bar at Scuppers.

Sometimes when he and Captain Boyd knocked off early, he strolled downtown Willisport while he was waiting for the ferry and admired the seascapes that hung in shop windows.

His mother never had any pictures in their house. The only thing she hung on the wall was a red neon bar sign with a clock on it. It had large letters that said "OPEN." There was a switch to make it flash . . . faster or slower. When he was little, he used to sit in the kitchen waiting for his mother to come home, trying to match the flashing of the neon sign to his breathing. He remembered staring out the window on winter nights, mesmerized by the reddish glow the sign cast on the snow. In the summer, flying insects followed the red light and found their way inside the house through holes in the screens.

He was deep in thought when Sander Gaines walked in and said, "Good morning."

Startled, Faron stood quickly and banged his knee on the low table near the couch.

"Sorry, didn't mean to sneak up on you." Gaines sat at his cluttered desk. "Go ahead . . . sit.

"Before we get started, there are a few guidelines I'd like to go over. The expectations are simple. We give people the benefit of the doubt, so you'll have a lot of freedom, unless you abuse it." He looked Faron in the eye. "Follow your schedule and respect everyone. No drugs or alcohol. One slip and you're out. You can use the phone in the downstairs lobby of the administration building any time before lights out. And don't leave the grounds. Questions?"

"No."

The sunny morning had suddenly clouded up and a light rain fell. Water splashed in the bird feeders. Gaines put on his glasses to check his watch. "You'll see me every day the first month, and you'll have a group session with John Holzer twice a week. I don't think you've met him yet. He's one of the counselors.

"And, as I said yesterday, you'll have a job—in the mill, laundry, kitchen, orchard—wherever you're assigned. It changes frequently, depending on the need."

He noticed Faron looking at the paintings. "Quinn mentioned you like to draw." He waited a moment to see if Faron would say something. When he didn't, he continued. "We've got a great art studio here. You can use it whenever you want. There's usually someone there to help. His name is Del. A nice man. I think you'd like him."

Gaines took off his glasses and brushed a strand of hair away from his forehead. "There are other counselors on staff if you want to talk with someone besides me or Holzer. You'll get to know them." He looked out at the rain. It was coming down harder. "Anything you'd like to ask me?"

Faron shook his head, 'no'. Except for grunts and nods and one-word answers, he didn't have a lot to say. He was glad not to be in jail for the dumb thing he did, but he didn't want to be here either.

Sander Gaines glanced at his watch again and they sat without speaking while the wind picked up and a slanting rain pelted the windows.

CHAPTER 21

THE NEXT DAY, everything was still wet from yesterday's rain. A smoky-gray sky. Faron walked through the dripping birches to Gaines's office, where he sat on the couch, saying nothing and inwardly admiring the paintings. The faces and figures on the canvases seemed to come to life in the warm light of the room.

Gaines gazed out the windows at an array of birds that ventured from their dry hiding places and hovered around the feeders. "Look. A ruby-throated hummingbird. A male. They have the red throat. You see it?"

Faron kept his mouth shut, but he looked more closely at the little bird darting about the garden. It was nearly impossible to see, so small and quick.

"Their backs are emerald green. The females aren't as brightly colored," Gaines said.

It went this way for the first rainy week—the two men sitting in the softly lit quiet—Gaines occasionally musing about what was going on outside the window. Faron was impressed with how many birds Sander Gaines could identify: summer tanagers, larks, wrens—and more.

He was different from most men Faron knew. He didn't smell of fish or diesel fuel or alcohol. He looked strong, like a workingman, but with good teeth and clean fingernails. He reminded him of Quinn, except without the worried look Quinn often had.

On Monday, the first sunshine in days blazed through the office windows. The patio was covered with twigs and soppy leaves, left over from a week of windy rains. A hawk screeched somewhere beyond the woods.

Gaines's chair squeaked as he swiveled in the direction of the sound. "Good to see the sun."

Silence.

"Have you ever seen anyone before, like this? Just to talk?"

Faron slumped on the couch, rubbing his temples.

"Are you all right?" Gaines asked.

Faron had awakened that morning with a pounding headache. "Head hurts." He put his hands over his ears and pressed as hard as he could to ease the throbbing pain. His ears were ringing . . . and Gaines's voice sounded like a paint scraper on a peeling aluminum hull.

Gaines watched as Faron held his head, rocking back and forth to try and soothe himself. He was struck with the childlike attempt to stop the discomfort—to make it all go away.

The following sunny afternoon they were staring out the window in mutual silence when a crow swooped down, cawing threats and scattering the assortment of smaller birds circling the feeders. A second crow joined the first, perching atop a low-hanging chokecherry branch at the edge of the garden, flapping its wings and making a racket.

After a while both birds flew off, but not before one of them rammed into a hand-blown glass feeder, sending it crashing onto the slate patio. The clear liquid inside the feeder spilled and ran in a slow-moving trickle, stopping when it hit the base of a ceramic planter.

Before Gaines could react, Faron asked, "What do you feed the hummingbirds?"

Gaines was careful not to appear surprised. He kept his attention on the smashed feeder. "Sugar water." He answered matter-of-factly, not wanting to betray his excitement at the shattered silence. "I boil a cup of water and mix in an equal amount of sugar until it dissolves. Then I add about three cups of cold water. That feeder—the one that broke—holds exactly four cups."

Faron shifted in his chair. "Mary, Quinn's wife, once made a basket of flowers for the hummingbirds. I remember she wove it from willow fronds and filled it with fuchsia. Begonia and sweet potato vine too. She hung it outside the kitchen window."

"Do you like flowers?"

"Sometimes I draw them."

"I'm asking because I'm impressed you remember the names of the flowers that were in the basket. How long ago was that?"

Faron didn't answer.

"Was there something special about the basket?"

"I knocked it over. Mary made me go with her to buy more plants. Begonia. Fuchsia. Sweet potato vine."

"Was she angry?"

"I don't know."

"How did you knock over a hanging basket?"

"I got a ladder and climbed up to catch a hummingbird. The basket fell on my way down."

Gaines was afraid to ask the next question. "And the bird?"

"I put it in a box and listened to it."

"Then what?"

"It died. It was an accident. I was just a kid. I never did that again."

"What did you do?"

"I already told you. I listened to the bird in the box."

"After that. After the bird died."

Faron was getting annoyed. *Hey, box boy . . . what's in the box?* Billy Gallager's voice popped into his head. He glared at Gaines. "Why are we talking about this? It happened a long time ago."

"And that," Sander Gaines answered, "is exactly why we're talking about it."

Things were different after the day crows knocked over the hummingbird feeder. The ruby-throats had headed south, and Faron opened up.

"Do you remember how you felt when you took the girl?" Gaines asked.

"Scared . . . but I didn't actually take her. It was her idea."

"I know." Gaines waited.

Faron chewed off a fingernail and spat it out. "I was nervous."

"About what?"

"Having sex. She said we could if I went along with her plan."

Gaines was surprised. He stepped in a little deeper. "From what you've told me about women flirting with you, it sounds like you could have slept with any one of them. Why her?"

"I don't know."

"Really? You don't know why you said yes to her but turned down sex with women who weren't asking for anything in return?"

"No, I don't."

This was the part Gaines didn't like, when he had to come right out with the hard truth because the other person couldn't quite get to it. "Do you think maybe it's because you couldn't believe someone would want you just for who you are, without asking you for favors?"

Hey box boy, your real mother didn't want you. For a moment Faron felt as though he couldn't breathe. What he didn't know was that, at the same time he was being suffocated by shame, a part of him was set free.

It didn't take long to meet all the other residents—twelve men and five women. Aside from the four talkative alcoholics he'd met on the first day, he knew little about the rest of them beyond what they felt safe parting with. Faron was cautious too.

He told the men in his group how he missed the ocean. Seabirds and whitecaps. He described the evening breeze by the bay and the salty smell of seaweed at low tide. He told them about the fishermen—the way they talked in clipped sentences, or not at all—dirt and engine grease ground into their lined hands, even on Sunday morning when they sat in the smooth wooden pews at church, next to their frowzy, overweight wives. Unattractive wives, he said, not pretty, like his mother.

"That's why they worry when she comes to town," he told the group. "She's the prettiest." His tall, thin mother whose skin glowed in the island light and who men followed with their eyes. He talked as if she were alive, so at first everyone thought she was.

"How did you like working on boats?" A chipmunk darted into a hole at the base of a stone wall in the garden. Sander Gaines stared at the moss-covered rock wall. Scanned the length of it, waiting.

Faron was sitting on the sofa, knees apart, relaxed. "I like it, but sometimes I close my eyes."

"What do you mean?"

"When we're hauling traps, and they're just below the surface, I always think of my mother . . . down there in the water.

That's when I close my eyes." Faron didn't admit how vividly he saw her—waterlogged and bloated, terrified. Cotton dress floating loosely in the ocean. The same image every time, rising with the traps. "I open my eyes when the trap breaks water." He stopped talking, distracted by the sudden taste of salty spindrift, and realized it was tears.

CHAPTER 22

COLD WIND WHISTLED through the yard, ripping brightly colored leaves from tree branches. Quinn stood by the fireplace with the phone to his ear. "Are you sure?" he asked when Owen Batch stopped talking.

"The tests are quite accurate. Ninety-nine percent."

The fire Quinn started earlier had burned down to bright orange embers and fading heat. "But . . . I was so certain. . . ."

"Listen, maybe it's better this way, less complicated."

Quinn reeled with disappointment, suddenly wishing he hadn't left Owen a message saying he was ready to find out the results of Faron's paternity test. He heard Mary coming down the stairs. The antique oak treads creaked loudly in the quiet morning. She saw him hang up the phone and lower himself slowly into a worn chair near the fire.

"You're pale as milk," Mary said. "What's wrong? Who was that on the phone?"

Quinn almost cried, but caught himself and told a small lie instead. "That was Sander Gaines. We can see Faron this week, if you want." He wiped his eyes. "Smoky in here. Must be the downdraft."

Mary walked past him toward the kitchen to make breakfast. He heard her pull a skillet out of a drawer.

"You want eggs?" she called to him, voice as lukewarm as the smoldering logs from his morning fire.

He wasn't sure why, but he got up from his chair and went into the kitchen and told her everything—told her about one night long ago, after a church potluck, when she stayed to clean up and he drove Nanny Doyle home—Nanny holding a foil-covered dinner plate on her lap because her old man was laid up with a broken ankle and couldn't walk, let alone drive the wife around. After dropping Nanny off, Quinn saw Alison Goss staggering along the side of the road. She was smoking a cigarette, a flimsy, faded dress clinging to her, showing everything underneath. Buttocks. Breasts. He offered her a ride. A sweet relief from the perfumed scent of Nanny Doyle and baked beans.

He drove Alison through the dark with the windows open, the night air loaded with the smell of spring and the ocean. Mayflies hatched on nearby ponds, swarming by the thousands. He was thirty-four then, been married eight years already, back on the island for seven of them. His older sisters had left the island for college and never returned. His mother died when he was in high school and his father moved away a few years after Quinn took over as pastor of Good Shepherd.

Quinn was a fisherman's son. His father, distant and gruff, was only ever home long enough to keep his mother pregnant—the four girls and one boy. He was proud of his virility and judged Quinn for the lack of it.

"Figures," his old man once said, still pissed off that his only son had chosen God over fishing, "married a woman who can't get knocked up. Or is it you?"

The night Quinn drove Alison home, she invited him inside. He said no, but put the car in park and sat there with the engine idling, staring straight ahead. Alison slid across the vinyl seat. Touched his thigh with one hand and turned off the ignition with the other.

She unzipped his pants, swung her right leg over his lap and straddled him. After one long, deep kiss they were both ready. When she climbed off him and stretched across the seat, head in his wet lap, he realized it was the first time he ever noticed the smell of sex, and he liked it.

Later, driving home and feeling guilty, he told himself it was her fault—she forced herself on him. When he got to the rectory it was dark, his wife already sleeping. He stood in the shadows outside the bedroom door, breathing in the scent of Alison that clung to him like sea spray. He showered before getting into bed with Mary, but the smell lingered in his mind.

That night with Alison was the first and last. He caught an occasional glimpse of her in town or along the roads, and sometimes he drove past her house, windows rolled down, sniffing for her.

He heard the rumors, too.

"Alison's on a binge," the fishermen's wives scoffed, huddled over fried fish platters at Scuppers, their thick fingers clenching forks and knives while they mocked Alison.

First time he heard she was pregnant was from his wife.

"Did you hear? Red Sedgwick says he saw Alison Goss in the post office. She's out to here," Mary said, holding her hands a foot in front of her own belly, to make the point. Judgment in her voice, envy in her eyes.

When he did speak with Alison again, her swollen stomach was buttoned under a wool coat, but you could still tell. It was November, and she was walking across an icy parking lot carrying a bag of groceries. He had just gotten out of the Chevy—going into the store for chowder crackers. Alison smiled when he took her grocery bag and carried it the rest of the way to her rimwracked car.

"How are you?" he asked. Both of them braced against a gust.

Alison wasn't much for small talk and that day had been no different. She opened the driver's side door so he could put her groceries in. "Don't worry," she said, sliding the brown bag out of her way and tucking herself in behind the wheel, "it's not yours."

"How do you know?"

"I just do."

"But . . ."

Alison closed the car door and started the engine. Lowered the window and lit a cigarette from a new pack.

"Listen," she said after two puffs, "I forgot about that night a long time ago. You should too. Doesn't much matter to me who the father is, unless he's going to take this kid off my hands." She blew smoke and looked at him. "You going to do that?"

A stiff wind blasted through the asphalt lot. Burned his face like the guilt in the pit of his stomach. His eyes watered.

She didn't give him more time to answer. "I didn't think so."

He didn't see her again until after the baby was born.

Since he was clergy, he felt obligated to pay her a visit at the hospital, but it took him four days to work up the nerve and she was discharged by then.

It wasn't until months later that he ran into her at Beaudry's Wharf. She had the baby in the crook of her arm and was standing at the register digging change out of her purse to pay for red-skinned potatoes and a hunk of cod. Faron was wrapped in a tattered pink blanket, a thatch of fine black hair sticking out, screaming at the top of his lungs. Not much bigger than the sack of spuds his mother was paying for.

A few years after that, Faron started to look like someone. Could have been anyone. More than a few men on the island silently worried they saw themselves in Alison's boy—same shape of the jaw, their nose or eyes. Something familiar in his boyish mannerisms. The dark hair and slender frame. Their wives had the same concerns. So did Quinn.

Until this morning he'd been convinced he saw himself in Faron Goss, even as his own wife miscarried twice and every month thereafter sloughed off the lining that could have borne a resemblance to them.

The whole time he was talking about Alison, Mary stood at the stove cooking his breakfast. The eggs were fried just right. Soft in the middle and crisp around the edges, the way he liked them. She scooped them up, slid them onto a plate, and set it down in front of him, then pulled on a sweater and went outside for a long walk through the windblown leaves.

She went to visit her parents on the mainland the next day. Stayed for the week and came back as if nothing happened. It would be a while before they both knew how much Quinn's confession had hurt.

CHAPTER 23

In September, John Holzer introduced a new man to the eleven o'clock group. Faron had seen him earlier in the day, getting out of a Washington County government car in front of the main building. His name was Laric Rudd, a twenty-five-year-old lobster fisherman from Addison, with sinewy forearms and rust-colored hair—a gaunt face, dark circles under his blue eyes. He told them everything during the first session, just to get it over with.

He was raised by his mother and had no other relatives.

"She got killed in a car crash three weeks ago. Too drunk to walk, but managed to drive long enough to swerve off the road into a tree less than a mile from home."

After the funeral Laric went on with his routine, until last week, when he stayed out all night on his boat with a livewell full of scratching lobsters. Another fisherman found him the next morning, aground in the lee of a small inlet, huddled in the stern, hungover and crying. An empty bottle of booze banging against the bulkhead.

Laric and Faron became quick friends. Knotted together like traps on a trawl. They sat with each other at meals and talked about things they both knew—dead mothers and fish stew. Bait bags and tides. Long winters and strong currents.

They were fortunate to get a job assignment together in the cider house, breathing the sweet steam that thickened the air when apples boiled down.

Near the end of the season they worked outside, gathering the last of the apples. There were legions of bees buzzing in the orchard, gorging on fallen fruit while the two of them tilted ladders against the trees to pick bittersweets and sharps.

"You crush the apples to make pulp," Laric explained over the steady drone of bees. "Then you wrap the pulp in cloth and press it to extract the juice. If you want, you can filter it. My mother used to make the best cider. That's how I know."

They filled two large baskets with apples and took the long way back to the mill, walking along the edge of the property on a trampled path between the trees and uncut meadow.

That night they drank fresh, strong cider just the way Faron liked it: cloudy, with pieces of orchard still floating in it. Afterwards, in bed, he dreamt of bees—so many of them crawling over browned and mushy apples on the sticky grass under the trees that the ground itself seemed to move.

When he woke in the morning, he could still taste cider and he longed for more. It made him wonder whether his mother, and Laric's—and maybe Laric too—had earth-moving dreams of whiskey that left them wanting more.

After the apple harvest, Quinn came for a visit. It was a dreary day, bludgeoned by rain. He met Faron in a small enclosed porch at the back of the main building, overlooking the fields. It had been a tedious drive along winding roads. Quinn was tired, and out of sorts this far from the ocean, hemmed in by the soggy acres of farmland and hills.

He took some rain-splotched papers out of a pocket and hung his dripping slicker on a wire rack in a corner near the radiator. He and Faron sat in silence at first, watching the storm blow the last shriveled leaves off the apple trees.

Quinn thought Faron looked good—well rested, and with a fresh haircut. "Here." He held out the papers with one hand and a pen with the other. "Sign these. I'm going to sell your place. Got a buyer already. Summer people. They'll pay a good price and I'll put the money aside for you. It'll be yours to do what you want with when you leave here." He wiggled his toes in his wet shoes. "I think it's for the best."

Faron took the papers. The year before coming here, when he was living alone on Puddle Cove, he'd been unhappy, but now he had second thoughts about selling the place. "It's all I have to remind me of her."

"I know." Quinn put a hand to his mouth to cover a cough. His throat was sore. Maybe a cold coming on. "But there are some bad memories in that house too. It might be best to leave them behind." He knew, of course, that Faron missed his mother, but he also had the impression Faron hadn't particularly liked living in the house alone. No need to sugarcoat things now.

"I guess." Faron signed the damp papers and handed them back to Quinn.

The summer people did buy the house, but they never moved in. One week after the closing, a hellish storm tore through and blew the roof off. The walls were splintered beyond repair. The new owners took it as an ominous sign, and instead of rebuilding they sold the ruins to the town and bought a larger piece of land closer to Preble Point. What was left of Alison Goss's old house was razed, and the town let the property on Puddle Cove grow wild.

CHAPTER 24

QUINN CAME OFTEN to see Faron but Mary didn't, preferring to send along food and other gifts with her husband.

On one such visit Quinn handed Faron something wrapped in brown paper and twine. They were in the dining room, drinking hot tea and looking out at a sky that threatened flurries.

Faron put his cup down and took the bundle. It was soft, like a pillow. His eyes gleamed when he unwrapped a thick woolen sweater, deep green with specks of crimson and ochre.

"Mary knit it for you," Quinn said between sips of tea. "She thought it might help keep you warm when you're outside tending to the animals, or whatever else they've got you doing here. She worked on it a long time."

Faron held the sweater against his face. The wool was soft, not the scratchy kind that made your skin itch or that was so stiff you couldn't bend your elbows. This was a one-of-a-kind sweater that you couldn't buy in a store or mail-order catalog. It was special.

Sander Gaines noticed the sweater the first day Faron wore it. "That's very nice. Did someone knit it for you?"

"Yeah. It's handmade. That really means something."

"Yes, it does." Gaines nodded in agreement, trying to see beyond the stockinet.

Faron wore the sweater every day in the wintry weather, pretending it was Alison Goss who cast it on and finished it. At night, in bed, he pulled it snuggly around himself. He closed his eyes and imagined his mother, sitting for hours by the lamp in the living room on winter evenings, lovingly knitting every stitch, needles clicking, while snow fell on the harbor and anchor lights twinkled in the crisp air.

He smiled as he thought of her calling to him from across the room, asking him to stand in front of her so she could hold the partially knit sweater against him, checking with her eyes to see if it measured right. Pressing the wool to his bony shoulders and spine with her warm, slender fingers. Stretching the sleeves along his arms, deciding when the length was just right, then working the ribbing at the cuffs.

Some nights he fell asleep to the make believe sound of his mother counting stitches, and after a while it seemed real. *Go ahead, try it on.* And she ran her hands across his chest to smooth out the wool, stepping back to admire the perfect fit.

Faron filled small sketchbooks with drawings of bees. It never occurred to him to work in the studios, but after the cider house closed for the winter and there were no more bees in the orchard, he got curious.

"You should go," Laric said when Faron mentioned it to him. "I think your bee drawings are great. Maybe there's something else to draw over there. I'll come with you, if you want."

The studios were on the first floor of a two-story brick building, a short distance through the pine trees. A maze of small, dark rooms had been transformed into four large, airy studios. The smaller one was for ceramics and the other three were used for painting and drawing.

On the second floor there was a good-sized kitchen with a refrigerator, sink, four-burner stove, some cabinets, and a table with chairs. The rest of the upper level was for storage.

Laric and Faron went into the first room they came to. An array of apples and empty glass bottles was set up on a cloth-covered crate. A shaft of morning light beamed through large windows, highlighting the Ida Reds. There were only two people working, intently painting the still life. The instructor, a graceful man with thick, silvery hair, stood between them.

Faron and Laric were at the back of the room, enjoying the unfamiliar scent of turpentine and oil paint, when the older man walked over to them, hands in the front pocket of a paint-smeared apron. He introduced himself in a whisper. "I'm Del," he said, offering his hand. A sparse growth of white stubble sparkled on his suntanned jaw. He pointed to the supply shelf. "Help yourselves, if you feel like it."

A few minutes later, Laric and Faron chose some paintbrushes, mixing palettes, tubes of oils, and small pieces of canvas board. They found seats and easels in a corner of the room and sat with a small, sturdy table between them.

Laric, who had never tried drawing or painting before, jumped right in, concentrating on the still life display and doing his best to reproduce it on his canvas.

Faron didn't begin with recognizable images, only shapes and colors. He sat at the edge of his seat, biting his lower lip, engrossed in what he was doing. When he didn't like something, he dipped a small cotton rag in turpentine and wiped the paint off the canvas and started again, until the painting began taking the form he wanted.

He worked carefully. He knew he had ability, but he'd never been one to stare out classroom windows, enchanted by shadows on the lawn or the simple shapes of trees. He'd been too busy immersing himself in schoolwork, fortifying himself with facts he could count on to stay the same year after year. Now it felt like he was seeing things for the first time.

"Very nice," Del said, standing behind the two newcomers. His melodic voice floated through the air like a dandelion seed on a spring breeze. "Don't think in terms of color. Only light and shadow. Squint your eyes and look for the shapes. Later, if you want to, you can fill in the color."

Laric leaned back in his seat, craning to have a peek at his friend's painting. "Wow. That's really good."

Faron returned the compliment, "Yours too."

"That was fun," Laric said later, when they walked to their rooms to get ready for supper.

Faron agreed. He couldn't wait to go back.

There were more people in the studio the next time he went, all of them sharpening pencils and mixing paint.

Del was there, arranging cut flowers in a glass vase and filling an enameled bowl with fruit. When Faron came in, Del looked up and smiled, hands full of oranges. "Welcome back. Where's your friend?"

"He couldn't make it." Faron chose a seat on the outside wall, his back to the windows. "Nice smell," he said, breathing in the linseed-loaded air.

Del grinned. "It sure is." He finished setting up the still life and stood back to admire it. The colors were brilliant against the white walls. Green stems and dried purple flowers. Yellow petals as bright as light. Pears and oranges overflowed the bowl.

When Del stepped away, everyone began sketching, but Faron just sat there, contemplating the colorful arrangement of fruit and flowers, unable to see it the way the others did.

He overheard Del talking to someone, scraping paint off their canvas. "There. That's better. Wipe off the rest and start again. Just use burnt umber and white, or indigo. You'll be amazed at the range of tints and hues you can get."

Faron stared at the display a bit longer, until he finally picked up a piece of charcoal and started making marks on the canvas. Short, straight marks, then longer lines that wandered and connected. Angles softened and shapes formed, almost as though he had no control over his own hand. He brushed paint into the blank spaces. Most remarkably, there was no sense of passing time, or any awareness of what went on around him.

Del walked by twice, but knew enough not to speak. He recognized an expression of intensity when he saw it and didn't want to interrupt.

At eleven forty-five he told everyone to stop for lunch. There was a sudden burst of conversation and Faron felt as if he were coming out of a trance.

"Have you painted before?" Del stood next to Faron, swishing dirty brushes in a jar of murky turpentine.

"No. Just some drawing."

Del eyed Faron's painting. "It's quite good, you know."

It was a wasp. Boldly drawn in charcoal pencil and partially filled in with varying shades of burnt sienna, ocher, and titanium white. He had worked from memory, thinking of the sleepy queen wasps who staggered along the wooden floor in his old bedroom at the rectory, awakening from their winter sleep.

One time he found a hibernating queen in the folds of an embroidered curtain Mary had sewn for him and hung in his room. He was sitting on the edge of his bed, putting on a shoe, when the wasp dropped to the floor, nudged awake by the season but still too sleepy to fly.

Faron lifted it with a scrunched-up sock and put it

in one of his cigar boxes. He listened to it for a while then carried the box outside and opened it on the woodpile, where the wasp stumbled clumsily and disappeared between the logs.

Faron sat alone in the empty studio and gulped down a sandwich. By the time everyone else returned from lunch, he was already back at his easel, reworking his wasp drawing with charcoal sticks, darkening lines he'd accidentally smudged. Before adding more color, he dipped a thin, pointed paintbrush in black paint and traced over the charcoal to outline the image.

He was pleased with the finished painting.

"Take it with you," Del said. "Or you can keep it here. I hope you'll come back."

"I will," Faron said as he took the painting and rushed out.

He hung it in his room and was admiring it when Laric knocked on his door.

"Time for supper. Hey, that's really good," Laric said when he saw the painting. "Why did you paint a wasp? Wasn't there a still life set up?"

"Yes, there was. I'm not sure why I didn't paint it. I was watching everyone else and I thought there was something wrong with me because I just couldn't see it."

"What do you mean?" Laric sat on the bed and leaned back on his elbows.

"It's hard to explain. I saw it, just not the way everyone else did, I guess." Faron slipped Mary's hand-knit sweater over his head. "Come on, let's eat."

He went to the studio frequently after that, sometimes with Laric, sometimes alone. Del usually had a still life set up, but Faron didn't always paint it, preferring to work from his imagination.

"You know, Faron," Del suggested, "you can teach yourself a lot by drawing from life. One of the biggest challenges is looking at something and drawing it as it is, not as you imagine. Really seeing it—from all angles, inside and out. Touch it with your eyes. Feel it. You haven't truly seen a thing until you do."

Del learned a lot during his long life. He knew about painting fat over lean, and how to sculpt from stone. About intaglio printing and lost wax casting. But mostly he knew about seeing and feeling. He worked in a factory downstate for forty-five years until he moved up north, away from it all, determined to see what he missed, and to finally use his hands to make something more beautiful than welded steel.

He and his wife bought some land with a small house on it, next to Gannon Mill. They put in a vegetable garden and pulled out bunches of carrots and radishes the first summer, Del thinking they were the most gorgeous things he'd ever seen.

"Paint them," his wife urged, seeing the appreciation for loveliness in his eyes.

Amazed at what you could create without a blowtorch and metal, he built himself an easel and set it up in the spare bedroom. He spent wonderful hours painting things he had never even noticed before. His wife helped him see the point of it, until she died the second year into his retirement.

Nothing made much sense for a long time after that, until one afternoon when the banging of hammers and the buzz of chainsaws jarred him from a grievous sleep and he forced himself out of bed and over to Gannon Mill to see what was going on. That was when Sander Gaines was renovating the art studios. He and Sander became good friends and when the studios were finished, Del painted there, instead of in his empty house.

His wife had saved his old work shirts, faded from weekly washings and riddled with solder spark burns. They were folded and neatly stacked in a cedar chest. He cut them up and carried them over to the new studios to use as painting rags. There were several boxes full. By the time they were empty he had learned how to see the point of things again.

CHAPTER 25

DECEMBER BLEW IN with a two-day storm that dropped nearly three feet of snow. Between shoveling paths and other work assignments, there was plenty to keep Faron busy, but he still found time to paint.

Del filled an empty wooden crate from the orchard with an assortment of leftover apples he kept in cold storage: Cortlands, Macouns, Crispins, Baldwins, and Golden Delicious. It was the largest still life Faron had ever seen, and he spent several days painting it, patiently trying to recreate the varying shades of reds and greens.

The radiators in the studio put out a tremendous amount of heat that warmed, and slowly rotted, the apples. Before long the room took on the same sweet scent as the cider house. Faron and Laric couldn't believe their luck. They told Del how pleasant it was to work in the apple-filled studio.

"You know," Del leaned back in a chair, hands clasped behind his head, feet up on a table, "I once read about a poet—German, I think—who kept rotten apples in his desk drawer because he thought the smell inspired him. I was so interested that I did a little research and found out that there was something to it. Some scientists—at Yale, if I recall correctly—did a study and concluded that the odor of apples had a positive effect on people's moods."

•

During their next session Faron told Gaines about the apples. "Del says it can help you mentally."

Gaines smiled. Faron was jumping right in. "Does it?"

Faron crossed his arms and slid down lower in the chair, a thoughtful expression on his face. "I always feel good in the cider house."

"Is there a time of year you feel better or worse?"

Faron was slow to respond, but he knew the answer. Summers had been the worst. His mother worked on the island then, keeping house for families on the Point. Since she wasn't commuting back and forth on the ferry to Willisport, she was usually home right after suppertime, often with a man—a summer visitor or someone on the island as hired help for the season. Less frequently, they were locals. Once it had been Billy Gallager's father and Faron always wondered if Billy had known, and if that was why he used to pick on him when they were kids. *Your mother's a whore who washed ashore.*

"In the summer my mother used to bring men home more than other times." Faron spoke so quietly Gaines could barely hear him.

"That's when I started listening to insects buzzing. I kept the lights on and they came in through the window. I concentrated on the beetles and moths banging on the screens, so I wouldn't hear my mother when she was with a man."

Faron squirmed. It was unpleasant thinking back. Winters had been better. Even though his mother often got home late, she was usually alone. The few times she did bring someone home during the winter, Faron sat in his room listening to the loud whir of a metal fan.

And the colder it was, the nicer she seemed, as if her angry moods went into hibernation with the drop in temperature.

"Winters were best. My mom was more quiet. I don't think she liked cold weather much, and she didn't have as much company at night, and I liked that."

"Do you think she was sad?"

"Maybe. She used to sit on the couch, smoking cigarettes and staring. She didn't yell as much either."

A spasm of guilt spread through Faron when he realized how much happier he'd been when his mother was unhappy. In a 'sog,' she used to call it: *Leave me alone, I'm in a real sog,* she'd say, but not in an angry way. She sounded tired. He remembered a time when she let him climb up on the couch to sit beside her; both of them snuggled under her grandmother's old quilt. "Once, she let me sit on the couch with her. Right next to her, under a quilt."

Gaines's voice softened as he pushed. "Once?"

Faron glared at Gaines and clammed up. He leaned forward, wanting to blubber. There was a spider crawling along the carpet. He concentrated on it. *Don't cry.* It crept onto his right foot. His eyes watered. *Don't cry.* He reached down and gently nudged the spider to a safe place under the couch.

Gaines watched, focusing on the elegance of Faron's sunbrowned hands, imagining him as a small boy, chasing moths in the island dusk, taking extra care not to rub the powdery scales off their delicate wings.

CHAPTER 26

SMALL BIRDS HOPPED through a tangle of juniper in the quiet aftermath of a snowsquall. Quinn Gage carried an armful of firewood up the steps of the back porch and stomped his feet to shake off the snow.

Mary was waiting for him, wearing only a sweater, bony wrists sticking out a chilly inch past the cuffs, arms wrapped around herself for warmth. Her words burned through the puffs of steam her breath made in the cold air. "I'd like to talk with you."

She was leaving. Already packed. It wasn't only about whether or not they still loved one another, she told him, or about his one night with Alison Goss, or his devotion to Faron. It was all of that—and everything else that added to the emptiness that grew inside her where nothing else did. *The will of God*, Quinn reasoned each month she bled. But as the years passed she noticed there was less disappointment in his eyes.

Mary left in the waning light of afternoon. Blue shadows stretched across the snow as she drove to her parents' house on the mainland and settled back into the neat white clapboard farmhouse she grew up in.

Quinn kept things to himself at first, not telling anyone that Mary had left him.

But a week later, when he stood at the pulpit in front of his congregation, he could see they already knew, because the island people were strayaway folks whose own weather-beaten lives taught them to follow the lines in someone's face and come to the right conclusions.

Twenty-five years ago, when he had returned to the island after seminary school—a well-read intellectual with a young wife from the mainland—he considered most of his island neighbors to be people who were uninformed. Backwards. He tried enlightening them with his sermons.

"You think your geese are all swans. Just you wait and see," his scornful father warned him one Sunday morning, after Quinn gave a particularly boastful, condescending sermon.

Turned out his old man was right. Quinn wasn't so puffed out any more after a few winters back on the island. The everyday realities faced by his parishioners—poverty, harsh weather, loneliness, sickness, and more than their share of bad luck—helped him remember his own childhood there. Helped him see their difference as strength. Life was hard, especially here. He stopped his church-mauled sermons and became one of them again, but never more than now.

A warm March. The month melted away fast. In April, winter cracked. Crocuses popped up alongside the driveway. Quinn was amazed at the patches of yellow, sprung up overnight. He was standing barefoot on the cold kitchen floor, looking out the window and admiring the flowers, when the phone rang.

It was Mary, the first time he had heard from her since she left. He'd tried calling her several times, hoping they could hang on to something from their years together. One or the other of her parents always answered the phone, polite, but firm. "She's not ready yet. Give her time."

But Mary didn't have much more time. Quinn flopped in a chair while she talked, hearing only part of what she said. "... a lump ... my breast ... I thought you should know."

They made plans for him to drive to the mainland the next day. When he hung up the phone, he suddenly had to take a leak but couldn't make it to the bathroom. He sat at the kitchen table and sobbed, shivering in his own urine, dripping tears and snot, trying to pray, but wondering if God still listened.

He took Mary to several doctors and they all said the same thing. "Might be in the other breast, too. We'll know more once we get in there."

The day before the surgery, Quinn drove Mary and her parents to the Maine Medical Center, down in Portland. She was scheduled for eight in the morning but got bumped because of an emergency. She trembled with cold and fear for three more hours, until they finally came to get her.

"Make that a double," the cocky surgeon said in the operating room, finding bad news in the second breast. "Uh, oh. Got to take the nodes too ... on both sides." Mining deeper, "Jesus ... will you look at this?"

Quinn got Mary's parents a hotel room and he stayed overnight in the hospital on a foldout chair by her bed. The surgeon gave her the news the next morning while she was still drugged and groggy.

"They like to do it that way, so they don't have to deal with the emotional side of things," Mary's devastated father confided to Quinn.

After a week in the hospital and a few more recovering at home, she started chemotherapy. When Quinn suggested he could move into her parents' house to help her through the treatments, she didn't object.

CHAPTER 27

SUMMER SNEAKED IN EARLY, attached to a stream of balmy May air that quickly became an oppressive swelter. Sander Gaines and John Holzer perspired in their shirts and ties as they climbed the stairs to the upper level of the studios, the heat rising with them. Faron had a private workspace on the second floor and they were on their way up to see his paintings. When they reached the top, they stood out in the hallway a moment, mopping sweat and catching their breath. The door to Faron's studio was open.

Faron was sitting on the window ledge, as still as a slack tide, scrutinizing his paintings. Canvases of all sizes leaned against walls. There were some portraits of people and animals and some pictures of the orchards, but most of the paintings were monochromatic images of butterflies and moths. He'd remembered the advice Del had given—squint and find the shapes and shadows. Work with a basic palette. The results were powerful.

Holzer unknotted his tie. He pulled it through his button-down collar and stuffed it in his pants pocket. "Del says you've done a lot of new work. May we take a look?"

"Sure." Faron dusted off a couple of chairs. "Have a seat."

They were quiet for a while, all of them engrossed in the spectacular array of paintings.

Holzer got up and walked around, standing in front of each canvas for minutes at a time. "They're lovely. It's hard to believe you never painted before. So expertly drawn, and with such respect for the natural world. Remarkable."

Gaines agreed. "You really have talent, Faron." He went to have a closer look at a painting of a moth. Faron had managed to convey a sense of determination. A fearless little creature in the vast darkness. "These paintings really look believable," Gaines said, picking up the moth painting and examining it more carefully, "and yet, they're almost not like insects at all, more like organic shapes that just happen to have images of insects in them."

"Like fossils," Holzer interjected, looking over his colleague's shoulder to admire the same painting.

"What?"

"Like fossils."

Gaines stared at the canvas. "You're right. Like faint images of insects pressed into rocks. Caught between layers of earth and time." He took off his glasses and aimed his blue eyes at Faron. "Like carefully excavated memories."

"Del says you can't really see anything until you feel it," Faron said, "and that you can't feel it until you look at it from the inside and paint your way out."

Gaines grinned. "Del may be right." Sometimes he thought he should be running the studios and his friend Del should be running the sessions.

CHAPTER 28

QUINN TOOK GOOD CARE of Mary. He changed bandages and cleaned her oozing chest wound. He sat with her on the bathroom floor while she clung to the cold rim of the toilet bowl and vomited. When she woke up one morning and found her pillow covered with tufts of hair, he shaved his head, then hers, and they laughed and cried like never before.

But after a month of treatment, they found out it wasn't working.

"You can keep trying if you want," the doctor said unconvincingly when they asked what was next.

"What do you think?" Quinn asked him.

"It's in the bones . . . the spine." The doctor looked at Mary. "That's why you're having back pain. The chemotherapy may slow it down . . . or you could stop and we could manage the pain."

They stopped, but the cancer kept going—spreading as fast as purple loosestrife at the edge of a pond, choking out everything in its path. Pale flesh seemed to fall off Mary's bones pounds at a time. Sunken cheeks and startled eyes—her face all ears and teeth. A worrisome smell seeping from her pores as she rotted from the inside.

"I'm sorry, Mary," Quinn said, sitting at her bedside in her childhood room, feeling as much guilt as loss.

Her parents waited in the gloaming, helpless in the background, watching their daughter die ahead of schedule. But she was calm, her pain and fear knocked flat by faith and morphine.

At the end, Quinn held her hand when she closed her eyes and put her regrets to rest in a way life never could.

Faron took it hard. He had seen Mary a couple of weeks after her surgery, and again in June, the month she died.

She was feeling better during his second visit and they were able to spend some time alone in her parents' potting shed, puttering and talking.

"You've changed," she said to him, pressing loamy soil into a peat container. "You seem more relaxed. I can't remember when I ever heard you talk so much." She smiled, brushing rich brown soil off her shirt.

"Quinn says painting's good for me."

Mary agreed. "He's probably right." She looked tired and thin, arms like a scarecrow's—twigs, with gardening gloves stuck on the ends. Her hair hadn't grown back and there was a bright red kerchief wrapped around her head. "Artists are fortunate they're able to express themselves through their work. Do you read about other artists?"

"Yes," said Faron. "My friend Del loans me books."

"Quinn's mentioned him. He sounds like a nice man."

"He is."

Faron helped her move bunches of seedlings from sunny spots near the windows to the shade just outside the shed door. Suddenly, he remembered watching her do the same thing when he was a boy. Hardening up, she called it—starting plants inside, then gradually getting them accustomed to the outdoors so they'd survive in different types of weather.

"Hardening up?" he asked her.

Mary stopped what she was doing and looked at him. "You remember that?"

He nodded. "You used to plant seeds in the kitchen and keep them on the window ledges, then move them to the porch after they sprouted. I'd forgotten, until now." He handed her a flat of basil. "I remember you once told me that childhood was like hardening up. I didn't understand it then, but I do now, and I realize how much you did for me."

Mary smiled weakly, uncomfortable talking about their past. She focused on the seedlings and tried changing the subject. "Well, it might be a little late in the season for these guys, but we'll see how they do."

Faron touched her shoulder. "I hope it isn't too late to say I'm sorry . . . about the cat, and everything else."

Mary pressed the small of her back with both hands. "Let's go outside, it's chilly in here." She pulled off her gloves and they walked out the door, around to the back of the shed to sit on a stone bench in the sunlight.

The warmth of the sun eased the ache in her bones, and she tried to find the energy to comfort him. "It's okay, Faron. I know it wasn't easy for you, and I always knew I couldn't take the place of your mother." She leaned against the splintered wooden shed, turning her head sideways to look at him. It had rained that morning and there was still dampness coming off the bench, working its way up her aching back. "I only hope you can forgive me for the times I seemed distant. I did my best. I guess we were both just desperate for the real thing."

"I know." Faron sensed her weariness. He stood and helped her up.

While they walked back to the house, he held her elbow to steady her. He told her he'd like to come back the following week and talk some more, but she said no.

"It won't be long, Faron. I swear, I'm half what I was yesterday." She took his hand. "Thank you. Today was lovely. Now go paint."

CHAPTER 29

"Why do I feel so awful?" Faron asked after Mary died. "We were never that close."

It was a hot day. He and Gaines were sitting out on the patio. The hummingbirds had been back since May and were looking for something sweet, zipping around the potted geraniums and zinnias that were neatly spaced on top of the stone wall.

"Closer than you realized, perhaps." Gaines stirred his iced tea and took a long, cool swallow. "You may also be experiencing some delayed grief," he suggested quietly. "Having to do with your mother."

"But I was sad when my mother died."

Gaines swatted at a mosquito. "I know. But maybe you never fully grieved for her. Sometimes people act out in other ways, to avoid grief."

Faron had that helpless look he got when he didn't understand. "What do you mean?"

Gaines filled in the blanks. "Like when you let yourself get stung by bees."

Faron wasn't convinced. "Why would I do that?"

"Maybe you were angry."

"About what?"

Gaines wasn't going to let him off the hook this time. "You mean, at whom."

"At Mary," Faron blurted out. "She wasn't my mother and I wanted her to stop acting like she was. She tried to treat me better than my mother did."

Gaines pushed. "That's right. When you went to live with the Gages, you weren't only upset because your mother died, but because Mary treated you kindly. To accept her love might have felt like a rejection of your mother, and an acknowledgement of what you didn't get from her."

"But it wasn't my mother's fault," Faron insisted loudly. "She couldn't help who she was."

"No, she couldn't. But you're out of sequence. First you have to express your anger at someone, then forgive them. If you don't . . . if you try forgiving first . . . the rage may stay inside you.

"Sometimes it's hard to admit when a parent hurts us. We want to think the best of them—to protect them. It was easier to be angry at Mary, and at yourself, rather than at your mother." Gaines paused a moment to let that sink in. "But there's no resolution without truth."

"But I accepted Quinn."

"That's different. There was no one to compare him to. You never knew your father."

In the weeks after Mary's death, Faron lost interest in painting. Not only that, he decided none of his previous work was worth saving.

He was in the studio cutting his canvases into pieces when Del walked in. "Why are you doing that?" Del asked.

"They aren't any good."

Del leaned a bony shoulder against the doorframe. "You sound like Edvard Münch. He didn't take good care of his paintings either."

Faron stopped, scissors in midair. "Who?"

"Edvard Münch." Del stepped into the room. "Mind if I sit?"

"No, go ahead."

Del cleared a spot on a tabletop and sat down. "Münch was a Norweigan painter. He didn't cut up his paintings, he weathered them."

Faron looked interested. "What do you mean?"

"He left them outside. Hung them in trees, propped them up in the garden. Rain, snow—it didn't matter."

"Why?"

"He was testing them. Wanted to see what they could endure—if they were good enough to stand the test of time. He called it a 'kill or cure.'

Faron was calmer now, and intrigued, as he usually was when Del was talking.

"Like seedlings," Faron said, putting the scissors down. "You have to harden them up before planting them outside, so they gradually get used to the change in temperature."

Del was quiet for a moment, thinking back to the summer he and his wife had planted their first garden. "I see your point."

CHAPTER 30

APPLES RIPENED in the orchard. Magicicadas emerged from the ground to live out the last weeks of their lives in the light. Some of them had been waiting nearly seventeen years—ever since they were nymphs, who fell from branches and burrowed their way underground to grow in darkness until they were ready to mate for the first, and last, time.

Faron got an early start walking over to the studios. Cicada husks littered the ground like empty shotgun shells. The mating songs of the males could be heard a half mile away. A chirp so loud it drowned out any thoughts he had in his head.

It was the first time in a long while that he felt like painting. He'd spent weeks building stretchers, mitering the corners instead of butting them together, perfection being a form of procrastination.

This morning he climbed the studio stairs to the kitchen and put on a pot of coffee. While he was waiting for it to brew, he sat crooked over a magazine.

Del came in, rolling up his sleeves. "I thought I smelled coffee." He sat down at the table. "Do you mind?"

"Uh-uh."

"What are you reading?"

"Nothing. Just looking at the pictures."

"Stretching more canvas?"

Faron closed the magazine. "No. I'm going to paint."

Del got up and poured them coffee. "If you're interested, a friend of mine has volunteered to model a long pose this morning. Forty-five minutes on the platform, one fifteen-minute break in between. He'll be here around ten thirty."

Faron didn't draw the long pose, but he broke his slump. What began with a single mark on canvas that morning turned into weeks of intense painting.

His best work was done quickly, in the first twenty minutes. He had learned, after ruining many paintings by overworking them, when to stop. He had Del to thank for that. The one thing that drove Del crazy was watching Faron destroy a painting by going too far. He'd stand in the back of the studio and yell, "Faron . . . STOP!"

"I don't know how to finish it," he complained to Del one night when they were both working late in the studio. He hunched over a painting of a bumblebee, clutching a number one brush, struggling with what to do next. "It doesn't look right. Maybe I should paint more hairs on the abdomen."

"Maybe." Del sighed loudly, with exasperation. "Or maybe you've said all you have to say."

Finally, Faron got it.

The orange October light coming through the windows shone on Del's face, making him look twenty years younger. "Your work is changing, Faron. It's more atmospheric—but not enough to dilute the essence of the insects. I like these fuzzy images in the background." Del pointed to specific areas on the unfinished canvas that Faron stood in front of. "They give the work a sense of place." He put one hand on his hip and the other to his chin. "What do you think?"

The work may have changed, but Faron still thought his paintings tied him to the past. "I'm not sure what I'm doing." He poured muddied paint thinner through a paper filter and wiped his hands with a rag. "I feel stuck."

"That's normal," Del reassured him, "when you're on the verge of a breakthrough, which I think you are."

"I'm not trying to have a breakthrough. I just want to enjoy painting, like I used to."

"No one tries to have breakthroughs, it just happens, and being stuck usually precedes it. I've seen a transformation in your paintings, similar to their real-life counterparts."

"What counterparts?"

"The butterflies and moths. They metamorphose into another stage, like your work is doing."

Faron squeezed cerulean blue from a tube, added iridescent white and a drop of linseed oil, and blended it with a brush while he listened to Del.

"Do you remember telling me that Sander said your work is like excavated memories? Well, you're beyond that now. You dug up old bones and sifted through them. You're in the realm of the living now."

CHAPTER 31

FARON SAT with his knees together, confident and smiling, balancing a cigar box on his lap, arms fully extended across the back of the couch.

Gaines pointed to the box. "Anything in there?"

"A moth—a wavey-lined emerald. I'm going to paint it."

Gaines nodded his approval. "Good. I hope you'll show me the painting when it's done. I think the green moths are especially beautiful."

"Me, too."

Gaines tilted back in his chair, mimicking Faron's relaxed posture. "How do you feel about going home?"

"For good?"

"Yes, but not right away. In December, sometime before Christmas."

Faron picked at a dried lump of cadmium yellow on his pants. He wanted to go back to the island, but he felt nervous.

Gaines noticed the discomfort. "It won't be much different. Most of your time here has been spent painting and you can do that anywhere. If I didn't think you were ready for the next step, I wouldn't let you take it. Do you believe that?"

"I'm not sure what I believe, but I guess I'm going to find out."

"There's more." Gaines sat straighter in his chair. "Laric is leaving tomorrow."

"What?" Faron gripped the cigar box with both hands. "How can that be? He hasn't said anything to me about it."

"That's because he just found out today."

"I don't get it. No one leaves that suddenly."

"You're right, there's usually a transition period, but we've got a strict rule here: if you drink alcohol, you're out—immediately. No exceptions." Gaines scrutinized Faron's reaction to see if he could tell whether or not he'd known what Laric was up to. But Faron looked genuinely shocked. "You had no idea?"

"None."

Concern creased Faron's brow.

"I know saying goodbye won't be easy," Gaines said.

"I'm worried about being here by myself, without Laric."

"That's not surprising. The two of you really connected, but if you're ready to leave—and I believe you are—then you're ready for his leaving."

Faron half expected Laric to skip supper that night but he found him in his usual spot, already partway through his meal. "You heard?" he asked as Faron set down his tray and cigar box and pulled out a chair.

"Yep." Faron felt a twinge of betrayal. "Why didn't you tell me?"

"I just found out today."

"Not about leaving, about the drinking. Maybe I could have helped."

"I doubt it." Laric chugged cold milk. "It's not something you can be easily talked out of. But you wouldn't know that . . . since you haven't got the problem."

"You say that like you're sorry I don't."

"No, that's not what I meant. But I guess I do envy you a little."

Faron shoved his uneaten food to the side. "I'll miss you."

"Me too. But we'll keep in touch." Laric pointed to the box. "Got something in there?"

"A green moth."

"Can I see it?"

Faron lifted the lid just enough for his friend to peer in.

Laric lowered his head for a closer look. "It's pretty. Nice color. Are you going to paint it?"

Faron nodded. "I've already done the preliminary sketches." The moth throbbed in the box. "I'll let it go later."

After supper, they walked to the edge of the moonlit orchard and set the open box on a stump to wait for the moth to fly away. It fluttered frantically for a moment, green wings gleaming in the moonlight, then ignored the star-filled sky and doubled back toward the bright lights of the cider house, and even though Faron knew releasing it was the right thing to do, it was hard letting go.

CHAPTER 32

THE WIND HOWLED the day Quinn brought Faron home. There was snowy weather in the forecast and the sky grew darker as they drove along the narrow, winding roads to the coast.

Quinn had brought the old blue Chevy, thinking Faron might enjoy driving it. It was good in snow, but the heater gave out a few minutes into the trip and now the vinyl seats felt as cold and hard as ice. Quinn hung on to the door handle, trying not to slide off the warm spots when Faron took the curves a little faster than he ought to have.

Halfway to Willisport an icy rain began falling. Quinn held on a little tighter when the car skidded around a turn. "Whoah. Careful. The roads are slick."

Faron slowed down to a crawl when the rain turned to snow. Visibility was poor. The windshield wipers weren't much help and after stopping for a third time to tap ice off them, Quinn spotted a gas station and told Faron to pull in. The small white building was nearly obliterated by snow, but it was strung with Christmas lights that blinked like a beacon in the storm.

Faron drove beyond the pumps and parked near the entrance. Snow stung their faces as they dashed to the front door. There was a woodstove blazing inside and when the door slammed shut behind them, they were embraced by radiated heat.

Quinn brushed snow off his shoulders. "Ahh. It feels great in here," he said to the disinterested attendant sitting behind the counter. "Got anything hot to drink?"

"Over there." The bleary-eyed man lowered the magazine he was reading and lifted his hand in the direction of a large candy rack. "Help yourself. It's on the house."

Quinn poured himself and Faron some strong coffee from a grungy glass pot that was overheating on a two-burner machine. It looked like it had been sitting there since morning, but it didn't matter. It was steaming hot, and a good dose of sugar and canned milk sweetened the burnt taste.

Snow fell steadily while they stood in front of the stove, noses dripping as they thawed. Wind rattled the thin glass windows and seeped in around the sashes.

Quinn looked at his watch. "Should be home by six, maybe a little later."

They were in no hurry to leave the warmth of the stove, but Quinn knew they had to get going if they wanted to stay ahead of the worsening storm. "Guess we should get a move on," he said, refilling his coffee cup. He covered it with a plastic lid and hoisted it in the direction of the cash register on the way out. "Thanks!"

"Just have to dump it down the drain later anyway," the clerk answered, not bothering to look up.

When Faron pulled into the church driveway nearly three hours later, a huge gust buffeted the car and rocked it sideways. "Home just in time," he said, turning the engine off and pocketing the keys. He followed Quinn as they tramped up the walkway, through the back door and into the mudroom.

A look of satisfaction turned up the corners of Quinn's mouth. "I never get tired of the smell of cold air and wet wool," he said as they hung their hats and coats on brass hooks. Snow melted off his hair and dripped down his neck. He kicked off his boots. "Come on, let's eat."

They were both starved. Quinn rubbed his hands together and finished with a final clap, reaching for spoons and bowls. "I made fish chowder yesterday. I'll heat it up." He grunted as he bent down to get the soup pot from the bottom shelf of the refrigerator. "Got some fresh baked cornbread too. One of the ladies from church brought it over."

Faron noticed a photograph of Mary on the counter, near the cookbooks. It hadn't been there on his last visit. A lot of her things were gone but Quinn had kept the kitchenware, some of her quilts, embroidered linens, and there was still some furniture in her upstairs sewing room.

Quinn noticed Faron looking at the framed picture. "I love that. Took it the year before she left. Recognize the place? We were over on the Point, near the lighthouse, digging clams. It was a brilliant day. Late August, I believe. She was happier than she'd been in a long time. Almost like when we were starting out."

"I guess you must really miss her."

"Yes, I do." Quinn stood at the stove, stoop-shouldered from years hunched over sermons and carrying other people's burdens. He stirred the chowder with a wooden spoon. When it reached a gentle boil, rising steam warmed the air. Quinn set the spoon down and lowered the flame under the pot. "You know, when she first left I felt so angry. I guess I was mad at her for leaving me. But the longer she's gone the more I see my part things. She was a fine woman." He gave the chowder another stir. "All I remember now is her goodness, and I miss her terribly—and, as long as we're at it," he said awkwardly, "I guess I haven't completely forgiven myself for any way I may have gone wrong with you either."

Faron pulled out a chair and sat down. Even after all the time he spent talking with Gaines and Holzer—and his friend Laric—he still felt uncomfortable talking about himself. "You and Mary were good to me. I know you both did the best you could. It just took me a long time to realize it. All I want now is to settle back into life on the island and put things behind me."

"I understand," Quinn said, after a pause. He stopped talking for a moment and listened to the sound of soup bubbling in the pot. "You know, after you visited Mary the last time, she was so pleased. She said you were changed, more grown up. She was right."

He poured chowder into their bowls and served it with a clattering of spoons. They sat at the table, buttering thick slices of cornbread and enjoying the hot soup, eating without talking while the storm surged outside. Snow drifted against the doors and piled on the window sashes. The steeple bell clanged in the strong bursts of wind that blew around the spire.

Faron ate quickly and got up to get himself more. "Want any?"

Quinn shook his head. "No, thanks." He stared at his chowder. "You know, I think it's when men are alone in kitchens—like now—that they miss women the most. Know what I mean?"

"I think so." Faron went back to the table with his second bowl of soup. He knew exactly what Quinn meant. Even in her absence, Mary's presence lingered, much as the memory of his own mother stayed with him.

CHAPTER 33

SUNDAY MORNING the storm quieted down, but there were still thin flurries and a solid gray sky. A foot and a half of new snow lay on the ground. Quinn was out early with his snow shovel, clearing a path for the parishioners. Most of them came to church every Sunday no matter what the weather. Cut their teeth on snow and ice. He just made it a little easier for them.

Faron sat in the front pew, welcomed home with Revelation 21:4: *And God shall wipe away all tears from their eyes; and there shall be no more death, neither sorrow, nor crying, neither shall there be any more pain: for the former things are passed away.*

The place was packed. It was one of Quinn's best sermons and nearly everyone stayed awake. Faron enjoyed being surrounded by so many familiar faces: Jarry, Brenda, Owen Batch, Clayton and Stan Jewett, Connie Ebel, Hodie, Emmett Paisley and his wife, Betsy—even Sheriff Paisley, who usually skipped church, showed up.

After the service, there was a sit-down breakfast in Faron's honor. The congregation clustered around him in the annex, pushing platters of food in his direction and reminiscing.

"Hey," Hodie Ebel said, spewing pastry crumbs as he spoke, "what about the time you set your own head on fire? Now that was something!"

"Wasn't it though?" Myron Sprague agreed with a snort as he layered bacon strips between two halves of a bran muffin. "Next he'll be cutting off his ears—he's an *artist*, now, you know . . . our own Faron Van Goss!"

While everyone laughed, Faron massaged his forehead. He had the dull beginning of a headache, but he took the kidding in stride, glad to be home. He was finishing a homemade blueberry waffle when an elderly woman dropped a steaming slice of lobster pie on his plate. It was Minna Beaudry, the lady who used to work behind the register at the Wharf. Her family owned the place and her son, Clyde, ran it now.

"So. I hear you're going to work the stern for the sheriff's brother . . . what's his name . . . Emmett." Minna poked Faron with a gnarled finger. "Shove over." She sat down next to him and scooped out a wedge of pie for herself. "Go on. Eat!" she ordered.

"That's right," Faron answered, chewing a spoonful of the buttery pie. "I start with Emmett next week."

Quinn overheard the conversation and sat next to them, smiling at Faron with paternal pride. "There's no one better to work for than Emmett Paisley." He spoke louder, into Minna's good ear, "Isn't that right, Minna?"

"Yup." Minna was nose down to her lobster pie, feeding herself with a trembling hand, juices dripping down her chin as she ate. She licked her fingers, swallowing the last of the meat-filled pastry. She wiped bits of piecrust off the front of her crocheted sweater and leveled her cloudy eyes at Quinn. "Your old man would be proud, having a sternman in the family. Does he know about Faron—not being your real boy, and everything?"

Quinn smiled at the woman's indiscretion and touched her frail shoulder. "Yes, Minna, he knows. In fact, I'm expecting he might get down here for a visit some time this summer."

Quinn's father was pushing eighty but still fishing. He didn't come to the island much, not since he remarried and moved way up coast near Canada, with a domineering second wife who didn't let him wander too far, especially to see his son, an Episcopal priest—she being a dyed-in-the wool atheist.

Minna narrowed her eyes at Quinn. "A visit? We'll just have to wait and see if that no-good Canadian wife of his lets him out of her sight."

CHAPTER 34

EMMETT AND ALDEN PAISLEY were as different as two brothers could be. Alden could sweet-talk a skunk all night long. Emmett was a man of few words. He pared down his paragraphs into one sentence and had little patience for people who couldn't do the same.

"Just peel the damn thing back and get to the pit," he said to anyone taking too long to make a point. He liked things summed up.

Looking at them, you would never know they were related. Alden was tall and weighed two hundred pounds at his lightest. You could add fifty to that these days. He had been sheriff for over twenty years and the free hunks of pie from Eileen's, and a habitual lack of exercise, showed. His belly hung over his belt and he made no bones about his chronic case of hemorrhoids, from sitting in a patrol car half his life.

As a younger man the women were after him, crazy about the combination of the uniform and six-foot-plus blond good looks. Back then it wasn't unusual to see his cruiser parked on a side road, him wooing an attractive tourist on a summer fling. He also wasn't above keeping company with a wayward Menhaden wife now and then. His woman-chasing tapered down some over the years, but he never did marry.

His brother, Emmett, was the opposite in every way. He was leaner and shorter than Alden, with weather-toughened skin. His auburn hair was considerably thinned by age twenty-seven. He married a high school classmate, Betsy Herrick, when they were only eighteen because he had sex with her one night in the woods behind the school and got her pregnant. Her father all but held a gun to Emmett's head until after the I DOs. Seven months later they had a baby girl.

Betsy's family is one of the oldest on Menhaden—got a cove named after them. Always headstrong, she walks around with a permanent scowl, giving wide berth to other people's opinions. With their grown daughter married and moved away, she and Emmett spend a lot of time hollering back and forth to each other from different rooms of the house. They're an oddly matched pair in all ways—she being big-boned and nearly a foot taller—but they've come to terms with their differences and found the good in one another.

After the marriage, Emmett went to work fishing with his uncle Blake, a stubbornly independent fifth-generation lobsterman—a curmudgeon who got jilted by a girl from away when he was twenty-two and swore off females the rest of his life. Named his boat the *B. Paisley,* after himself.

He had a profitable business but it could have been better if he wasn't always haggling over lobsters prices and tossing them back into the drink when he didn't get what he wanted.

He always said he'd never retire and he'd die on his boat, and that's exactly what happened, and when it did, Emmett took over.

Running a lobster boat alone is hard work, and no one knows that better than Emmett. Help is scarce. Sons fish with their fathers or uncles. They only work for someone else if they're having a family rift, and that doesn't usually last too long once they find out that working for relatives is a lot easier than setting traps with a ballbuster like Emmett Paisley.

Sometimes Emmett gets one of the rich summer kids to work his stern, and occasionally Alden or Betsy. But Alden's the leading half of a two-man police force and chief of public works, which doesn't leave him much spare time, and Betsy . . . well . . . enough said.

When Faron Goss came home, Alden told Emmett he should hire him.

Emmett wouldn't have considered it on his own, knowing Faron's past, but if Alden had one thing, it was good sense when it came to people. He could size someone up with one look and know if they were a keeper or a short, so Emmett took his brother's advice and hired the kid. From day one it worked out.

CHAPTER 35

THE MONDAY MORNING after New Year's glittered like a gem. A seamless blue sky. Emmett's house overlooks Herrick Cove and has a good stretch of lawn sloping down to the water. You can't see the place from the road—the trees are too thick—but the exterior is a pleasant mint green and pink, the same as the *B. Paisley's* buoy colors. Betsy always told Emmett that the cheerful color scheme helped offset his uncle Blake's grumpiness. As it turned out, the colors were a good fit for Emmett, too.

Faron slowed the blue Chevy as he turned into Emmett's long dirt driveway.

Betsy was up early, in the yard throwing table scraps to a large spotted dog. "Go on in!" she shouted to Faron as he got out of his car. She dumped the remains of last night's dinner on the ground for the dog and walked towards the house, following Faron inside.

"Emmett's in the kitchen," Betsy said, hanging her coat on a wooden peg behind the door. Voice as sharp as an ax. Cigarette dangling from her mouth. "Breakfast is made. Sit down and eat."

Faron found his way to the fifties-era kitchen and pulled up a chair to a table with a scratched porcelain top. A place was already set for him and there was a warm pan of eggs and a stack of buttered bread in the middle of the table. Another dog, smaller than the one outside, sat on the linoleum floor with its wet, black nose in Emmett's lap.

"Have some eggs," Emmett said. "She scrambled them with ham. There's coffee on the stove. Over there." He pointed with his fork.

Faron stood up again. He took off his coat and draped it over the back of his chair, poured himself coffee, and sat back down. Spooned a pile of eggs onto his plate while Emmett talked.

"You worked a boat on the mainland, right? Must remember some things. Let's see how you do." Emmett ate and talked at the same time. "I want you to run into town after breakfast. Over to the General Store." He reached in his top chest pocket. "Here's a list. Get it exactly. If they don't have the ten gauge wire panels, don't get any. And it's got to be blue. Everything else they usually have. Order the wire if they're out of it. Eight panels."

Emmett ate the last of his breakfast and put the plate on the floor for the dog. "There's a shed out behind the house—that's where'll I'll be when you get back with the list. We'll start going over all our gear—make repairs and such. Want to be ready to launch early. Be good if I'm the first one in, for once."

He left Faron sitting there with the dog sniffing his crotch and Betsy in the next room sorting laundry and calling out orders to pick her up a newspaper and gallon of milk—the low-fat kind.

When Faron got back from town, he put the milk in the refrigerator and left the paper on the kitchen counter, then went out to the shed.

He'd snuck into the Paisley's yard lots of times when he was younger, chasing the cabbage whites that frequented Betsy's garden, but now the shed seemed bigger than he remembered. It was built solid, and insulated. There was a woodstove cranking out heat and new windows that still had stickers on them.

Emmett noticed Faron admiring the row of double-hungs that looked out to the cove. "Nice, huh? Installed them myself the day after Christmas, with a little help from Alden."

Emmett sat at a long table, painting a buoy. "Get everything?"

"Yup." Faron put the wire and a cardboard carton onto the table—bait bags, hog rings, head netting, a new lobster gauge, clips, and a pair of oversized rubber gloves.

Emmett shoved the gloves back toward Faron. "Present for you. Sit down."

For the next few hours Emmett showed him how to replace netting and other components. Faron had seen it done before, with Captain Boyd, but Emmett had his own way of doing things. Wanted it just so. "No one else's method'll do," he said when he saw Faron tie a strange knot.

At noon they stopped working and went back to the house for lunch. The wife had made lobster bisque and coleslaw. Sourdough biscuits on the side. She didn't eat, but sat at the table with them, smoking a cigarette.

She'd been putting away two packs a day for as long as anyone could remember. Back in high school her friends nicknamed her Butsy because she smoked so much. Emmett still calls her that on occasion, but he's the only one who can get away with it.

"Here." Emmett handed Faron a hefty ceramic bowl. "Have some slaw. No one makes it like her." They took a stab at conversation while they ate. Neither man had much to say and Betsy just frowned at both of them.

Emmett did ask about Faron's painting. Had some interest since his cousin's kid over in Deblois liked to dabble some. "See that, there?" he asked, pointing to the wall, aiming at a faded watercolor of a pine tree. "The cousin's girl done that. Not bad, huh?"

Faron agreed that it was pretty good.

Betsy ground out her cigarette in a pattern of yellow violets on a chipped china saucer. "I'm not keen on it."

"Didn't ask you," Emmett grumbled.

"Well, since I have to look at that picture of a spindly tree day in and day out, I think I'm entitled to voice my opinion, especially as long as we're having this artsy discussion and you're sitting here eating the food I made for you."

Faron couldn't figure out if they were arguing or not because the both of them broke out laughing and Emmett said, "Whatever you say, *Butsy*."

They ate in silence after that, until Betsy decided they were done and started clearing the table.

Emmett headed for the door. "Time to skedaddle."

Faron stood and pushed in his chair. He hadn't seen much of Betsy growing up, but now he remembered that he'd always been a little scared of her the times she'd come into Scuppers. "Thanks for lunch, Betsy," he said timidly.

"Well, there's that, then," she answered, on her way out of the kitchen, both dogs trailing her.

The two men worked in the shed a while longer, until Emmett called it quits. "Don't like putting in too many hours when the boat's out of the water." He opened the woodstove and poked around with a twisted piece of galvanized sheet metal strapping. "Not unless I have to."

It went that way the rest of the winter. Some days they were over to Gallager's yard working on the *B. Paisley*, puttering in the dim light inside the boat, where what little talking they did got blotted out by the sound of loose tarps flapping in the wind. Other days they didn't work at all and Faron stayed home and painted.

Quinn cleared a space for him in Mary's old sewing room. "Is this going to be okay?" He separated Mary's hand-sewn curtains and peered out the window. "She always liked the view."

"It's fine," said Faron. He remembered Mary spending a lot of time in this room. The cat used to keep her company, pawing at bits of cloth that fell away from the patterns she cut.

Quinn cracked open the window. "I'll get Myron Sprague's plumber nephew to hook up running water and a sink for you. Let me know what else you want moved out of here. We can put it in the basement . . . or maybe," Quinn added, "it's time to get rid of it."

Faron put in a long day over at Emmett's—much of it doing chores for Betsy. It was just getting dark when he got home and went upstairs to his studio.

He switched on the light and unwrapped a corned-beef sandwich Betsy insisted he take with him—left over from the St. Patty's Day bash that the church hosted the day before.

"It's more than me and Emmett can eat," she said when she thrust the thick sandwich into Faron's hands. "And God knows Quinn can't cook."

Faron bit into the tasty bread and meat and contemplated his recent paintings. They'd been on his mind most of the day. His eyes flitted from one to the other—moths, butterflies, and other flying insects—in midair, or perched on flowers. The paintings weren't as tight as his earlier ones. These images were slightly blurred, similar to the impressionists he'd recently begun to admire.

He finished his sandwich and was wiping his hands on a napkin when he heard Quinn downstairs.

"You there?" Quinn called out.

"Up here!" Faron answered. He really wanted to be alone tonight, but Quinn was already halfway up the stairs and a moment later, standing in the doorway.

"Have you eaten?" Quinn asked.

"Betsy made me a sandwich."

"Okay. I'll just grab something and head out. Minna Beaudry's down with a bad back and I promised to stop in for a game of checkers."

Faron listened as Quinn went downstairs and rummaged through the kitchen. When he heard the back door close, he relaxed. Now it was just him and the paintings. It was good to be home.

CHAPTER 36

One warm day this far north doesn't mean spring. The day after a snowmelt a frigid rain hammered the island. Lasted three days. Further south daffodils split the soil with bright-yellow cheer. Tree buds faintly green, downstate.

On Menhaden Island, cars veered and slid on frozen rain. Fishermen shivered, mending their gear in chilly sheds. But at the end of the second week in April, there were five straight days of blue skies and bone-warming sunshine. Spring had arrived.

Saturday morning, Faron opened a window in his studio and breathed in the mild sea air. The gulls were brash in the warming weather and he could hear them squawking down in the harbor.

Emmett called earlier and said Monday was going to be a busy day. "Season's about underway. Got to finish rigging the boat—do some last minute maintenance. Come by the house in the morning. Six o'clock. The wife'll fix breakfast."

Faron knew that once the boat was in the water he wouldn't have as much spare time, and he wanted to make the most of this last weekend before the fishing season started. He and Quinn had knocked out part of the north wall in his sewing room studio, and today they were finishing the mouldings on a large window they'd installed.

The room was brighter with the new window, and there was a wider view of the harbor. Faron could watch the boats come and go and there was a direct view of Emmett's mooring. When the light was right, he could see the tidemarks on the pilings in Jarry Gallager's boatyard.

Quinn walked in and saw Faron staring out the window in the direction of Gallager's docks. "Maybe this wasn't such a good idea," he said, following Faron's gaze. "I could move in here and you could paint in the back room, if you like." Quinn had skipped his usual morning walk and was dressed for business. He looked down at his polished black shoes, hands clasped behind his back, waiting for an answer.

"I'm fine here," Faron said.

Quinn looked doubtful.

"Really, I am."

Emmett was ready to launch on Tuesday morning, but the first order of business was a huge breakfast at Scuppers. He and Faron sat at a table with Arvis and Abby Cutter, two old-timers who had been friends with Emmett's uncle.

Nobody could find lobsters the way the Cutters did.

"Hands down, they're the best on the island," Blake Paisley used to grudgingly admit. He'd always been in competition with them and now his nephew was no different.

Abby and Arvis still made their own traps from scrap wood, and the scuttlebutt on the island was that they spent more time replacing broken slats than fishing, although they had the last laugh, considering how much money they saved. Both of them are in their early eighties, with twisted, arthritic fingers and crooked backs, but they could still catch lobsters better than anyone.

Every spring there's a long-standing tradition of choosing a day in April for all the lobstermen to gather together in the harbor and help each other out with last-minute preparations before launching. After that, it's every man for himself.

The Cutter brothers always skipped the group work party and launched early, like they were doing today.

"We like to beat the crowd," Arvis explained to Faron.

"That's right," Abby agreed. "Seems every year there's more and more knuckleheads out here." He cleared a wad of phlegm from his throat and swallowed it. "Pass the sugar, will you?"

Emmett exhaled frustration. He'd told Faron when he hired him that this year they'd be ready before the Cutters. But they weren't. Abby and Arvis had a way of knowing when someone was about to launch and they always managed to beat them in, although today was a close call, which made it all the more exasperating for Emmett.

Except for a last minute problem with the *B. Paisley's* bilge pump, he might have been in before them, but he wasn't taking any chances by putting the boat in the water with a faulty pump.

"Too bad, Emmett. For a minute there it looked like you might be first this time." Abby roared with laughter and Arvis joined him.

Emmett rested his chin in his hands and stuck out both middle fingers, which only made Abby and Arvis laugh louder.

Faron knew it was good-natured teasing, but he was feeling apprehensive about his first time out on Emmett's boat, and the noisy banter added to his jitters.

He'd learned plenty during his time fishing with Captain Boyd and he was good at what he did. The work kept him in great physical shape, and he enjoyed the sounds and sensations of being underway. But he dreaded hauling traps—he always closed his eyes, afraid of seeing his mother's face rising with the trawl. It was worse when the sea was flat and he saw her rippled image surfacing with the traps. Sometimes it was so vivid he gripped the muddy rail, fighting the urge to jump off the boat and swim away.

"Hey! Wake up!" Abby snapped his fingers in Faron's face. "You look like you seen a ghost."

"Better get it out of your system now. There'll be no day-dreaming once you're on board," Emmett growled, depositing his leftover bacon onto Faron's plate. "Here, eat some more . . . it's good for you."

It was seven o'clock when they finished breakfast and headed for the door.

Scuppers was filled with latecomers. "Slowpokes," Arvis said, nudging Faron so hard he lost his balance and had to steady himself on the back of someone's chair. "Laggards won't be in the water for weeks," Arvis scoffed.

The foursome made their way over to Gallager's yard where Jarry and Billy were waiting for them. "Who's first?" Jarry smirked in Emmett's direction, already holding the lines on the Cutters' boat.

Emmett scowled. "Come on, Faron, we've got a pump to fix."

The repair went quickly and they launched without any glitches. For a moment Emmett considered joining the work party to help his fellow fishermen, but decided against it. After stowing some gear and sprucing up the deck, he looked at his watch, then at the overcast sky. "What the hell. It's only ten thirty. A little rain won't kill us. Let's take her for a spin and shake out the kinks."

They couldn't have picked a worse day as far as Faron was concerned. Even the Cutters had decided not to leave the harbor until tomorrow.

"That sky's breeding a storm, Emmett Paisley!" Abby screeched on his handheld radio.

"What's the matter, grown nervous in your old age?" Emmett chided as the Cutters rowed past them, back to shore.

Faron looked upward. The sky had turned downright black, and judging by the way they were rolling on their mooring, the swells further out must be a good size. He could see whitecaps at the mouth of the harbor.

While he rummaged through his sailbag for a flannel shirt to put on top of the one he was wearing, a cigar box fell out.

Emmett knew all about the boxes. "What've you got there?"

Faron tensed. "Just my gear."

"Not that." He pointed to the box. "That."

When Faron didn't answer, Emmett felt sorry for him and didn't question him further. "Just as long as it's empty. We don't need no distractions out here." Emmett steered for open water. *No use making a big deal of it,* he thought. Besides, he was stuck with the guy, distractions or not, because Betsy had decided she was fond of the boy, which for her, was saying something.

CHAPTER 37

In spite of being haunted by what lay below, Faron's first summer on the *B. Paisley* passed quickly, and the next five fishing seasons went even faster. He could empty and bait pots as well as any sternman on the island, though there was still that problem when he hauled a trap.

"You about to puke?" Emmett asked when the color drained from Faron's face. "Keep them eyes open!" He'd heard about the eye-closing thing. The gang had quite a laugh about it a while back.

When he wasn't on the boat or painting, Faron wandered along the shell-flecked beaches and pungent marshes that he explored as a child, but his favorite spot was where he first listened to the pacifying thumps of little brown moths—the small meadow that sprouted where his house used to be.

It wasn't unusual to see him sitting on the overgrown sliver of land, watching insects soar through the rue and feed on the white and yellow flowers. Seaside dragonlets, slaty skimmers, and violet dancers zipped through the air at Puddle Cove, their iridescent wings beating so fast they seemed not to move at all. Monarchs fluttered from blossom to blossom, on their way to Mexico, and nothing soothed him more than the hum of chunky, fuzzy bees, bending stalks of goldenrod as they gorged on sweet nectar.

When the weather was bad, like this morning, he took his sketchpad to Scuppers, where Connie Ebel was still one of the regulars. Being Hodie's wife got her the prized table—the largest one, with a sweeping view of the harbor, as well as the front door, so she and her lady friends could monitor the comings and goings by land and by sea.

Faron hadn't quite outgrown his interest in her, and Connie always made a point of saying something nice. She and her friends were just finishing breakfast when Faron sat down at another table and opened his sketchpad.

"Not bad," Connie said, looking over his shoulder on her way to the register. "You make good pictures of bugs. You still catching those things?"

"Only so I can draw them. Then I let them go."

Ninety-one-year-old Clara Duncan stood up as straight as a woman her age can do and poked her head in the middle of Faron and Connie for a closer look at the drawing. Clara could see terns diving for small fish halfway across the harbor, but everything up close was a blur. "That's real nice," she told Faron. "I like bats—they eat the skeeters."

"It's not a bat," said Faron.

"Tell you what." Clara dug in her pocket and pulled out a crumpled dollar bill and a handful of change. Laid it on the table. "I'll buy it from you—put it on my fridge. I like bats."

"It's not a bat, Mrs. Duncan."

Clara squinted at the drawing. "It's not? What is it, then?"

"A moth."

"Well, so it is," she said, now holding the sketchpad up against her nose. "Nope. You better keep it." She put one crooked hand against the edge of the table and swept her money into it with the other, then shoved the cash back into her pocket. "Let's go, Connie."

All the other ladies at their table had gotten up too. One of them took Clara's arm. "Hey, Clara, I know you can't see very good, but this boy looks just like the great-grandfather."

Clara's weak eyes got a faraway look. "Don't need to see it, I can sense it. Could always tell when Zed Goss was in the room."

Not too many people on the island were old enough to remember Zed in that way, but several of the retired fishermen who were on the hard at Scuppers that morning turned their stiff necks towards Faron and felt a twinge of the old resentment at being second fiddle to Zed Goss.

After Connie and her group left, Faron continued drawing. In fact, he became so absorbed he wasn't aware of the time passing, neither did he notice several women who came in and sat at the next table. It wasn't until he heard laughter that he realized they were there.

One of them was Evie Belden, Menhaden Island's only realtor. She didn't have an office and conducted her real estate business at Scuppers, giving Red a piece of the action in return, although not too many houses changed hands on the island and Evie was more likely to be seen straightening shelves at the library, where she worked part-time.

Faron didn't recognize the other two women. One was near Evie's age, the other much younger. He only saw her profile, but it was enough to know she was attractive. Plain, with long, auburn hair pulled back from her face. He couldn't see her eyes but knew they must be sparkling with her laughter—a laugh as refreshing as a sea breeze through an open window. Not a cackle or a howl, not a giggle or a guffaw. More like a chortle, coming from deep within, though not raspy. The kind of sound that makes everyone else smile.

He pretended to keep drawing as he listened in on their conversation, which he only managed to catch part of—but it was enough to know they were interested in a particular house on the island, though he didn't hear which one.

As they were leaving he still couldn't get a good look at them but he did hear Evie call out, "Have good trip back to New York!"

CHAPTER 38

THE FLEET WAS GROUNDED by a fog as thick as white school paste. As usual, many of the fishermen were waiting it out at Scuppers, Faron among them.

When an attractive woman from Preble Point walked through the door, conversation ebbed. Faron hunched lower over his plate of eggs and snuck a peek at her.

He heard other women making comments, keeping their voices low: *She's got kids. Comes out here all summer without the husband. Will you look at what she's wearing?*

Her bare legs and thigh-length red mackinaw made it seem as though she wore nothing under it. Her tanned face glowed. She didn't sit. Just asked for something to go, elbows on the counter until Red came back with her order.

Faron waited a few minutes after she left, then got up.

"Where're you going?" Billy Gallager hollered when he walked in and Faron bolted past him.

"Got things to do." Faron grabbed his wet foulies off a hook near the cash register and hurried out the door.

He drove slowly along Sheepscot Road, feeling his way through the fog. There was no hurry, he knew where she was going. He went about a mile before he saw the red blur of her car tail lights. He hung back and followed until she turned into her gravel driveway out on the Point and drove past the main house to a shabby outbuilding in the thick pines.

Faron's heart raced as he stepped from his car.

The dank cottage smelled moldy and dead insects crunched under their feet as she led him to an unmade bed. It was still morning but he smelled alcohol on her breath when she wrapped her legs around him and whispered in his ear, "Don't tell anyone."

It wasn't their first time. They made love there whenever she came looking for him—mice running across the floor and squirrels scratching in the eaves. He liked it best in foul weather, when rain pummeled the roof and mixed with the sounds she made when she was right on the brink.

They didn't need clean sheets or swept floors. And late one night when headlights caught him, pants pulled down to his knees, deep inside her, he didn't need to know if it was her husband who sat outside in an idling car, afraid of seeing the truth through a cottage window.

"People are talking," Quinn warned one night when Faron came home late. He wasn't as prudish about such things as you might expect him to be, but he still didn't like it.

"We're just friends," Faron lied.

Quinn frowned. It wasn't the first time there'd been rumors about Faron and summer women. He almost said something else, but remembered his own night with Alison Goss and avoided the hypocrisy.

Faron kept seeing her until she left the island at the end of October, the same day he and Emmett hauled the *B. Paisley*. Emmett had heard the talk, too, and he'd seen her board the ferry when he was coming out of Scuppers that morning. Her kids had gone earlier in the week, with the husband.

"Betsy says you'll have pot roast with us tonight. Celebrate the hauling," Emmett said as he and Faron were finishing up for the day.

A nod from Faron, his hands full of twisted trap lines.

At supper, Betsy groused about the looming winter, and Emmett home for the whole of it. "Drives me crazy every year," she complained to Faron, standing over him and holding a plate heaped with plump buttermilk biscuits. She plopped herself down.

Faron reached for a biscuit and spread it with butter while Emmett and Betsy sparred.

"You could go see your sister this winter," Emmett said, chewing pot roast.

"I suppose I could," Betsy said, pushing her plate away, "if I didn't need to be here and boss you around." She slid a bowl of carrots in Faron's direction. "Eat these, they'll help you see things more clearly." She sounded pissed off.

Emmett sighed. He'd wondered how long it'd take her to get around to Faron's personal business.

But she didn't pursue it. Saw the mistake in what she said right away.

Faron eyed his food. He supposed he knew what Betsy meant—about seeing things clearly—but people view things differently and he never did see things the way most folks did.

CHAPTER 39

Walter and Lydia Dodge gave their daughter, Alva, a name she'd grow into, not out of. Always an eye-catcher in a plain sort of way, she still had striking good looks at age thirty-seven. She favored slacks to dresses and often wore her thick, wavy hair pulled back with her grandmother's ivory barrettes.

She wasn't vain but did express surprise when she recently glimpsed her reflection in full sunlight and noticed deepening laugh lines at the corners of her mouth.

"Too much time outside looking at birds," her father said. "Ruins the skin." He never understood why someone as affable and beautiful as his daughter wasn't married, though he guessed it had something to do with her strong opinions, which his wife said came from him—a former sergeant at Normandy who barked orders that kept most of his men alive after their platoon leader got blown to bits.

Alva loved birds. She carried a pocket-sized pair of binoculars everywhere she went. When her parents retired to upstate New York and bought a wild piece of land chock-full of the feathered creatures, she followed, happy for the chance to tromp through their property with a sightings log, searching for a rare one.

Walter sidled up to Alva's desk and looked over her shoulder at the title of the magazine she was working on. "*Watch The Birdie*? Who the hell thought that one up?"

Alva worked from home, editing bird magazines, or, as her father said, 'wasting her time looking for other people's mistakes.'

"Dad, do you mind?" she asked impatiently, nudging him toward his reading chair in the living room. "I'm working."

She was at her desk in a large enclosed sunporch at the southern end of the house. It was a splendid day to sit in the bright room, working among the specks of dust floating in the sunlight.

When her father left her alone, she stared absent-mindedly out the window at the assortment of birds zooming back and forth to the feeders. She was in the middle of a daydream when the phone rang.

"It's for you!" Walter shouted to Alva. It was Evie Belden—a real estate agent from Menhaden Island—calling to say that the house Alva's grandparents' once owned was for sale. The last time Alva and her mother visited the island they met with the realtor, but never really expected anything to come of it.

"Go on up and have a look. You don't have to buy it," Alva's mother coaxed.

"Buy it? Damn crazy if she does." Her father disapproved, padding with stockinged feet into the sunporch to see what was going on. "Don't put those ideas in her head, Lydia."

"Don't think she hasn't already thought of it on her own," Lydia rebutted. Her husband had never been particularly fond of the place, but she and Alva were.

The likelihood of purchasing the house was slim, but after thinking it over, Alva called the realtor back the next day to arrange a visit.

"Get on the car ferry in Willisport," Evie instructed. "It's about a one-hour crossing. You got a schedule? Oh, will you listen to me. . . . you already know all that. I'll meet you at the local watering hole, like last time."

Alva pictured the realtor's directions clearly. Even though she didn't get back to Maine often, she did still know her way around Willisport and Menhaden.

"Want to come?" she asked her parents after hanging up the phone.

Before her mother could say anything, her father answered for both of them. "No. Have fun." He stomped into the living room, plunked down in his reclining chair, and put his nose in the newspaper, wondering where his daughter got such crazy ideas.

CHAPTER 40

AT THE END of a fast-moving thunderstorm, the sun highlighted huge, billowy clouds. Alva couldn't recall when she'd seen such a beautiful sky. She was admiring it when Walter and Lydia came outside.

Walter couldn't believe she still hadn't left. "Stop gawking. It'll be tomorrow by the time you get there." Whenever he took a car trip he was out of bed and on the road before daylight, no matter what the weather was. For the life of him he couldn't understand his dawdling daughter.

Alva tossed her purse into the car and kissed her parents goodbye. "Don't worry, Dad, I'll be there before dark."

Her father was right, she should have gotten an earlier start, but she always dreaded traveling anywhere and put it off as long as possible, and this trip was no different.

Other than the short visit to Maine last year with her mother, she hadn't been anywhere since volunteering to record piping plover nesting sites on Long Island, and that was three years ago. It was also the last time she'd been with a man—a fellow birder who swooped down on her like a hawk on a vole, or at least that's how she remembered it now. She cringed at the recollection.

"I think he might be the one," she'd gushed to a friend on the ride back to Dutchess County. But he wasn't. Turned out his bird-watching interest was a ruse to flush out one of the many women he knew he'd find during Audubon bird counts. That ill-fated affair still stuck in her craw.

Now, she sped north, leaving the Empire State behind her, entering Connecticut, then Rhode Island and Massachusetts. It was a beautiful ride. Trees were just starting to fill in. She opened the window and took a deep, full breath, inhaling the spring green landscape.

She made several stops throughout the day—once to eat lunch and twice more to stretch her legs. At a rest stop in the Granite State she stayed longer than she should have, watching a glossy-feathered crow hop slowly sideways along a fence to steal a chunk of bread from a squirrel.

By late afternoon she wove through the maze of inlets along the road leading to the narrow streets of Willisport, feeling the same bittersweet tug she always did in Maine.

She parked the car at the ferry landing and squinted against the sun sparkling on the water. She had planned to head straight for Menhaden and meet the realtor this afternoon, but now she reconsidered. She was tired and hungry and thought it might be better to wait until tomorrow.

Alva phoned her parents to let them know where she was, then bought a soda at a small store next to the ferry landing and called the realtor. "I'm in Willisport, but I'm exhausted. Can we meet in the morning?"

"Where did you say you are? Willisport? There's a decent hotel there, two blocks up from the ferry dock—well, you must know it—been there forever. New management though. The rates just went up. Have a good night and I'll see you in the A.M. What time?"

"I'll be there by ten." Alva hung up the phone and got back into her car and drove to the hotel, an old but recently painted building that took up an entire block. She parked around back and walked through a garden along a brick pathway to the sunny front lobby. The fresh scent of the bay wafted through a propped-open window.

After checking in, she went to the restaurant across the street for an early supper. The place was loud and the service slow, but the steamers and beer were worth it.

She topped off her meal with a stroll along the beach, where the Menhaden locals sometimes went on summer weekends to blend in with the tourists. Fancy shops had sprung up where fishermen's sheds and a sardine factory used to be. She kicked off her shoes and walked barefoot in the sand, looking out across the water, straining to make out the islands that she knew were there in the salty darkness.

In the morning, Alva was too excited to eat breakfast. After checking the ferry schedule, she hopped in the car and turned on the low beams for the short, foggy ride to the landing.

The ferry was right on time. Alva followed a line of cars being waved forward by a wind-burned crewman. Once aboard, she climbed the stairs to the upper deck and steadied herself against a metal railing, watching the water churn as they left the dock. The smell of fresh paint and diesel fumes tainted the sea air. Boisterous gulls swooped overhead. When the wind got too strong, she went below to sit by a window.

The string of smaller islands that were obscured last night were now slightly visible through the fog. Years earlier, during family outings to Willisport Beach, she used to love watching sailboats tack back and forth between the pine-studded islands.

Alva closed her eyes and fondly recalled playing in the surf within shouting distance of her grandparents, yet feeling so completely alone when suntan-lotion-laced breezes blew the sound of their voices out to sea.

She was deep in her memories when one of the ferryboat crewmen sat near her and started yammering, doing some reminiscing of his own.

"Your first crossing? Good to get out early in the season, before the damn tour boats ruffle the water. Too many people from away mucking things up," he complained. "Can't even remember the last time the river had a good alewife run. Habitat's disappearing."

Alva knew what he meant. It was the same thing in upstate New York. Large, sprawling houses where there used to be sunny stands of white birch and thickets of arrowwood and buttonbush. She went into a silent rage every time she passed a field and saw developers pacing it off with tape measures. Nobody gave a hoot about the environment anymore.

"There's Johns Island . . . out over that way," the man said, pointing past their reflections in the salt-encrusted window, "and right across from that is Gray Senny Rock. Those are the two largest islands, except for Menhaden. There's a bunch of smaller ones, too, and lots of birds and seals."

Alva listened politely to the man until the ferry shifted gears and lurched to a noisy stop at the Menhaden landing, where she bid a pleasant goodbye to her unofficial tour guide.

Evie Belden was waiting for her in front of Scuppers. "What say we just go directly to the house?" Evie suggested. "We can come back here later for lunch."

CHAPTER 41

THE REALTOR JIGGLED the key in the lock and opened the front door. The place smelled of damp woodsmoke and dust. Sections of wall had been removed and debris was scattered on the floors.

"Not as clean as your grandparents kept it, I'm sure," Evie noted apologetically. She lifted a foot and brushed sawdust off her shoe. "The last owners started renovating and . . . well, as you can see . . . they got overwhelmed.

"Divorced right after the husband finished ripping out the plaster in the dining room. A shame, really. They were a nice young couple. She's still in town, with her folks. Don't know what happened to him. Wasn't from around here."

They moved quickly through the front entryway, the realtor chatting the entire time. "The roof's still good—will last another twenty years. Plumbing's brand new three years ago, all copper.

"There's a woodstove and a brick fireplace," Evie chirped. "Previous owners had a space heater installed. Used it for years until someone recommended against it—said it was unsafe—so they pulled it out and put in the stove. Works like a charm. Can heat the house all winter. The woodshed's filled. The husband split the oak himself before he took off. Three cords. Comes with the house. Boiler works, too, if you get tired of lugging wood."

The living room was overcrowded with two sagging sofas and an assortment of threadbare chairs. The knotty pine walls that Alva loved so much as a child were darkened with age. Someone had begun pulling up the kitchen floor and several layers down there were remnants of her grandmother's speckled linoleum.

"Come on out back," Evie said. "There's a new deck over the well."

At the end of the wooden walkway that led from the house to the well, a fresh coat of gray paint gleamed. Beyond, there was a small meadow bordering a freshwater marsh.

"Even though the house isn't on the ocean, it's near enough that a person in good shape can easily walk the distance there and back," Evie pointed out. "Oh. There I go again. Keep forgetting your family used to own the place."

Alva shut her eyes, taking it all in.

"Ah, well." Evie mistook closed eyes for disinterest. "There's another place not too far from here—on the upper island near the harbor. I think it might be just right for you. There've been some major repairs made to it and the structure's solid. On an acre of land, set back nicely from the road. It's bigger and closer to the water—got a seasonal view from the back—you might even be able to cut down some trees to expand it. Have to check with the town board on that. What do you think?" There was a touch of impatience in her voice. "Want to have a look?"

"No," Alva said decisively. "I want this one."

"You did what?" Walter Dodge was fuming. Worried, really. But when he worried, he fumed. "Why'd you do such a stupid thing? You can't move up there! Jesus Christ, Alva, at your age you should be moving closer to civilization, not further away. That island's miles out from the mainland. What the hell are you going to do there all by yourself? Those people never accepted your grandparents and they lived there fifty years!"

"Forty-two," his wife corrected.

"What's the difference?" said Walter.

Alva had just gotten back to New York and told her parents the news. Now she and her mother were trying to calm her father down. It wasn't easy. He just couldn't understand why she was buying back the same house he sold decades ago.

"Don't worry, Dad. It'll be fine. It's in good shape. Just needs a few repairs and a coat of paint. It'll be a great summer house for us—you, Mom, and me. I'll still live here."

"I don't get it," Walter grumbled, "you're going backwards, buying that place."

"No, Dad, not backwards . . . in a circle." Alva made a loop in the air with her hand. "I'm coming full circle, just like everything else in life—seasons, relationships . . . besides, it's a good investment. I'm buying in a down market. It'll increase in value."

He made faces at the full circle hogwash, but that last part got his attention: a good investment. When she told him the purchase price and he calculated how much the house would appreciate over the next five years, it started to make a little more sense.

CHAPTER 42

THE FIRST WEEK IN JUNE, Alva packed her car and drove to Maine to begin working on the house with a carpenter the realtor recommended. By the end of August, they were finished and she went into town to buy paint for the walls.

A dangling cowbell jingled a greeting when she opened the door to the General Store. She'd been in before and had admired the sardine memorabilia on the walls: signs, knives, photographs—there were even pieces of the wire flakes that held fish during the cooking.

"All that stuff came from a fish processing plant on the mainland after it shut down," said the older man behind the counter when he noticed her interest.

He got up from his comfortable spot at the register. "Name's John Brady. Aren't you the gal who moved into your family's old place, over by Keeps Pond?"

Alva smiled. She'd only been on the island a short time and already everyone knew the details. "Yes, I am," she said, shaking his hand. "I'm Alva Dodge."

"My family knew your grandparents, Jack and Milfred. I was just a kid, but I remember them. Nice folks." His eyes drifted to the past. "I think I knew you, too, but you probably don't recall me."

"You're right. I don't remember many people out here," Alva replied, a lump in her throat at the mention of her grandparents from someone who actually knew them. "It's good to be back though. I've been in here several times but I haven't seen you, only the fellow with the beard."

"That's my son." The storekeeper sat down again, took off his glasses and wiped them clean with his shirttail. "I'm the owner but he's taken over the day-to-day. I just show up once in a while to make sure he's not running the place into the ground."

Alva laughed. "You sound like my father."

"Well, that's someone I'd like to meet."

"Oh, you will. He used to love this place, years ago—when the Thompsons ran it." Alva gestured toward the surrounding shelves that were filled with dusty odds and ends that looked as if they'd been in the store since her grandparents' time.

"Old man Thompson. What a character he was. Now that's going back some!" Mr. Brady declared. "As you can see, the place hasn't changed much."

"No, it hasn't," Alva said. "I'll bring Dad by when he and my mother come up to visit."

They made some more small talk, and then Mr. Brady pointed her in the general direction of the paint supplies. "Third aisle on the left. Midway down for the buckets and brushes. Paint's against the back wall."

Alva found the buckets and was trying to decide between metal or plastic when there was a commotion behind her at the back of the store. She turned in the direction of the racket and saw a bird, a barn swallow—*Hirundo rustica*. It flew past her at high speed, grazing her left cheek with the tip of a wing. It startled her so that she was knocked off balance and fell over, taking a shelf of steel pails with her, which landed on the hardwood floor with an earsplitting crash.

Mr. Brady jumped up to help but retreated when two other men ran over to her. "Just leave the mess!" he shouted. "I'll get it later!"

"You all right?" one of the men asked, biting his lower lip as if trying to suppress a laugh.

"I think so." Alva guessed it was a funny sight, her on the floor amid the buckets. Embarrassed, she grabbed the stranger's outstretched hand and hefted herself up. "What was that all about?" she asked, still wobbly.

"A bird. Must have been trapped in here all night. Took off when I grabbed something from the shelf. You should have ducked." He had a hand over his mouth but she could tell by his eyes that he found her predicament amusing.

Alva dusted herself off. Humiliation tinted her cheeks. "I didn't have time to duck," she said, sizing him up. He was short. Windburned. Had a quickness about him that reminded her of birds darting to and from a seed patch.

The second man seemed more sympathetic. He was younger than his friend. Probably younger than her, too. And the most handsome fellow she'd ever seen. He stood quietly, holding a coil of bright pink line, staring at her with eyes as dark as a grackle. She figured they were both fishermen and swore she could smell the sea on them.

Then they were gone. She heard the register open and close. "Take care, Emmett. You, too, Faron," the owner called after them.

Alva picked out some paint and brushes, grabbed a metal pail from the jumble on the floor, and went up front to pay, trying to remember if there'd been a wedding ring on the younger man's hand.

CHAPTER 43

THINGS DIDN'T GO exactly as Alva planned.

One evening, after cleaning paint rollers and brushes, she went to the local library to attend a lecture called "Maine's Endearing Winter Resident: The Black-Capped Chickadee." The place was filled to capacity with islanders laughing it up and cracking the same old joke about the black fly being the state bird, not the chickadee.

The guest speaker was from the Maine Audubon Chapter. "Black-capped chickadees," he began enthusiastically, "hide seeds to eat at a later time. They store them in hundreds of different spots and can remember every single hiding place."

"Kind of like a lobsterman, eh?" a man in the audience called out.

"Excuse me?" the confused lecturer said.

"Like a lobsterman! We know where every pot is set, even without those new fangled GPI's. We eyeball it. Why don't you give a talk about that?" he kidded.

"You mean GPS, you old Black-Capped Lobsterman!" another man shouted.

Someone between the shelves in the agriculture and gardening section started doing their best imitation of a chickadee and the whole place broke out in raucous laughter, birdcalls, and some unmentionable phrases.

The speaker was a good sport, and once he realized it was all in fun, he laughed along with everyone else. Before long he got the evening back on track, explaining eloquently about the chickadee and all its charms.

Although she was already well acquainted with the antics of the chickadee, Alva enjoyed the talk immensely. She hung around afterwards for refreshments, mingling with the locals and sharing her thoughts on their state bird. Even though most of the attendees were only there for a night out and the free snacks, and could have cared less about the fluffy black-and-white bird, they humored her with nods and grunts in response to her enthusiastic interest.

Driving home along Sheepscot Road with the windows wide open to let in the aromatic night air, Alva felt wonderful. She had no doubts that buying her grandparents' house was the smartest thing she'd ever done, and the chickadee lecture cinched it—she wanted to be a year-round resident.

The next day, when she called her parents and told them the news, her mother answered the phone, but she heard her father in the background say, "I told you so, Lydia!"

Thanksgiving Day, Alva and her mother cooked their first turkey dinner together on Menhaden Island. Her father had, grudgingly, made the trip with his wife, not trusting her to make the drive alone. They were walking off bourbon stuffing and pumpkin pie in a misty rain when they ran into Faron Goss on Harbor Street.

It wasn't the first time Alva had seen him since their awkward meeting in the paint aisle. They'd stolen glances at one another several times since, at the General Store, and down at Beaudry's Wharf—and once, when she ventured into Scuppers for some take-out food, she'd seen him sitting at a table with a bunch of older women. But tonight, on the narrow sidewalks in town, they spoke for the first time.

While her parents wandered down the street looking at the Christmas decorations that already adorned the town's few buildings, Faron mustered his courage and asked Alva to have dinner with him the following weekend.

A heavy snow fell the day of their first date. By late afternoon, there was more than a foot on the ground.

"Going somewhere?" Quinn was stooped over shoveling new snow off the walkway when Faron came out the back door

"Yes," Faron answered. He was freshly showered, steam rising off his damp hair in the cold air. Traces of rose madder and viridian green still under his fingernails. "Sorry, I won't be here for supper."

Quinn straightened up and tipped the shovel against a tree. He sniffled and wiped his nose with a snowy sleeve. "That's okay. I have some calls to make this evening. Where're you going?"

"Remember that woman I told you about . . . at Brady's store?"

Quinn thought for a second. "The one that got knocked over by a bird?"

Faron flashed a quick smile. "That's the one."

It was thirty degrees and falling. Both men stomped their feet to keep warm, hands tucked under armpits.

Quinn was glad, but surprised that Faron was going out. He didn't think Faron had any female friends—well, except for Connie Ebel and her crowd . . . and those summer women.

With Emmett's traps pulled for the season, Faron had more free time and spent most of it alone in his studio. Quinn knew that was a good thing, but so was socializing.

The studio was untidy, too—spider webs in the corners and dead flies on window ledges. It reminded him of the way Faron kept house on Puddle Cove. In fact, he was so concerned about it that he'd called Sander Gaines . . . and been embarrassed when Gaines said, "For goodness sake, Quinn, there are dead flies in my own house this time of year too."

Quinn took off a glove and scratched his neck. Snowflakes melted under his collar. "Where are you taking her?"

"Scuppers. She didn't like the idea of a ferry ride to Willisport."

"Can't say I blame her . . . in this weather." Quinn put his glove back on and reached for the shovel. It had been snowing in fits and starts all day, but it was really coming down now. "Be careful on the roads," he said, then bowed over and went back to work clearing a path.

CHAPTER 44

Alva shivered against the leather seat of her car. She didn't know if it was from the cold or from a case of nerves. It had been a long time since she'd been out with a man. She was surprised when Faron asked her to dinner, but something hopeful in his voice gave her the courage to say yes.

She clutched the steering wheel with both hands as she turned into Scuppers. It was her idea to meet there, rather than have him pick her up. This way, she could leave whenever she wanted if things didn't go well.

Faron was already sitting at a corner table by the window at the far end of the main dining room, where there was a good view of the harbor, as well as some privacy.

He rose to greet her. "You look nice."

"Thank you." She thought he did, too, but didn't say it.

He was dressed in jeans and a tweed jacket. There was a small speck of dried blood on his chin where he must have cut himself shaving.

He waited for her to sit, a half-finished beer in his hand. "Can I get you a drink?"

"That looks good," Alva said, eyeing the bottle of amber brew he was holding.

Faron waved in the direction of the bar and Jeannie Ebel came over to their table with her order pad and two sauce-stained menus. She'd been working at Scuppers since graduating from the Culinary and Baking certificate program at Washington County Community College. Even though she was younger than Faron, she always acted like it was the other way around. She did that with everyone. A regular Miss Smarty-pants. She flipped through her order pad for a blank page and gave Alva a curious look.

"We'll have two of these." Faron hoisted his beer bottle to get her attention.

Alva glanced at the menu while they waited for their drinks. Seemed like battered and fried was standard fare. "I'll have the fried chicken," she said when Jeannie returned with their beers.

"Dressing on your salad?"

"Oil and vinegar."

Jeannie raised her thinly plucked eyebrows and looked at Faron. "And you?"

"Fried shrimp and a baked potato. No salad." He handed her the menu.

Jeannie closed the order pad and stuck her pencil behind her ear but didn't leave. "Aren't you going to introduce me to your lady friend?"

Faron's face reddened. "Jeannie, this is Alva."

"Pleased to meet you," Jeannie drawled, hoping for more information. "Can I get you two anything else?"

"No. Just that." Faron deliberately looked down at the tablecloth until Jeannie realized he wasn't playing along, and went to place their orders.

"Friend of yours?" Alva asked.

"Not really. Just someone I grew up with."

"She's pretty."

"I guess. I never really thought of her that way."

They struggled to find something to say until Jeannie came back with their food. "Here you go." She plunked down their meals and Alva's salad—a wooden bowl of wilted iceberg lettuce and two slices of mealy tomato, soaked in dressing.

Alva should have known better than to expect fresh vegetables offshore this time of year. But the crispy chicken made up for it. The batter was light, with just the right amount of salt.

Conversation came easier with the hot food. Heat rose in the room and condensed on the paned windows as they ate and talked. Alva felt at ease in the cozy restaurant, although she wondered why the younger man was interested in her. Never one to mince words, she asked him, "Why did you invite me to dinner?"

"I don't know. You just seemed so . . . approachable."

"You mean lying flat on my back in the store?"

Faron blushed. "Yes."

Alva laughed.

"I like your laugh . . . and this isn't the first time I've heard it."

"What do you mean?"

"I saw you once. You were sitting over there with Evie Belden." He pointed to the far corner. "I was at the next table. Evie must have said something funny, because you laughed."

Alva was taken aback, but before she could say anything, Jeannie headed toward them from the direction of the bathroom, pulling at her apron to straighten it. "Want dessert?"

Faron couldn't help noticing Jeannie was being more attentive than usual, probably hoping to overhear something juicy so she could blab it all over the island.

"I think I'll pass." Alva looked at her watch. It was still early but the roads were slick coming over and she was afraid it might be worse on the way back. Faron was staring at her. She hoped he wasn't insulted that she'd checked the time. "I'm worried about the weather," she explained.

"That's okay." Faron reached for the bill Jeannie left on the table.

Red took his money at the register. "Everything all right tonight?"

"Yup. As usual."

"Drive slow," Red advised. "Roads are bad."

Faron held the door open and Alva stepped outside. It was snowing hard. Too cold to stand and talk for long, but before Faron strode away they made plans to meet at Scuppers again, the following night.

CHAPTER 45

ALVA GOT THERE FIRST. She parked around back in the neatly plowed lot and waited with the engine running. It hadn't snowed all day, but it felt twenty degrees colder than yesterday. She glanced out the window at the starless sky, trying to quell her nervousness. They were supposed to meet at six and it was ten after. She waited a few minutes more, then went inside.

The place was busy and she had to stand by the door while Jeannie Ebel cleared a table. "You alone?"

"No, there're two of us."

Jeannie pursed her lips and dropped a second menu on the table. "You want a drink?"

"I'll have a Chardonnay."

When she looked up from her second glass of wine thirty minutes later, Faron was rushing in through the door. "I'm sorry I'm late," he said, pulling out a chair.

Lucky for him Alva was feeling the drinks and let him off easy. "Don't worry about it," she said with slightly slurred forgiveness.

Faron's sigh of relief was audible. "Emmett—my boss—asked me to go over to Willisport and pick up some traps. It took longer than I figured—then I had to wait for the ferry. Sorry."

Alva waved off his apology. "It's okay. It's been nice sitting here looking at the harbor."

They ordered hamburgers and more wine and sat in silence. Faron had a nervous habit of shaking one leg and his knee kept banging the underside of table.

Just when the lack of conversation was beginning to become unbearable, Jeannie returned with their drinks and burgers. "Medium rare?"

Faron raised his hand and she put a plate down in front of him and gave the other one to Alva. "Anything else?" Her eyes watered as she suppressed a yawn.

Alva figured she better order another drink now, considering how long it took to get the first two. "I'll have more wine."

Faron held out his glass. "Me too."

When Jeannie returned, she didn't say a word, just left the drinks on the table and put a cigarette in her mouth as she ambled away.

Alva glanced at the *No Smoking* sign over the bar and watched Jeannie blow smoke rings in the air. "I thought there was no smoking in here."

Faron chewed a French fry and dipped another in a gob of ketchup. "There isn't, but Red lets her."

"Why?"

"She's the harbormaster's daughter and it doesn't hurt to be on his good side."

"What for?"

"It can get you first dibs on a mooring, among other things, or reserved spots to tie up boats in front of Scuppers."

They ate the remainder of their meal without saying much. When Alva ordered tea, Faron did the same.

He stirred milk and sugar into his cup, feeling completely relaxed. Maybe it was the wine, but suddenly he was very talkative and he told Alva everything—about his mother, the bugs, the fake kidnapping, and his painting. It didn't really matter. She'd find out soon enough. God knows Hodie and Jarry like to tell the story of how they pulled Alison Goss out of the water just before lunch, and people still talked about the Lobster Queen incident.

He glanced toward the bar. And that Jeannie Ebel's got a big mouth too. You just never know what she'll say. There was an often-repeated saying on the island that news is like Sheepscot Road: it makes a continuous loop. Quinn Gage had always referred to that loop of news as gossip, but most everyone else simply thought of it as sharing information.

While Faron told Alva about himself, he watched her for a reaction. If anything he said bothered her, she didn't show it.

There was an icy rain dribbling down when they walked outside. The neon signs in the restaurant windows cast a purple hue on the plowed mounds of snow in the parking lot. Muffled strains of music and Jeannie Ebel's smoky laugher drifted out from the bar as Faron and Alva stood in the wet cold.

Faron pulled up his collar. "Where'd you park?"

"Around back," Alva said, jutting her chin in the general direction.

Faron took her hand and walked with her, both of them a bit unsteady from the wine.

When she unlocked her car and turned to say goodnight, he kissed her and pulled open the rear door. The two of them tumbled in and stretched across the back seat. There were voices outside. Truck doors slammed shut. Footsteps crunched the frozen snow. But all they heard was their own breathing quicken. Alva moaned when Faron lifted her skirt and slid on top of her. He smelled of booze and cold air. She knew that afterwards her face would be red and blotchy, burning where his whiskers scraped her chin, but she didn't care. She put her arms around his neck and raised her hips to meet his.

CHAPTER 46

SOME DAYS, after working in his studio, Faron went to Alva's, a vague scent of linseed on him. Other days he went to her house straight from Emmett's shed, bits of wood and rope fibers clinging to his shirt, a bracing whiff of cold air on him. Either way, Alva thought love smelled good.

The stars loomed close the crisp January night she stood over her bathroom sink reading the instructions for a home pregnancy test. Faron was in the kitchen washing dishes, thinking it was a chore Alva should really be doing, when he heard her shout, "It's positive!"

A minute later she was standing beside him waving something that looked like a thermometer. "Did you hear me? It's positive." She could see by his expression that he was confused.

"I'm pregnant," she explained.

Faron was speechless. He stared at his hands in the warm suds.

"Aren't you going to say anything?"

He had an uneasy feeling that the starry night sky was closing in on him. "I don't know what to say. I never thought about something like this." Actually, he'd thought she might be too old to get pregnant, but he knew better than to say it.

"I know, it's a shock for me too. I guess I'll go see a doctor to confirm it." She put a hand on her stomach. "But I'm pretty sure."

Faron's apprehension lifted when he saw how calm Alva was, and how her eyes shone. "Does this mean we have to get married?" he asked.

Alva's father always said that she wasn't happy unless she got her way, but this was almost too easy. "Yes, it does."

The three of them sat in Quinn's kitchen drinking hot chocolate. It was another snowy Sunday. Quinn had met Alva twice before when Faron surprised him and brought her to church. He'd done the same today.

"What will you do?" Quinn looked from Faron to Alva, then back to Faron. He was concerned, but the news came as no surprise. He remembered what doctors had told him and Mary all those years they were trying to have children: the more sex the better your chances. Judging by the amount of time Faron had been spending at Alva's, their chances were pretty high.

"We're getting married." Alva put her hand on Faron's to let him know she was doing the talking. The gesture didn't escape Quinn.

He didn't know much about the woman, only that her grandparents had lived on the island. He vaguely remembered them from his childhood. Catholics, who went to church on the mainland.

He knew she was a bit older than Faron. Something about birds, too—she liked going to the Audubon lectures at the library and there were feeders all over her yard.

It was obvious why Faron was drawn to her. She was attractive and bright. But Quinn wondered if Faron had told her everything about his past, and if so, why it didn't matter to her. Not that he didn't think Faron had a lot to offer, it's just that he thought it was rather an odd pairing.

Then again, Alva wouldn't be the first woman to find him irresistible.

Maybe she just wanted a baby. Maybe it's what all women want. Mary had. He never really understood the depths of it.

Quinn swirled a spoon through the dollop of whipped cream in his hot chocolate. All he wanted was someone who'd be good to Faron. "Well, I suppose if your minds are made up it's too late for advice."

Alva squeezed Faron's hand. A different signal, meaning he should speak up.

"It seems like the right thing to do, since she's pregnant," Faron said on cue.

"Well, it's the honorable thing to do, but what about love?" Quinn knew there was no stopping the marriage, but he still had to ask. "Do you love each other?"

Alva didn't hesitate, "I love him very much, Father Quinn."

Quinn could see from her expression that she meant it.

"Me, too." Faron looked down at his hands and scratched at a paint stain. His face flushed. He thought about the time he buried Mary's cat without telling them. He remembered being questioned by Quinn, shamed by what he'd done. It felt a little like that now.

Quinn wasn't convinced. He and Mary had done their best to give Faron a loving home, but eight years with Alison Goss left an impression and he wouldn't be surprised if, now, Faron was confusing sex with love. But there was nothing he could do about it. He could only hope for the best.

Quinn got up to pour himself another cup of hot chocolate. "Anyone want more?"

"I'd like some," Alva answered.

He took his time at the stove, thinking about Alva and sneaking glances at her. She seemed like a nice enough person. Folks at church liked her, although he did overhear a few remarks about her being from 'away' and looking a little 'old' for Faron.

"Thanks," Alva said when Quinn handed her the cocoa. She took a thoughtful sip and, as if reading his mind said, "I know it's sudden, and you're probably uncomfortable with our difference in ages, but I'm choosy about men—" she paused and looked lovingly at Faron, "—and I know he's the right one."

Quinn watched as Faron slung his arm around the back of Alva's chair and kissed her on the cheek. It was a perfectly normal response to her sentiments, but he simply could not imagine Faron married or raising children. "Have you thought about when you'll have the wedding?"

"The sooner the better," Alva piped up, cradling her stomach with her hands.

"And we'd like you to perform the ceremony," Faron added. "Me and Alva already talked about it."

"I should hope so," said Quinn. "It wouldn't be right not to have a church wedding."

CHAPTER 47

THE DATE WAS SET for March third, Alva's father's birthday, and what turned out to be an unusually warm day, considering there was still two feet of snow on the ground.

Her parents drove up from New York the day of. Stomped snow off their feet on the front steps of the church. Walter gave his daughter away and he and Lydia sat awkwardly during the rest of the service.

"Is it me," Walter whispered to his wife during the vows, "or does he look a little young for her?"

"Hush," Lydia murmured, "just pay attention."

Laric was best man. Came alone. "Wouldn't miss it," he assured Faron. When he got to the church, he stood off by himself most of the time until things got started. Needed a haircut and some meat on his bones. Had a brooding look in his eye.

After the ceremony, the entire congregation went to the annex for a potluck reception.

"Congratulations!" Emmett slapped the groom hard on the back. Across the room Alva and Betsy were deep in conversation. "Have a look at that, will you?" Emmett directed Faron's attention to their wives. "Aren't those two hens a pair?" Emmett snickered. "Oh, boy. Are you ever in for it."

Laric made a meandering toast that ended with a quote from Ralph Waldo Emerson: '*Do not go where the path leads, go instead where there is no path and leave a trail.*'

"What's he talking about?" Abby Cutter asked out loud.

The whole room shrugged.

Minna Beaudry shuffled up to Abby and squawked in his ear, "That's the boy's best friend . . . from you-know-where."

"Ahh. Got it." Abby held Minna's spindly elbow. "Come on, there's cake."

The bride and groom cut into the wedding cake Lydia made for them. Two layers of chocolate with vanilla frosting, Alva's favorite. *Congratulations Alva and Faron*, in blue icing, her mother's handwriting squeezed through a pastry bag. Yellow buttercream rosettes around the edges. Alva, already craving, wolfed down three pieces.

Her father tended the fireplace and stacked logs. It was easier than talking to strangers. By five o'clock, he and Lydia were ready to leave.

"Maybe we'll go see Ethel," Walter said, trying to make an excuse for leaving early. Ethel's mother had been a friend of Lydia's mother. The Dodges had lost contact with her some time back, but the thought of seeing her now cheered them.

"Ethel Fennessey?" Alden asked, cheeks stuffed with cake. "She's dead. Backed out of her driveway into a snow plow. Quite a mess."

The bluntly delivered news stunned the Dodges.

"Sorry to be the one to tell you," Alden said, wiping yellow buttercream off his mouth with the palm of his hand.

The Dodges wanted to ask for more details but Alden was already preoccupied with another hunk of cake.

Walter helped Lydia on with her coat and shook his new son-in-law's hand. "See you tomorrow at breakfast."

Alva hugged both her parents goodbye. Her father smelled of aftershave and woodsmoke. He held his daughter tightly and whispered in her ear, "I hope you know what you're doing."

Two days after the wedding, Quinn helped Faron load his things into the back of Emmett Paisley's pickup truck and haul them over to Alva's.

The new wife's house had three bedrooms—the larger one for them and the spares for Faron's studio and a guest room. The studio was smaller than at Quinn's, but it would do. When the kid was born, they'd have to rethink the space.

Quinn dropped a carton of clothes on the floor near some other boxes in the master bedroom, where there was a view of a meadow. You could see the length of it now but it wouldn't be quite the same when the trees filled in. Not unlike most things, he thought. Everything changes.

He walked back down the hall to the living room and looked around. He'd been in this house before, when he was a boy delivering newspapers. He recognized the paneled walls and could clearly recall a mounted deer head that used to hang above the couch.

He closed his eyes and pictured Alva's grandmother—the snow-white hair and twinkling eyes. At Christmastime she used to run out to greet the school bus and give candy canes to all the children. Her husband had been ill—in a wheelchair. When it got so bad that he had to be put in a nursing home, they sold the house and moved to New York to be closer to their daughter.

Quinn was still deep in thought when he heard someone coming up the back steps with more boxes. He scurried into the kitchen and held the door open for Alva, who had her arms full. "Need help?" he asked.

"No, thanks," she snapped, barreling past him.

She kept going, down the narrow hallway toward the bedrooms, and Quinn went back outside to see what was left in the truck.

Faron juggled a large cardboard carton filled with painting supplies.

"Need a hand?" Quinn asked.

"Nope. I got it. But you can get that other one . . . behind the front seat. That's the last of it."

"What's wrong with Alva?" Quinn made a sour face as he reached in the truck for the box. "I offered to help her carry something and she nearly bit my head off."

"Sorry, Quinn. I guess it's hormones. She's kind of cranky."

"That's an understatement."

Faron laughed and shook his head. "I know. But Lydia says it's temporary." He walked past Quinn and up the steps to the back porch. He pushed the door open with his shoulder, put the heavy carton down on the kitchen table, and caught his breath.

It felt strange seeing his things here. As many times as he'd been in Alva's kitchen before, it all seemed different to him now.

A small pair of binoculars hung on the wall near a shelf of birding books that he hadn't noticed before. He leafed through a notebook with lists of birds in Alva's handwriting: *evening grosbeak, summer tanager, hermit thrush, wood thrush, pine warbler.* . . . He remembered seeing a similar list in the bedroom. . . . *laughing gull, osprey, common grackle, swamp sparrow.*

Quinn came up behind him with the last carton from the truck. "What's that?"

"Some kind of birding diary, it looks like," Faron guessed, wrinkling his brow.

Quinn rested the box he was carrying on the back of a chair. "You look baffled. Everything all right?"

"Yup, fine." Faron closed the notebook. "I guess I just didn't realize she's such an avid bird-watcher."

Quinn patted Faron's arm. "You'll find that. No matter how long you're married you won't know everything about each other." He hoisted the carton onto his shoulder and left

Faron standing there. *And*, Quinn thought on his way down the hallway, *I bet she doesn't know you keep insects in cigar boxes next to tins of oil pastels in your studio*.

Spring finally burst from a gusty squall, winds spreading out low to the ground, scud on the underside of shelf clouds. Hail the size of quail eggs. Thunder rumbling in the distance sent dogs under couches with tails between their legs. Then sunshine. A rainbow.

May. The month of mud and black flies.

Faron and Alva put on high rubber boots and walked out back across the wet meadow into the woods and stood among the speckled alders, listening for returning birds.

"This is a good spot for warblers," Alva told her new husband.

"It really is beautiful back here." Faron couldn't believe his luck. A woman who liked walking outdoors as much as he did. "Look!"

"What?"

"Over there . . . in the marsh . . . dragonflies!" He pointed to a colorful haze of pond damsels and darners zooming in circles above the water.

Alva aimed her binoculars. "Uh-huh, I see them." She held the binoculars steady. "And there's a red-winged blackbird . . . *Agelaius phoeniceusa* . . . uh-oh."

"What?"

"It just ate a dragonfly."

Faron stared at her. His wife. A pregnant bird-watcher who had her head in the toilet most mornings. Until now, the irony that birds eat bugs had escaped him.

CHAPTER 48

THE HARBOR TEEMED with noisy flocks of gulls lured by the scent of fresh bait. Emmett and Faron launched the *B. Paisley* late one morning after some last-minute preparation, amid friendly chatter with other fishermen who were rowing or motoring to their moorings in battered skiffs.

The early birds had set traps in April, including the Cutters, who were first in, as always. This year Emmett had to settle for launching his boat even later than usual, thanks to a bent prop that had to be sent out for reconditioning, and which took longer than expected.

He seemed to take the late launch in stride this time. "What's the use?" he confided to Faron. "Seems the Cutters are always first no matter how much I break my ass."

At noon they dropped their mooring ball with a shiny length of new chain and tied the boat off.

Standing in the bow admiring his work, Emmett said, "Let's eat. I'm starved."

Scuppers was crowded. Not an empty table in the place. Someone put change in the old jukebox and sang along.

"It's goddamn noisy in here!" Emmett complained as they searched for a seat.

Jeannie Ebel was shouting out orders to Red and he shouted back when they were ready. Between that, the music, and the caffeine-fueled jabbering of fishermen, the noise level was off the charts.

Faron pulled at Emmett's jacket. "Over there."

At the far end of the room, Alden was signaling them to join him and Stan and Clayton Jewett. The three men shuffled hats and newspapers to make room for the newcomers.

"Good thing I'm not as big as you," Faron kidded Alden as he crammed in beside him.

Alden ruffled Faron's hair, "Damn good thing . . . for you. I only pick on guys my own size."

Faron chuckled. He took a dose of friendly teasing from the other men about being an artist and fielded some winks and questions about the new wife.

Then Alden said, still joking, "Hey, Emmett. Betsy tells me you're thinking of joining the co-op."

"What? I never said any such thing."

When he saw his brother's exasperated reaction, Alden regretted his joke and tried retreating from the topic. "I'm kidding. Betsy didn't say anything." But it was too late.

Emmett was furious. "Co-ops don't work. No loyalty. Men come and go for the lowest price."

He was referring to the group Myron Sprague started. There were still only three members: Myron—who couldn't catch his own weight in lobsters in a year—and the Cutter brothers, who wanted to counteract their age by being 'modern,' so they joined the co-op.

Menhaden fishermen either sold their catch at the Wharf or on the mainland, depending on their mood and the price. But Myron got it into his head that they could save a lot of money if everyone banded together and pooled their resources.

Minna Beaudry's son, Clyde, who ran the Wharf, let the three-man co-op use a small alcove opposite the bait room, thinking that his generosity could be good for business. Besides, he figured there wasn't a chance in hell their little operation would get legs.

"You never know when a bit of hospitality might pay off," he explained to his mother when she bitched about him giving away something for nothing.

The alcove was just big enough for the three members, a few chairs, and an octagonal poker table the Cutter brothers hauled over in their downtime. So far, the only resources being pooled were the bets wagered during their poker games.

"I'll tell you," Emmett lamented, "that Butsy doesn't know what she's talking about. Ain't no way I'm joining any co-op. Isn't that right, Faron?" He jabbed his sternman with an elbow.

Faron was only half listening. He was tired. Been awake since two in the morning when Alva puked off the side of the bed. He mopped it up while she scuffed into the kitchen and leaned on the countertop, watching the last of the night fade. When the birds started their morning chorus, Alva said their names aloud . . . *robin, ovenbird . . . chipping sparrow* . . . then cooked his favorite breakfast: bacon crisp and eggs runny.

CHAPTER 49

ON A SWELTERING NIGHT in June, Faron was alone in the house. Alva went to a lecture over at the library—something about endangered species. He stayed home with a promise to vacuum, because her parents were coming for the July Fourth weekend. At eight o'clock he finished eating the beet and onion salad she left for him, and was filling the sink with soapy water when the phone rang. It was Del.

"A friend of mine wants to give you a show. He owns a gallery in Portland. He was up visiting the other day and saw one of your paintings in the studio. The one you framed for me before you left—the monarch on beach plum. He couldn't believe it when I took him to the storage room and showed him your other paintings. Wanted to buy one, but I told him I had to talk with you first. It's your choice, Faron, but I think having a show's a great idea. Not just for the money either. It'd be a tremendous accomplishment for you."

Faron's stomach clenched. He missed being in the studio. "I'm not painting much these days. I'm on the boat all week, or busy around the house." He held the phone with one hand and put his supper plate in the sink, up to his elbow in soapsuds, watching the warm dishwater turn beet red . . . alizarin crimson.

"That's okay. He wants the ones you left here," said Del. "He thinks they're fascinating. Says you'll make a fortune. He'll frame them. Mount the whole show. You'd have to come to the opening, of course."

"Would you be there?"

"Wouldn't miss it. Gaines and Holzer, too. What about your friend, Laric? You still see him?"

"Not since I got married, but we talk on the phone once in a while. I'm pretty sure he'd come to the show." Faron unplugged the sink and rinsed the dishes, wedging the phone between his ear and shoulder as he grabbed a towel to dry his hands. "I'll think about it and get back to you."

As he hung up the receiver, he heard car tires grinding gravel on the driveway. Headlights flashed on the kitchen wall. Minutes later, Alva slammed through the screen door with a stack of bird books balanced on her pregnant belly. She was out of breath, sweat rolling down the sides of her face.

"Did you know there are more than three thousand coastal islands in Maine and hundreds of them are nesting sites for endangered birds?" She dropped the books on the kitchen table and eased herself down into a straight-back chair, still talking. "Our islands are the only breeding places in the country for *Fratercula arctica*. That's the Atlantic puffin, you know . . . the one with the orange beak. Razorbill auks, too. Where the hell would they be without the Maine islands?"

Faron hung the dishtowel on the rim of the sink and sat next to her, waiting to get a word in edgewise, as usual. Out of the corner of his eye he watched large moths gather around the porch light. Pitch blackness behind them. Thought it would make a good painting.

"There was a guy there tonight," Alva continued, "a seabird expert who works for the Fish and Wildlife Service—something to do with the coastal ecosystems program, I think. Forgot his name—but you should have heard him. He says there are so many people moving to Maine that bird habitats are threatened. Half of the seabird islands aren't even protected. People hike there now—I mean, not during nesting season . . . but still—and some people actually want to build on them, can you believe that?" She stopped for a minute, her hand moving in a circular motion on her bulging stomach. Fire in her eyes.

"He says birds, like roseate terns and peregrine falcons, come to the islands to get food for their babies. And migrating birds stop in the mudflats to eat and rest. You know the picture hanging over the bar at Scuppers? The waterfowl? That's *Branta bernicla*, the Atlantic brant. It was almost kaput until environmental groups saved it. It needs those islands."

Then, just like that, she changed the subject. Wanted to know how he liked the salad. Said she got the beets fresh this morning off the mailboat. The captain dug them out of his garden for his old friends Arvis and Abby Cutter, but they'd turned their noses up at the vegetables and given them to her since she just happened to be walking by on her way to the store.

"They're good for the liver," Alva said, yawning loudly. "Goodnight. I'm going to bed."

She slept with a bird book on her chest, rising and falling with each breath. Faron tiptoed into the room and switched off the bedside lamp. There was a moth beating its wings against the pleated linen shade, but it stopped when the room went dark. There was a time Faron would have stood there, hoping for the sound of thumping to resume, but he'd finally learned his faith was no match for that of a moth. Somehow, they knew that stillness would lead them back to the light.

CHAPTER 50

JULY FOURTH, fireworks and cold watermelon arrived on the morning ferries along with hordes of tourists who off-loaded by the dozens to stand along the narrow streets and watch Menhaden's homegrown parade. Afterwards, they clogged Sheepscot Road on their way to cookouts on Preble Beach.

The islanders had mixed feelings about the inrush of people. They didn't like the crowds, but they had to admit that the holiday was profitable. Anyone could buy lobster in the supermarket for a lot less than what a lobster dinner on Menhaden cost, but tourists were suckers for 'the real thing.'

It wasn't Faron's favorite holiday either. Although his escapade with the Lobster Queen happened long ago, it still loomed above his head like a storm cloud every year when Fourth of July rolled around.

Midweek he got the idea to invite Laric. They hadn't seen each other since the wedding and this might be a good chance to catch up.

"Can't," Laric said when Faron called. "Remember the woman from Gannon, the one who only stayed a month? Short blonde hair?"

Faron did remember her. Overweight. Pretty. Alcoholic.

"She's coming for the weekend. Sorry."

"I understand," Faron said glumly. "Maybe another time." He hung up the phone feeling disappointed, but there wasn't much time to dwell on it because Alva walked in and handed him a to-do list as long as his arm.

Alva stood in the broiling sun at the ferry landing. She'd taken a cool shower and washed her hair only an hour ago, but she was already hot and sweaty. She was waiting for her parents—thinking about how pregnancy seemed to increase perspiration—when she saw them. She took off her hat and waved it in their direction. "Hi, Mom! Dad!"

Walter drove off the ferry and parked near his daughter. Rolled his window down. "Didn't expect to see you here. Everything okay?"

"I'm fine. Just doing last-minute errands in town and figured I might as well stay to greet you." She scrunched down and peered through the window past her father. "Hi, Mom."

Lydia angled toward her husband, in such a way that she could see her daughter's face. "Hello, dear. Are you following us to the inn?"

Alva hadn't planned to but now that her mother suggested it, she thought it might be nice to spend a little time with them alone. Maybe have a cool glass of lemonade on the Newcomb Inn's wraparound veranda, overlooking the lush lawn and the ocean.

"You go ahead," she said to her parents. "I'll meet you there when I'm done shopping. We'll sit on the porch and have something cold to drink."

"Oh, that sounds lovely. See you soon," Lydia said.

Walter put the car in gear. "We're in the Admiral's Quarters. Top floor."

"Staying in style this time, huh, Dad?"

"Your mother's idea. Costing me a fortune."

Alva laughed, waving goodbye as her parents pulled away. With some difficulty she got back in her car and wedged herself behind the wheel. Her stomach was huge. When she and Faron went down to Portland in March for an ultrasound, they found out she was carrying twin boys. What a shock that was. Two heartbeats! She thought Faron would keel over. She couldn't believe her luck.

Supper was at Quinn's. Betsy and Emmett arrived early to help, since they knew cooking wasn't the preacher's strong point. Emmett brought dark-brown bottles of home-brewed beer—the result of a newfound hobby. Betsy baked a deep-dish blueberry pie.

"Hands down—the best on the island!" Emmett exclaimed as Betsy put the pie plate on Quinn's kitchen counter, although he knew his brother, Alden, secretly preferred Eileen's baking. "Where's everybody?" he asked.

"Faron and Alva aren't here yet, but her folks are out back." Quinn was slowly shaping hamburger patties and arranging them neatly on a platter. Even though he had a fan blowing, the room was sweltering.

"Godfrey mighty! It's hotter than the Devil's kitchen in here. No offense, Quinn." Betsy fanned herself with a potholder, already frustrated with the length of time it took Quinn to make one patty. "Let me do that," she said brusquely, shooing him out of the way. "Emmett! You help."

"It's all yours." Quinn took off his apron and rinsed his hands under the faucet. Even in shorts and a loose-fitting cotton shirt he was uncomfortably warm, and only too happy to turn things over to Betsy.

He grabbed one of Emmett's homemade beers and joined Walter and Lydia outside, where the three of them sat in the shade and shucked corn. In the short period of time he'd known the Dodges he'd grown fond of them. Their daughter too. Any misgivings he had at the beginning were gone. She was good for Faron, who didn't steep in silence as often since marrying her.

He mentioned as much to her parents while he yanked off pieces of husk. "Alva fits right in. Doesn't even seem to mind the insect thing." He didn't realize what he said until it was too late. It was a subject he usually avoided. *Must be the heat*, he thought.

Walter and his wife exchanged worried looks.

Lydia spoke first. "What exactly is the 'insect thing'? We've got some idea, but Alva doesn't say much."

Quinn put a stripped ear of corn onto a plate and glossed over the question, sorry he mentioned anything. He was on the verge of outright lying and he knew it was wrong, but if their own daughter hadn't filled them in on the details, why should he.

"It's nothing, really," he said. "Faron's always enjoyed catching insects—moths, butterflies . . . bees. When he was little he liked the sounds they made."

"Why?" Lydia asked.

"He just did."

Walter said, "We do know a little about that," he paused and looked at Lydia before continuing, "but the last time we were in Scuppers we heard someone talking about the kidnapping. I was wondering wha—"

Quinn cut him off, annoyed that people still talked about that, especially in front of Alva's parents. "That was a long time ago. Faron was a kid, and you know how they are. Besides, it wasn't a real kidnapping. It was staged. The girl planned it all to trick her parents into buying her a car. She convinced Faron to help her . . ." Quinn pulled stringy silks off the corn with a bit more force than he needed to, ". . . because she knew he's the kind of guy who tends to do what other people want. Look at him and Alva."

Lydia bristled at that remark.

"I'm sorry," Quinn apologized, "I didn't' mean to criticize Alva in any way. I think she's the best thing that ever happened to Faron. It's just that . . . you know . . . of the two of them, she's the strong one."

"But . . ."

"Now Lydia," Walter interrupted. "Our Alva does have a mind of her own. We've never been able to tell her anything. You know that." He turned back to Quinn. "You were saying?"

Quinn shrugged as though it were nothing. "The girl's parents were angry and didn't want to admit their own daughter would do such a thing. They insisted on filing charges."

"So, the time in the hospital wasn't because he had a breakdown?"

"A breakdown? Of course not. Where'd you hear that? And it was rehab, not a hospital," Quinn corrected. "Actually, more like an artist's retreat. It's where he started painting," Quinn added, trying to put a more positive spin on the facts.

Walter grabbed another ear of corn and started peeling. "What about the cigar boxes? He still has them, and I've seen him put bugs in there." He looked at the corn and not at Quinn. Didn't feel right questioning a priest, but it was his daughter he had to think about. He would have asked these questions before the wedding if he'd had any inkling then—not that Alva would have listened to anything he had to say.

Quinn stretched the truth some more. "He only catches insects to paint them. The cigar boxes were his great-grandfather's. They have sentimental value." He tried changing the subject. "I wouldn't worry. He's got a great job. Emmett's teaching him a lot. And he may make some money when he exhibits his paintings. I'll say it again—Alva's a good influence."

"I guess," Walter conceded, with a chuckle.

"What's so funny?" Lydia asked.

"Nothing—but you have to admit, Alva's sure taken charge of Faron."

Lydia wasn't so sure she liked that characterization of her daughter, but it was true. It was also true that Lydia was glad of it. Alva kept her new husband so busy around the house that he had little time for anything worrisome.

After midnight on Saturday, Faron got undressed and slipped into bed next to his wife. It was still unbearably hot outside and he sighed with relief at the sensation of cool sheets on his warm skin.

It had been a long day of cookouts and fireworks, and he was exhausted.

"You think you're tired now? Just wait until this time next year when you're juggling two babies and trying to flip burgers and hotdogs at the same time," Walter teased earlier that afternoon.

Walter's remark had filled him with dread, and a wretched flash of understanding: maybe his mother had felt the same way when he was born—scared. Overwhelmed.

Now, leftover bottle rockets and repeater cakes went off in the background. Kids out late—probably summer brats. Straggling day-trippers had left on the last ferry. Tomorrow the streets would be littered with bits of plastic, shredded paper, and sparkler wire. Alden and his Public Works crew would grouse, but not at the overtime pay.

Alva was still awake. She turned over and whispered in Faron's ear. "Did you know that smoke from fireworks is toxic? It's full of chemicals. Not good for birds, or anything else."

Faron rolled his eyes in the darkness and turned on his side. His wife was giving him a whole new set of worries, but maybe they'd help push aside the old ones.

CHAPTER 51

SIX FOOT SWELLS the afternoon Alva's parents left on the ferry. Blazing sun and dry heat—both of them looking for their sea legs as they held on to metal railings as hot as branding irons and waved goodbye, then went inside to the shade of the large cabin and settled in for the eight-mile crossing.

After days of fireworks bombardments, it was so quiet you could hear yourself breathe. Monday night, when everyone was gone and Alva and Faron were alone in their bedroom, lying naked in the dark, he put his hand on her stomach and told her about the day in Mabel Pinkham's yard. "I just stood there and watched while a fox killed the baby rabbits."

Alva wasn't sure she wanted to have this conversation. She realized the Fourth of July brought up some bad memories for her husband, but she'd been doing a pretty good job of blocking out that part of his past and she preferred to keep it that way. Besides, it was another stifling night and her hormones were raging. She was in no mood.

She unstuck his hand from her sweaty belly and dropped it on the sheets a couple of inches away, then lifted her head from the pillow, grunting as she propped herself up on her elbows. "So what? I had a pet rabbit when I was a little girl. Didn't feed it for a whole week—in the middle of winter. Kept it in a shed with a dirt floor, not even a bed of straw. It died of cold and starvation. Ever seen a rabbit that's been lying in ten-degree weather for a week? It was flatter than a frozen flounder fillet when I found it. The ground was too hard to bury it, so I just covered it with twigs in a field across from the house."

Faron couldn't believe how matter-of-factly she told her story, although something in her voice made him think she was trying to hide what she really felt.

He started to say something, but she cut him off. "Jesus, Faron. I beat myself up for years over that. But you know what? One day, not too long ago either, I realized . . . whose fault was it? I was just a kid . . . and maybe it was partly my parents' fault . . . they never reminded me to go feed the rabbit. They never built me a proper rabbit hutch. You see what I mean?" She looked at him.

He saw what she meant, and more. Even in the dark he could see her eyes were moist and that something that happened long ago still hurt. He was surprised to hear that Walter and Lydia may not have been the perfect parents he imagined. Maybe he and Alva had more in common than he thought. Quinn was right, about not knowing everything about someone.

"Forgetting to feed a pet rabbit is an accident, it's not the same as what I did," Faron said.

"To me, it is." Tears rolled down Alva's cheeks.

Faron put his ear to her stomach, listening. "Maybe," he quipped, trying to cheer her up, "we should have started with a puppy, for practice."

"Is that supposed to be funny?" Alva sat straight up. "What are you saying, that you're scared we might hurt the babies?"

Faron talked into her belly, "No. I'm just not sure I know how to take care of children."

He rolled onto his back and glanced sideways at his wife, suddenly reminded of the times he peeked into his mother's bedroom on steamy summer nights, barely able to make out her face in the glow of a cigarette. Sometimes a strange man was zipping up his pants, about to walk out the door.

Alva laid a hand on Faron's head. His hair was wet with perspiration and she felt him tense at her touch. "I'll tell you what," she said more kindly, "you keep an eye on me and I'll keep an eye on you. These babies aren't the same thing as rabbits, and we'll take better care of them. Now go to sleep."

But he couldn't sleep. Whenever he closed his eyes he saw things rising to the surface.

CHAPTER 52

THE ISLAND WOKE UP to a soft rain that sounded like the faint hum of a honeybee hive. Faron dipped his razor in warm water and scraped whiskers off his cheek.

Alva's parents were in for another visit and had already started their day.

"Where's Walter?" Faron asked when he scuffed into the kitchen, freshly shaven and starving.

"He's down at Scuppers," Lydia said.

"So early?"

"He wants to make sure the coffee's fresh," Alva said over her shoulder. She shifted from one foot to the other, stirring with a wooden spoon as she heated a pot of strawberry jam to a rolling boil. There were a dozen more pints of fresh berries on the kitchen table waiting to be cleaned.

She skimmed foam from the cooked jam and poured the mixture into jars, chatting with her mother. "Connie Ebel says canning's like nesting—says there's nothing like the third trimester to bring out the mother bird in a woman."

Connie would know. She's an avid bird watcher. Some of the refuge islands near Menhaden are off-limits to the public, but she makes Hodie take her out on the police boat and they float as close to the rocky shore as possible, while she surveys the landscape for birds. Sheriff Paisley is never too happy about that. He's not a big fan of using government property for personal pursuits, but like a lot of other things on the island, he lets it slide. Besides, Connie makes chowder like no one else can.

Lydia knitted her eyebrows together, watching Alva dump another pint of berries into the blender. She bought the contraption for her daughter to make homemade baby food. For now, Alva was trying it out on the berries.

Lydia put her hand to her lips, scrutinizing the rows of jars and boxes of fruit pectin lined up along the countertop. "If you don't mind me saying so, Alva, I think it's silly doing all this work. Store-bought was good enough when you were a child, and you turned out just fine."

"Mom, people do things differently now."

Lydia handed Faron a plate of eggs and kept her mouth shut.

Faron eyed the new appliance on the counter. He wondered how Alva would have time to make homemade baby food. She was busy enough editing that bird magazine and helping Emmett with the office end of things.

She'd boned up pretty good on the lobster business and showed Betsy and Emmett how to keep better track of expenses, making sure Betsy understood the complicated federal and state rules and regulations about lobster management as well as Emmett did, just in case.

"In case of what?" Betsy harrumphed when Alva insisted she learn more about the business.

"In case I go overboard and don't bob up, you can take over," Emmett kidded.

"Hells bells! If that ever happens, I'll take the insurance money and buy me one of those fancy condos down south in Kennebunkport," Betsy joshed.

Truthfully, she was grateful for Alva's help. With more outsiders trying to fish the Menhaden grounds and fewer lobsters to go around, she knew they had to keep a closer eye on their books.

Faron cleared a place for himself at the table to eat his breakfast, listening to his mother-in-law and his wife quibble.

"I think your mother's right," he chimed in after swallowing a forkful of eggs. "Store-bought baby food is probably good enough."

Alva made a face. "Why do you say that?" It was unusual for Faron to give his opinion on such things and she didn't appreciate his taking her mother's side. She focused her brown eyes on him.

Faron lowered his voice to barely audible. "Because you've already got enough to do taking care of the house and everything, and you just volunteered for the Maine Audubon Society." His hands were shaking a little and he wondered if all men were afraid of their wives.

On his wedding day, Red Sedgewick had taken him aside and said that women change for the worse as soon as you marry them.

"Trust me, you won't get as much sex as you used to and you won't be in charge of anything," Red enlightened him.

Faron pushed pieces of egg around his plate with his fork, waiting for a blast from Alva. But it didn't come.

"I'd forgotten about the Audubon thing," she said. Her first assignment was coming up soon, counting puffins on a small rocky island a few miles to the north. Betsy was going with her. Connie Ebel was supposed to join them but right now she had a bout of bad arthritis in her knees and warned them she might have to beg off.

They were going to look for nesting pairs, before the chicks fledged and the birds headed out to sea for the winter. The women planned to hitch a ride to the rock on the mailboat and the *B. Paisley* would pick them up when Emmett turned back for the harbor.

"Well," Alva concluded, scraping the last of the berries out of the blender, "I only signed up for two days of counting, so there'll be plenty of time for baby food."

Lydia bit her tongue and Faron took a bite of toast. He kept the rest of his thoughts to himself but wondered how Alva—pregnant as she was—would even be able to get off the boat and climb ashore, let alone squat, wedged between rocks, counting birds through a pair of binoculars. Hell, Connie Ebel and her bum knees might do better.

Lydia was thinking the same thing. "Your wife just doesn't know when to stop." She directed her comment to Faron, hoping for an ally. "The other day she dragged me out back to look at birds, and when she heard the frogs in the marsh she remembered that the watershed people need volunteers to record amphibian breeding calls and . . ."

"Mom," Alva cut in impatiently, "I told you, I decided not to do that."

Faron concentrated on his food, determined not to get in the middle of mother and daughter again. Then he remembered the phone call from Del. He already mentioned it to Quinn, who loved the idea of the art exhibit.

"Hey," he said to Alva, timidly changing the subject. "Come here. I want to ask you something."

Lydia finished screwing a lid onto a warm jar of jam. "That's a good idea, Faron. Sit her down and get her off her feet. I'm going in the other room to lie on the couch."

Alva poured herself tea, stirred in a good dose of Stan Jewett's honey, and sat with her husband. It wasn't too often he wanted to talk and she was curious. She thought he looked older this morning. Maybe impending fatherhood was wearing on him.

"The other night when you were at the bird lecture I got a call from my friend Del. He says a gallery in Portland wants to exhibit my work."

Alva blew at the steam rising off her sweetened black pekoe. She was surprised he waited this long to tell her, but not surprised he'd been offered a show. She thought his paintings were beautiful.

"That's wonderful! You said yes, I hope. Didn't you? When is it?"

"I told him I'd call back. I wanted to talk with you first."

"Did you tell Quinn?"

"Yes."

"What did he say?"

"He thinks it's great. Said he always knew I had talent."

Alva put her cup down on the table and gave Faron a hug. "He's right. Your work is amazing. You should call your friend and tell him you'll do it, unless you want me to call."

"Would you?"

Alva looked at the clock on the wall. "Leave me his number. I'll try him later, when the rest of the world wakes up."

She packed Faron's lunch and walked with him to the back porch. The air smelled like damp pine needles and the trees appeared gray against the greenish sky.

"Better put your rain gear on now or you'll be wet all day." Alva kissed Faron on the cheek and handed him an insulated lunch bag filled with enough sausage sandwiches and strawberry pie for both him and Emmett.

At nine o'clock she called Del to give him the go-ahead for Faron's exhibit. An hour later, while she was melting hot paraffin to seal jelly jars, the gallery owner called and they worked out the details.

"I'll arrange to have the paintings shipped here," he told her. "The gallery will oversee the framing, announcements, price setting, and reception—everything, for a forty percent commission." He insisted it was standard when Alva balked at the steep fee.

But when he wanted to open the show in September, she put her foot down. "Can't do it. I'm pregnant with twins and that's the month I'm due. It'll have to be later, after things settle down here."

"That's too bad. The next time I could do it isn't until January."

"That'll work. One more thing—you mentioned something about an evening opening?"

"Yes. Is that a problem?"

"Big one. My parents will probably be driving up from New York and making the trip back to Menhaden with us later that same day, so it has to be in the afternoon, to make it easier on them."

The art dealer let out a frustrated sigh, but gave in to her preferences. "I guess we can do that. I'll put a contract in the mail. The sooner your husband signs it, the sooner we can get started."

Once she finished her conversation with the gallery, she dialed Quinn's number. "Good news," she said. "I've made the arrangements for Faron's show."

The ringing phone jarred Quinn out of a deep sleep. He'd been called out in the middle of the night to the home of Kay Hamblyn, a blind parishioner who lived alone in a double-wide. Her guide dog had eaten some rat poison and when Quinn got to her house, he found bloody diarrhea all over the place and the dog still squatting, spurting out watery stool. Quinn called Owen Batch, who doubled as the island veterinarian.

Doc Batch couldn't drive out himself because he was tending to a seventeen-year-old cat that belonged to Jarry Gallager's brother-in-law. "I'm done in," he groaned when

Quinn called. "Been up half the night because a goddamn cat decided she wasn't letting raccoons come up on the porch. She's just about torn to pieces, and . . . well . . . you know how they are about this cat. But put that dog in your car and bring him right over. Kay would be lost without him."

Quinn had some trouble getting the one hundred ten pound German shepherd into the backseat of his Chevy Suburban—the pooch wasn't exactly what you'd call a ride-along dog, since his owner couldn't see to drive. But with some soft talk and a leg up, the sick mutt finally climbed in, turned in tight circles, and curled up on an old blanket.

Owen was waiting for them outside when they got there and quickly coaxed the whimpering, frightened dog out of the car. "Call me later," he said, holding the shepherd by the collar, "and tell Kay not to worry."

Quinn went back to Kay's to clean up the mess and was worn out when he got home, the stench of feces and disinfectant plastered to him like a rain-soaked shirt. He took a shower and fell into a well-needed sleep, until Alva's phone call startled him awake.

"Were you sleeping?" she asked, hearing the fatigue in his voice.

Quinn didn't bother to explain, just listened while Alva made a date with him for the following night.

"Mom and Dad would love to see you. I've got some beef stew in the freezer and I'll ask Mom to make that parsley salad you like."

Quinn's stomach growled at the mention of food. Suddenly he was a bit more awake. He hadn't eaten since yesterday. "And some stovetop brown bread?"

"You got it. And afterwards we can play cards and fight over baby names."

CHAPTER 53

ONBOARD THE *B. Paisley*, Faron and Emmett were hunkered down, steaming toward shore. The weather had turned for the worse. By lunchtime a driving rain battered them hard and the waves were building. The morning forecast called for intermittent showers in the afternoon, but when a later report was upgraded to a small craft warning, Emmett headed for home. It didn't matter. The morning had been a total loss—every pot came up empty.

While Emmett piloted the *B. Paisley*, Faron finished stacking traps and clearing the deck. It was slippery and he fell twice. The wind stiffened to twenty knots and they were being tossed about good. Not far past their turnaround point they heard a horn and saw the wavy blur of a light flashing in the rain. A man in orange foul-weather gear was at the helm of a fast moving boat.

It was the Maine Marine Patrol—Officer Tim Pruell. Emmett throttled down as the MMP boat overtook them for a routine boarding. Emmett wasn't surprised. Last week there had been talk down at Scuppers about poachers, and yesterday a couple of guys he knew from further north had called him and said someone had been meddling with their lobster traps. Poaching wasn't common these days, but every once in while a wise guy thought he could make some easy money, or act on a grudge.

Emmett put the *B. Paisley* in neutral and Faron dropped fenders over the starboard side so the two boats wouldn't knock together. He caught the Marine Patrol's bow line, then hurried aft for the stern line. It was pretty rough conditions for a boarding, but MMP never let that stop them. Poachers liked working under cover of bad weather, so sometimes the worst conditions were the best time to catch them.

"Afternoon, Captain." Pruell stepped on board and offered Emmett his hand. "Some ugly weather today, heh?"

They'd known each other a long time—eighteen years—ever since Tim had been assigned to the area. He took his job seriously and did a lot of routine boardings and safety checks. He was well-liked and respected by all the lobstermen, and more than once had rescued some of their asses.

This boarding was a quick one. Officer Pruell looked in the livewell for v-notched females and shorts. It was empty. "Nothing in your pots?"

"Nope. Just changing water all morning." Emmett turned his back to the wind and spit over the rail.

"That been happening more than usual lately?" Tim kept talking while he checked to see that there were life jackets on board, as well as some type of throwable flotation device.

"Now that you mention it . . . yes. Came up with a lot of empties last week. So did some of the other guys."

Tim knelt to check a loose bolt on the livewell. "You're looking good Emmett. Just tighten this when you get a chance." He made a note in his pad. "Seen anything else unusual?"

Emmett figured Tim was referring to poachers. "No." He stood aft, holding on to the patrolboat's stern line while Officer Pruell climbed back aboard his own boat. Cold rain trickled down Emmett's neck. He and Tim exchanged a few more words while Faron released the bow line and pulled the fenders inboard, pushing off from the other vessel.

Once in gear, Marine Patrol sped ahead of them, undaunted by the weather and quickly obliterated by the rain. Emmett and Faron stayed put a while longer, dripping in the wheelhouse, finishing off mugs of hot chocolate and the last of Alva's strawberry pie.

They were making ready to get underway again when the wind abated and the rain came to a sudden stop. Almost instantly a fog bank rolled in.

Emmett stood at the helm and instinctively looked overhead to check his electronics: depth sounder, radar, and a global positioning system—everything he needed to navigate through the pea soup when he couldn't see past the bow. He loved the strange, visceral sensation of motoring in the fog, piloting by his senses, but technology made it a whole lot safer, and his boat was equipped with state-of-the-art instruments.

Even with the electronics, there was still an element of danger in the low-visibility conditions. Emmett had slowed practically to a stop when they heard the steady blast of a horn somewhere in the distance. He maneuvered cautiously, keeping just enough way on to steer, watching the blips on the radar screen—another boat, maybe two. He glanced at the depth sounder as they glided over the deep water.

The VHF radio crackled—a Coast Guard transmission—to the same MMP officer who boarded the *B. Paisley* earlier. Emmett opened a section of his windshield and strained to see through the fog as he kept his boat creeping along. Two points on his starboard bow he saw a hazy flash of blue and red lights and carefully turned in that direction.

In a few minutes the broadside of a Coast Guard vessel was clearly visible, circling another boat that was slightly stern down and appeared to be on fire. Marine Patrol had gotten there first, and Emmett could just make out Tim Pruell's bright-orange slicker as the officer climbed onto the deck of the wallowing boat.

Emmett motored closer for a better look. It was *Triple Threat*. Belonged to Marvin Dreyer. He recognized the gaudy colors—cornflower blue with a yellow boot stripe—the only one like it in the harbor.

Dreyer was licensed for this zone, but as far as Emmett and the other men on the island were concerned, he was an interloper—a mainlander who moved to the island only a year ago. A loudmouth who knew nothing about catching lobsters and thought he had more rights than anyone else. Came to every town meeting and complained about everything from fishing regulations to the price of gasoline at the local pump. No one could stand him. The Menhaden lobstermen tried scaring him off, but they could only go so far—not like the old days.

Dreyer had stuck out a season of vandalized and stolen gear.

"Fish further out," the gang kept telling him.

He finally did, when he got it through his thick head that life was different here than on the mainland. Actually, Marvin Dreyer decided to fish on the other side of the island, which meant he didn't have to pass through these waters to get there. That's why Emmett thought it was odd that *Triple Threat* was here now, way out of its territory and deep into theirs.

Emmett shifted into slow forward and looked around. Red and white Cutter-brother traps bobbed in the fog nearby. They'd been having some bad luck lately, too, which was highly unusual for them.

When the *B. Paisley* got close enough to *Triple Threat* to hear the hiss as Tim Pruell doused the last of the flames with buckets of seawater, Emmett got a good look at the damage.

Triple Threat was burned halfway down the coamings on the starboard side, from amidships to the stern. The aft cockpit sole and the transom were charred, but the rest of the boat was intact. Emmett guessed the worst of the fire was put out by a combination of the downpour they had earlier and the surging waves. The boat had taken on some rain and seawater but was still afloat.

The Coast Guard crew launched an inflatable to look for survivors, but their captain stayed aboard the larger vessel.

"You know whose boat that is?" the captain asked as Emmett eased the *B. Paisley* along the Coast Guard boat's port side.

Emmett lowered the squelch on his radio. "It belongs to a guy named Dreyer. Marvin Dreyer. Out of Menhaden, same as us."

"How many crew are usually onboard?"

"Three—him and his two sons." Emmett was sweating under his foul-weather gear and pulled the jacket open. A fishing accident, even when it concerns a brazen outsider like Dreyer, was always somber news for the islanders. "Seen any of them?"

"No, sir." The Coast Guard captain fiddled with a boat hook. He was new this year. Young. Probably not even thirty. Came into Scuppers now and then with his crew, but was all business now.

Emmett was quiet. Scratching his head and thinking. The fire could have been mechanical, or maybe spontaneous combustion in the engine compartment—something that could happen if you got sloppy and left oily rags about.

Emmett offered to stick around and help with the search.

The Coast Guard captain was grateful. "Thanks. We can use the assist." He put down the boat hook and adjusted his life vest. "It'll give us a better chance of finding these guys."

Emmett pulled the microphone from the clip on his VHF and radioed in to Hodie Ebel to make sure he knew what was going on. There were offers to help from others who heard the transmission, but the Coast Guard didn't want anyone else coming out in the fog, which hadn't lifted and in fact, seemed thicker.

When the *B. Paisley* started drifting too close to the Coast Guard boat, Emmett put the engine in forward and steered clear while the captain shouted instructions to him.

"Run real slow! Keep your sternman aft to make sure there are no swimmers near the propellers! And shut down your engine every five minutes, so we can all have a good listen!"

"Aye, aye!" Emmett shouted back to the captain, but thought to himself, *Swimmers is overly optimistic. Bodies is more like it.*

They did that for the next couple of hours—motoring, then drifting and listening— hoping for any sign of a man. There was none, and Faron was glad of that. The whole time they'd been there his head was spinning and his lunch sloshed around in his stomach. He was afraid of actually finding someone.

They stayed until dusk, drifting through a small amount of floating debris: bait bags, polypropylene line, a life jacket—anything that hadn't been tied down—but no bodies. Emmett and Faron talked among themselves, speculating on what happened.

"Marvin and his boys smoked like chimneys—maybe it was a cigarette fire," Faron guessed.

"Nah," Emmett contradicted. "Probably mechanical . . . or combustion, and the crew jumped into the water. Amateurs would do that—panic and abandon the boat. If they were wearing boots and foulies, they'd sink to the bottom like lead weights, more than likely." He thought any fool would know enough not to jump into the water with all that gear on, but he kept that part to himself.

When the Coast Guard finally decided to give up the search and tow the scorched boat to shore, Officer Pruell agreed. "Nothing more we can do today." Pruell watched the Coast Guard crew attach a towline to *Triple Threat*. It wasn't often that there was anything left of a burning boat to investigate, and they were going to take full advantage of a unique situation.

Before heading in, Emmett punched the coordinates of the site into his navigation system and then wrote them the old-fashioned way—in a notebook. As helpful as the electronics were, he didn't trust them 100 percent. He and the other fishermen would come out again tomorrow and he wanted to be sure to return to the exact spot.

The harbor lights were a welcome sight to the *B. Paisley*. Fishermen know. It could just have easily been their boat at the other end of the Coast Guard towline.

There was a group of people gathered on the pier. In a small community like Menhaden, where many of the inhabitants are related to each other by blood, and all by weather and water, it's everybody's business when a fishing boat's in trouble, even in this case, where the missing men were outsiders who rubbed everyone the wrong way.

Emmett and Faron snagged their mooring and put the *B. Paisley* to bed, then rowed their dinghy to shore. A meeting was already underway at Scuppers, and there was unanimous agreement to call off fishing the next day so they could all go out and search for the missing men.

At four o'clock in the morning, everyone met at Scuppers as planned. Betsy and Alva helped serve breakfast to the overflow crowd, the two of them braying out orders to whoever would listen, although Jeannie Ebel was really running the show.

Coffee was on the house—Red's contribution to any disaster. He had the radio tuned to the weather channel. A bright clear morning was about to dawn. In a couple more hours sunlight would sparkle on the harbor, but the radio croaked a warning for heavy rains by midday.

After breakfast, an assortment of small craft left the harbor single file, with the *B. Paisley* leading the way. Emmett steered with his knees and thumbed through his dog-eared notebook to find the coordinates he plotted the day before, checking them against the electronic readout.

A mile and a half out there was strong wind and plenty of chop. Although they knew a storm was blowing in, the men figured they would have at least half a day of tolerable weather.

When they reached the site, they spread out a mile in each direction. It didn't look good. There were a lot of boats scouring the water, but except for some garbage and pieces of line that had floated off *Triple Threat*, nothing turned up. Around two o'clock thunderheads rolled in from the north, right on schedule, and the Coast Guard told everyone to go home.

"No point risking more lives," the young captain reasoned.

Beer flowed at Scuppers, but not conversation. The men were quiet, imagining the worst, and counting their blessings. When wives and kids started piling into the restaurant around suppertime, children's chatter filled the gaps and families lingered over their meals until well after dark.

The next day, none of the fleet went looking and that night the Coast Guard officially called off the search. There were the three Dreyer wives to consider, but otherwise, the islanders got back to normal more quickly than they would have if it had been one of their own who went missing. No one said as much, but it was the unspoken truth.

Weather-wise, it blew for several more days, washing everything ashore, including fishermen, who huddled in Scuppers, rehashing recent events.

There was a lot of suspicion on the fourth day, when the sun shone and the men went out and found lobsters in their traps. Everyone knew there'd been poaching activity in the area the week before, and three days of foul weather never stopped a poacher.

"The only thing that's changed is Marvin Dreyer's out of commission," Clyde Beaudry said. "Not to put too fine a point on it." He was in Scuppers with the rest of the gang, drinking beer and tossing darts. "Never did trust that guy. His sons, neither."

"He's right," Brad Sawyer said, throwing a bullseye. "I mean . . . I'm happy we all had lobsters in our pots, but it's no coincidence so many of us weren't catching anything and now we are. There's only one thing different, *Triple Threat* ain't here."

Brad had a point. The men had put their heads together and realized it wasn't just Emmett who pulled up empty traps the week before *Triple Threat* caught fire, and that caused them to suspect their pots had been tampered with. In their minds, their suspicions were pretty much confirmed when word got around that Marvin's livewell was filled with lobsters when his boat swamped.

CHAPTER 54

ARVIS AND ABBY CUTTER couldn't remember when they'd seen the ocean this flat. "Stiller than a cow pond in August," Abby said.

"Flatter than Grandma's chest," Arvis one-upped him, bending over the rail to inspect his reflection in the glassy surface.

"Ayuh," Abby agreed. "And that's wicked flat!" They both laughed.

It had been eerily calm since they baited up at four this morning—first ones to leave the harbor. Even the squabble of gulls that followed them out seemed more quiet than usual.

Days earlier they set several trawls, and now they were ready to haul them. Abby steamed up to a buoy and put the engine in neutral. He snagged the brightly colored buoy with a gaff, strung the line through the hauler, and hit the switch to raise the traps.

Arvis pulled the first trap aboard when it surfaced. It was loaded with seaweed, and heavy. There was one keeper in it and several crabs. The robust older man struggled with the slippery weight, but managed. The next trap had two eggers. He punched v-notches in their tails and tossed them back into the water. As Arvis worked his way down the string, he hit pay dirt—keepers in all the other pots.

When they finished hauling the first trawl, Arvis refilled the bait bags and dropped the string of pots back into the water.

Abby was singing as he steered the boat to the next buoy, hooked it and put the line through the hauler. This time when he started the hauler it ground to a stop after taking in only a few feet of line. "What the hell?"

"What's wrong?" Arvis asked impatiently.

Abby gave the rope a tug. Tried again. "Don't know."

Arvis joined his brother and fiddled with the hauler. They both pulled at the same time. It moved a little.

"I don't like this," Abby mumbled. "I'll put her in forward and see if we can shake it loose."

While Abby drove the boat, inching ahead, Arvis worked the hauler. The line came slowly until the tip of a yellow rubber boot was visible close to the surface.

"Hold up!" Arvis screamed. "We got a problem! A floater!"

"Holy sailor, call the water!" Abby idled the engine. "Bet it's one of them goddamn New Yorkers, caught in our frigging set!"

It was, too. Marvin senior. They pulled him the rest of the way up and dragged him over the gunwale. The trawl was wrapped around him, taut across his neck and chest. There was a lobster in the trap. Arvis reached in and grabbed it . . . a cock, and legal size. He put it in the livewell with the others—about thirty so far today—and then helped his brother untangle the floater.

Old man Dreyer seemed twice his normal size—like a bird with its feathers fluffed up against the cold. Small crabs crawled through his hair. There was a fire extinguisher hung up on his torn slicker. His skin was wrinkled from being submerged for so long. He'd been caught in the trawl in such a way that his head buffeted against the pot, which accounted for some ugly gashes in his face.

"Face is really mashed up," Arvis said. "Don't look too bad, otherwise."

"Yup." Abby took off his cap and wiped sweat from his forehead with the palm of his hand, thinking the cold, deep water must have slowed decomposition. "Well, no point in rushing back."

Arvis nodded in agreement. They shoved the body toward the stern and got back to work. After checking the remainder of the trawl, Arvis rebaited the traps and tossed them overboard, careful to stand clear of the line as it unraveled across the deck. After a few more hours of hauling and resetting traps, they got a conscience.

"What do you think?" Arvis asked over the whine of the engine.

"Huh?" Abby put the engine in neutral and walked aft to where his brother was standing over the body. "What'd you say?"

"What say we go back? I mean, I know Dreyer was a bastard . . . but . . . "

Abby cut him off impatiently. "You're right. Let's go in."

Arvis hadn't hosed off the deck yet. Sea fleas were crawling on the floater, and everywhere else. He hadn't noticed a smell when they first lugged the body aboard, but now, after several hours in the warm sun, it was rank.

"Phew. Some stench." Arvis held his nose to make his point. Between the dead man and rancid-smelling bait, the place stank.

Abby turned the boat for home. Black-backed gulls followed them in, skimming the water for wayward bits of mackerel and pogies while Arvis washed off the slippery, stinking deck. When he finished, he rinsed his hands in the engine-heated tray of hot water near the bait bin, then cracked open a beer each for him and Abby. He joined his brother at the helm. "Here's to keepers."

Abby knocked his bottle against his brother's. "Yup. And one dead man."

Although they'd been getting a better price on the mainland, Abby headed straight for Menhaden. "We'll do Clyde a favor today and sell to him!" he shouted to his brother.

They roared full throttle to the island, chugging through the breakwater slightly earlier than usual, due to the circumstances, barely slowing down when they entered the No Wake Zone.

Abby had called ahead to Hodie, who was waiting on the dock along with Alden Paisley and the wives of the missing men. The ambulance was there, too, and Brenda Gallager dripped perspiration in the heat, a gleaming stethoscope dangling around her neck, the stretcher already unloaded.

Alden was apprehensive. Seeing a dead man come off a boat was nothing new, but it was never easy—even if it was a windbag like Marvin Dreyer.

When the Cutters were close enough, Alden walked down the gangplank and waved at them to indicate where he wanted them to tie up. The three stupefied wives were up on the pier, and Alden hoped they stayed there. He hadn't wanted them here at all, but they insisted.

Abby maneuvered the boat into an empty slip near the launch ramp and Arvis tossed lines to men on the dock. Once the bow and stern were made fast, Sheriff Paisley stepped aboard. "Everyone else, stay put," he ordered when at least two onlookers started down the gangplank.

He winced when he saw the body . . . as much from the smell, as anything. It was Marvin the elder, all right. He wished Abby and Arvis would've at least covered the guy with something. He motioned for Brenda to come down with the stretcher.

"Where'd you find him?" Alden wanted to know.

"A few miles out, a little more, maybe," Arvis said. He looked at his brother. "Wouldn't you say?"

"That'd be my guess. He was tangled in one of our pots. Didn't drift too far from the scene of the fire, I'd say."

Alden scribbled something in his notebook. "Seems that way. I may call you later, if I have any other questions."

"That'd be fine, sheriff," Abby said agreeably. "After we unload we'll be over at Scuppers, same as always."

"Got lobsters?" Alden asked, as an afterthought.

"Oh, yeah. Plenty," Arvis said.

Alden peeked behind the men at the livewell. It was near full. He took a step toward it to have a closer look but stopped when he heard Brenda shouting to him.

"Give me a hand with this, will you, Alden?"

Alden closed his notebook and pocketed it and went to help her.

Brenda already had her hands under the dead man's armpits. She bent her legs at the knees, ready to lift. "You grab his feet, Sheriff. On the count of three . . . one, two, THREE!" They swung Marvin over the side onto the stretcher, both of them huffing and puffing. Brenda spread a clean white sheet over him and Alden helped her get the stretcher ashore.

Marvin's wife had gotten a good look from above and she was wan with grief at the top of the gangplank. Alden hustled over to comfort her, but she was already shored up by her daughters-in-law, one on each side.

Women spent that night cooking, and the next day they carried an assortment of foil-wrapped dishes to the widow, properly sympathetic but secretly relieved it hadn't been one of their husbands drowned in a trawl.

The Cutter brothers got their pictures in all the newspapers from Portland to Canada—boating disasters are always big news. It wasn't the first time Arvis and Abby had been in the headlines. In their lifetime of lobstering they'd seen their share of sunken boats and drowned men—about twenty in all, according to their account in the newspaper article.

Their own father lost his boat in a summer storm when they were boys. "He was fishing alone when he got caught in a williwaw and was pulled overboard by a triple," the newspapers quoted Arvis.

But their father had been lucky. With a lungful of air and a hip-tethered pocketknife he managed to cut himself free and swim to the surface. His boat didn't fare as well—it smashed to pieces against the rocks. Old man Cutter was found a while later, hypothermic and hanging on to a piece of the hull.

"That's why we fish a bit further out," Abby told the newspaper reporter. "No rocks."

Faron and Emmett made the papers too. They were interviewed about the initial rescue attempt with the Coast Guard. Emmett didn't feel too good about that. Thought it might be bad luck to talk publicly about another man's misfortune.

Faron didn't have much to say either, except to answer the reporter's questions in brief sentences. There was a photograph of him, though, resting on a bait barrel down at Beaudry's Wharf.

"It's a great picture." Alva yawned, stretched out on the couch, reading the paper and eating carrot sticks.

"You think?"

"Uh huh."

"You know, I didn't actually see the body."

"I know." She crunched another carrot with her teeth, turning the newspaper page to look at something else, hoping Faron would stop talking.

"I mean my mother's body."

Alva stopped chewing. "What's your point?"

"After hearing how Marvin Dreyer looked when they found him . . . it got me thinking about my mother and how she . . ."

Alva cut him off. "Stop right there. Do you see what you're doing? You're going backwards."

Faron shut up and watched Alva struggle to get up from the couch—probably to get something else to eat.

He knew that sometimes going backwards is good, but he wasn't going to argue with his wife. He held out his hand and helped her up. "I guess you're right, Alva. No use thinking about all that."

CHAPTER 55

FLAGS HUNG LIMP on their halyards in the scorching air. The breeze wafting off the ocean barely made a difference. Faron was concentrating on the stifling stillness when Alva suggested they have a clambake on the weekend.

"My parents will be here, and we can ask Quinn and the Paisleys." Really, she hoped the picnic might snap Faron out the rotten mood he'd been in lately.

On Saturday, after running errands for Emmett and going over to Beaudry's Wharf for quahogs and steamers, Faron grabbed a cold beer and went outside to join Walter and Quinn in the backyard, where Quinn was trying to persuade Walter to stay at the rectory instead of the Newcomb Inn. "I sleep downstairs. You'll have the entire top floor to yourselves, for free."

Walter hesitated. "Maybe. I'll have to check with Lydia. She likes to spend my money at that fancy-schmancy inn."

They made small talk about the Dodge's drive up from New York, then more serious discussion about the drowned fishermen. Quinn told them he visited the widow yesterday and she was pretty broken up.

"It's not easy losing a loved one," he mused.

No one knows that better than me, Faron felt like saying, but instead he swallowed everything he knew about loss and washed it down with a cool mouthful of beer. Maybe Alva was right about not bringing up the past.

Walter listened to Quinn, nodding his head solemnly, then politely changed the subject. He asked about Faron's upcoming gallery exhibit. "What are the paintings like?"

"They're similar to the ones I'm doing now, only bigger," Faron said.

The short answer satisfied Walter, who'd only asked the question because he preferred not to dwell on anything related to the hereafter. Their conversation quickly changed to politics, weather, and other things men were at ease with.

They were lamenting the high price of gasoline when Alva called out, "Anyone hungry?"

They went to Scuppers for the early-bird special, and as usual, the place was filled to the rafters.

Alva had called ahead to reserve a spot, and Red pushed together two small tables and the even smaller one from under the dartboard to accommodate them. He was putting the finishing touches on the makeshift seating arrangements when they arrived.

"It's the best I could do," he snarled when Walter griped about the close proximity to the bar. "Buy some drinks and you won't notice."

Red was right. After a few rounds, everyone forgot the discomfort. They all ordered the franks and beans special, which was more than any of them could eat, except for Alva, who devoured all of hers and some of theirs.

When the bill came, Lydia poked her husband, signaling him to pick up the tab. He did the math in his head, adding the total to the price of a night's stay at the inn, and changed his mind about their sleeping arrangements. "Quinn, I think we'll take you up on that offer to stay with you."

After church on Sunday, the Dodges, Faron, and Alva piled into Quinn's Suburban and headed for the beach. The men dug a fire pit, lined it with rocks, then threw on kindling and large chunks of wood and ignited it with a flaming wad of newspaper.

"We better keep those chilled," Alva suggested, pointing to the crate of clams.

She followed Faron to the water and sat on a driftwood log while he waded ankle-deep in the surf and wedged the crate between two large rocks and tied it off with a length of line. "I saw Doc Batch," she said.

Faron was surprised. "When?"

"Yesterday."

"Why didn't you tell me you were going?"

"I did. You forgot. Mom went with me. I fell asleep right after we got home from Scuppers last night, and this morning was hectic. This is the first chance I've had to talk to you alone."

"How did it go?"

"Fine. Doc said one baby's smaller but it's not unusual."

"You tell your parents?"

"Yes. They're worried sick. They already think we won't be able to handle twins." Alva tugged windblown hair out of her eyes. "I told them we'd be fine. We will, won't we?"

"Of course," Faron answered with false confidence. He looked at his wife. She was out of breath. No one thought she could get any bigger than she was last month, but she'd gained another few pounds and it was getting more difficult for her to move around.

He held her arm and helped her up from the log. The other night he wrenched his back getting her off the couch and now he felt a painful twinge as he pulled. He reached around to a sore spot at the base of his spine. Hauling his pregnant wife was a lot harder than hauling lobster traps. He'd be glad when she was back down to her normal size, although the guys at Scuppers said that might never happen.

CHAPTER 56

BETSY AND EMMETT slept late and their lazy morning disintegrated into an argument. They were still quarreling when they arrived at the beach.

Quinn stepped between them and handed Emmett a bucket. "Let's get some seaweed for the bake." He pointed to the rocky end of the beach. "Over there." Faron tagged along.

Betsy unfolded a lawn chair and sat with Alva and her parents, who were discussing the latest prenatal visit.

"Let's not worry," Walter said to his wife, "it's in God's hands."

"Dad's right," Alva reminded her mother, knowing her parents believed that's all it took.

Betsy yanked the pop-top off a can of beer, cursing when it sprayed the front of her shirt. She struck a match and savored the first puff of a cigarette "What?" she asked when everyone stared at her.

"I'm not saying a word," Lydia promised, tightening her lips together in an exaggerated show of silence. She'd tried convincing Betsy to give up smoking months ago. "You don't listen, anyway. You're just like our daughter."

Betsy and Alva had become instant friends when Faron

introduced them. Most mornings, after their men left for the boat, Alva drove over to Betsy's for her second cup of coffee, where the two of them sat around running their husbands' lives from the kitchen table.

"Someone's got to do it," Betsy liked to say.

Now she took a long swig of beer and let out a very unladylike burp. The two friends laughed until they cried.

"Peas in a pod," Walter said, grinning at them. He squatted to poke the fire, which had burned down to red coals. He dipped his hand in a pail of seawater and splashed some on the hot rocks. They sputtered.

"Sounds ready," Lydia said.

Walter stepped away from the fire. "I'll get the clams."

He was seventy-three years old and never thought he'd live to see his daughter marry, let alone have children. Except for being a bit of a know-it-all, she was a good catch. Kindhearted, and decent looking, too. He was relieved she finally found someone, although that Faron—he was an odd one—an artist who painted bugs. Walter knew it was none of his business. They seemed happy. He just hoped it didn't all fall apart when the babies came. They'd have their hands full.

He walked in the direction of the water, enjoying the sensation of warm sand on his bare feet as he neared the spot where Faron stashed the clams. The tide had risen but he could still see the crate poking out of the water.

He steadied himself on the rocks, crouching slightly as he made his way forward. There was something yellow off to his left. "What the hell?" he said to himself. He stepped further into the water for a better look.

When he saw what it was, he panicked and slipped on the rocks, falling sideways into the chilly water. He landed with a hard splash, scraping his elbow on the cobbled bottom, in surf up to his chest, too stunned to move.

"Walter!" Lydia yelled. She'd been watching from the beach—having second thoughts about him carrying the heavy crate on his own.

Everyone ran towards him when they heard Lydia scream. Emmett got there first. As soon as he saw the yellow rain slicker, he guessed it was one of the drowned Dreyer brothers. He plodded into the water and helped Walter to his feet. Faron and Quinn were right behind him.

"Betsy!" Emmett shouted, slightly out of breath and trying to keep his footing in the frothy water. "You got your phone? Call Alden and tell him to get over here."

Alva and Lydia walked with Walter back to the fire. The cuts on his arms were sore and bloody, but the salt water stung them clean. He was soaking wet and trembling, as much from fright as cold.

"Here." Lydia handed him a towel. "Take off your shirt and wrap this around yourself."

"Don't worry, Dad," Alva said, wringing saltwater out of his shirt. "The sun will be so hot in another hour you'll wish you were wet again."

Walter stretched his blue lips and forced a teeth-chattering smile while he dried himself with the towel, still at a loss of words from the jolt.

Emmett yanked in the crate and handed it to Faron. "Go ahead, might as well put them on the fire. It's what we came here for."

Faron didn't move. He was only a few feet from the body. It was face down but he imagined a pair of wide-open eyes.

"Go ahead," Emmett repeated, firmly pushing Faron in the direction of the fire.

Once they were alone, Emmett and Quinn dragged the body onto the beach.

"Looks like Warren, the younger one." Quinn kneeled in the sand, his face close to the dead man.

"Think so?" Emmett tried conjuring up an image of the young man rowing out to *Triple Threat* with his older brother and father, but he couldn't. He'd never paid much attention to them. He felt badly about it now, but his regret was tempered by the fact that the Dreyers had, more than likely, been poaching his traps.

Walter snugged the towel around his shoulders and knelt down to knock coals from the sides of the pit, happy to have something useful to do. Faron brought the clams and the bucket of seaweed and the women started layering food on the fire.

The steaming mound sizzled and popped, filling the air with a thick cloud of fragrant steam. But the sweet smell didn't help Faron's lousy mood. Seeing a dead man stirred things up—he couldn't shake the thought of his mother rowing across Puddle Cove on a balmy summer day, only to end up face down under Jarry Gallager's pier.

Alden was at the gas station filling the cruiser and cursing the heat when the call came in. When he heard it was a floater, he took his time responding. He'd learned years ago that there was no point in hurrying for something like this. If they'd been in the water long enough to bloat and float, they could wait a little longer.

He pulled up to the beach nearly thirty minutes later. His mouth watered when he got a whiff of roasting corn and potatoes. "Good morning, everyone. What's up? Betsy said you found something?" He slapped Faron on the back. "You look a bit green around the gills."

"We all are," Lydia responded grimly.

"Over there." Walter pointed toward the water where Quinn and Emmett were standing.

Betsy handed her brother-in-law a slab of pie. "It's one of the Dreyer's, we think."

Alden looked at her. "No kidding?" He took a bite of pie and washed it down with a soda he snagged from the cooler. "Delicious, Betsy." He ate the rest in two more bites and took the can of soda with him as he trudged across sandy patches of broken shells and small stones to see what the ocean coughed up.

Emmett waved to him.

Alden tipped his hat. "Emmett. Quinn. What have we here?" He bent at the waist, twisting his neck to get a better look at the dead man's face. "Uh huh. It's Warren, all right."

The ambulance siren shrieked in the background. "Jesus Christ!" Alden straightened up, pissed off. "I told them not to do that. And on a Sunday, no less. The last thing I want is a bunch of rubberneckers running over here gawking."

He drank the rest of his soda in several long gulps while the ambulance whined to a stop in the parking lot. The cool drink was refreshing, but he was sweating worse than a pig on a spit. Perspiration stains spread across the khaki police shirt that stretched snugly over his belly. He wiped his dripping forehead and scowled at Emmett and Quinn. "Come on, help me carry this guy up there."

They loaded the body into the ambulance and Alden told the driver to stick around. He had a hunch, and wanted to search the rest of the beach. He thought there was a good chance the third victim might have washed up in the same vicinity, since there had been a roaring three-day storm recently.

He was right.

•

"Over here!" Quinn climbed across the slippery rocks into the edge of a salt marsh. "I found him!"

Alden and Emmett plodded through the sand to join him in the tall reeds. The three of them made their way across the muddy bottom and pulled the body through the spartina to higher ground. They let him drip-dry there until they caught their breath, then lugged him up to the ambulance and hoisted him inside next to his brother.

"Damn," Alden wheezed, "I'm getting too old for this crap." He slammed the ambulance door shut. "Get going. I'll meet you at the hospital. And don't turn on that goddamn siren!"

Back in town the news spread quickly, along with the subdued cheerfulness that comes when folks are uplifted by any disaster that doesn't directly affect them. Lobstermen were relieved they wouldn't have to hold their breath anymore when they hauled traps—except for Faron, who always did, no matter what.

The next day, the mailboat delivered the drowned Dreyers and the grieving Mrs. Dreyers to the mainland. The women never returned, not even to empty out their house. They hired locals to pack and ship certain items but left everything else up for grabs.

Alva tried talking her parents into buying the place, but Walter and Lydia wouldn't leave New York, especially not to move into a dead man's house.

CHAPTER 57

Quinn switched on the Suburban's high beams as he drove along East Sheepscot on his way home from Connie and Hodie Ebel's, where he and some congregants spent the evening brainstorming a fundraiser for the church. They'd tossed around ideas but mostly they just diddle-daddled over second and third helpings of the delicious fish chowder and brown bread Connie prepared for them, their talk bordering on gossip—including speculation about Faron's impending fatherhood.

"Kind of hard to believe he'll be a father of twins." Connie ladled soup into heirloom china bowls.

"I'll say," Minna Beaudry agreed. "Seems like only yesterday he was a weird, skinny kid carrying a box of bugs everywhere he went." She blew on a spoonful of soup. "Just goes to show you."

Everyone looked at her. Minna was one of the island elders. She'd been around a long time and people listened to what she had to say.

Hodie piped up from the other room where he was watching television and listening in on their conversation at the same time. "Show what?" He asked the question they were all thinking.

"What's that?" Minna was stone deaf in one ear and not much better in the other.

Hodie raised his voice. "I said, SHOW WHAT?"

"Well!" Minna hollered, turning at the waist to compensate for her stiff neck. "If it isn't Mr. Big Ears, eavesdropping!"

Hodie yelled to be sure she heard, "Aw, come on, Minna. Just goes to show what?"

"It shows there's some good blood mixed in with the unlucky Goss blood and the boy's just fine. Married and all!" Minna chewed thoughtfully on a mouthful of haddock and swallowed. "Of course, his wife's from away, so God knows what she'll turn out!" Her voice was strained from the effort of trying to be heard in the next room.

"Her grandparents lived on the island!" Hodie yelled back.

"Not born and raised. Doesn't count!" Minna got the last word.

Quinn was tired and over-sated, belching up Connie's creamy chowder. He popped an antacid and drove with the windows down to help him stay awake.

He was thinking about what Alva said when she had stopped by the rectory the other day—that Faron seemed depressed ever since the three Dreyers were found. She also mentioned overhearing him on the phone with Laric, saying he wondered what his mother looked like after she drowned.

That caused Quinn a pang of regret. It was his idea not to let Faron attend his mother's funeral. At the time he thought it might be too hard on such a young boy.

Alva said she asked Faron what was troubling him, but he shooed her away like a housefly. Lately, Quinn saw more of her than he did Faron. She was in the habit of doubling recipes and bringing them over to the rectory, which is what she was doing the day she came by and they talked.

"He locks the studio, but I snuck in recently," Alva confessed, organizing food containers in Quinn's refrigerator.

Disapproval darkened Quinn's face.

"Don't worry, I wasn't snooping. I was looking for art supplies. I want to make him something special for his birthday."

"You're really planning ahead."

"I know. But after the babies are here, I might be too busy."

"That's true. What are you making?"

Alva's eyes brightened. "Have you ever heard of a hummingbird moth? It looks like a hummingbird. I had this idea that, since I like birds and he likes moths, I could paint the hummingbird moth on a picture frame. What do you think?"

Quinn was touched by her thoughtfulness. "He'll like that. Did you find what you needed in the studio?"

"No. A moth flew at me. Scared me to death. I tried catching it, to put it outside, but Faron walked in."

"Uh-oh. What did he say when he saw you in his studio?"

"He told me I should use a net to catch the moth, or else I might hurt it. Then he opened a window and it flew out. He didn't even ask what I was doing."

That was just like Faron, Quinn thought, quicker to stand up for a moth than himself.

Quinn was still lost in thought when he approached Keeps Pond and Alva's house came into view. The lights were on in the garage and the door was wide open. He and Faron hadn't spoken since they spent an afternoon installing a new hot water heater in the rectory, so he decided to stop in now for a quick visit.

Faron was sitting in a vinyl lawn chair under the bright overhead light, holding his butterfly net, looking up at a flurry of insects clustered around the blazing fixture—one of Zed Goss's cigar boxes in his lap.

"Evening," Quinn said, stepping into the garage. He looked up at the night fliers and pointed to a particular moth. "I like the markings on their wings . . . the black shape." He'd done a bit of moth research since seeing the distinctive mark in one of Faron's recent paintings—a symmetrical shape that resembled the Hebrew letter nun.

Faron's face radiated pleasure. "The Hebrew character moth—it's one of my favorites." He'd caught countless numbers of them since he was a boy. In fact, he liked thinking that the ones flying overhead now were descendants of the moths that knocked against the screens in his mother's house on Puddle Cove.

He never kept them for long—just listened to the thumping for a while and let them go—catching new ones with a beam of light on another dark night. More recently he put them in glass jars and made quick sketches before releasing them.

Quinn unfolded an aluminum-framed lawn chair and sat. Got to the point. "I'd like to talk with you, Faron. You seem preoccupied lately. Is everything all right?"

Faron twirled the net in his hands. He looked at Quinn, noticing gray hair and thickness around the waist for the first time. "I don't know. I've been thinking a lot about my mother lately."

"I'm not surprised, considering the three men that drowned recently. It's an unpleasant reminder of what happened to your mother."

"And sometimes I'm scared I'll do things."

"Like what?" Quinn asked.

"You know . . . the way I caught flies . . . with Mary's cat . . . and the girl."

Quinn shuddered. Occasionally he had the same fears, but didn't let on. "That was kid stuff. You're fine. You're just under a lot of stress. A new marriage, and children on the way. It's a lot to deal with. But if you've got things on your mind you can always talk to me, or Alva."

Faron gave Quinn a suspicious look. "Did she say something?"

"Yes, but only because she's worried."

Faron looked past Quinn to the throng of insects gathering around the light bulb. In the sixty-watt glow the moths appeared more red than brown, even prettier than they actually were.

When a moth separated itself from the rest, Faron scooped it into his net and gently dropped it into the cigar box. "Here," he said, handing the box to Quinn and switching off the light, "let's go inside and have a nightcap."

Quinn held the box with both hands, surprised at the strength of the vibrations the moth made when it moved. He looked down at the tattered, colorful cardboard container, smiling at the childlike thoughtfulness of the holes punched in the lid.

"Do you hear that?" Faron touched Quinn lightly on the arm and stopped to listen.

Quinn cocked his head, put an ear closer to the box. He had to admit, there was something nice about it.

At the top of the porch steps Faron took the box from Quinn and opened it. The moth was motionless in a corner. Faron knelt and tapped the cardboard lightly until the moth flew upwards and landed in the shadows above the dim light shining through the kitchen window.

Sunday, Quinn stood at the pulpit holding a glass jar. "You've all seen moths on summer nights, flying around your porch lights or campfires, but maybe you never took much notice.

"Well, I have one here." He held the jar high above his

head. "It's a plain, brown little thing—drab, some might say, but the mark on its wings is significant.

"It resembles the Hebrew letter nun. In the language of the Talmud, the letter nun means fish, a symbol of life. Some Jewish scholars say nun signifies a miracle. There are varying interpretations, but everyone agrees it represents faith—something we talk about all the time, here in church.

"Not only does the letter nun symbolize faith, but the moth itself is a powerful animal totem. They're truly special creatures, revered worldwide for their symbolic attributes, such as intuition and determination.

"They're nocturnal animals who—some believe—are guided by the moon." Quinn paused and admired the moth. He felt sorry it had taken him this long to appreciate the intriguing flutter of magnificence that meant so much to Faron.

He pressed the jar against his chest. "Does it not require tremendous faith for this little animal to forsake the lovely bidding of the moon and fly through darkness towards man-made lights and unknown dangers?

"I'll tell you . . . we all could take a lesson from the moth, not just by showing more faith in God, but by having more faith in ourselves—more determination to fulfill whatever it is He put us here for. *I am come that they might have life, and that they might have it more abundantly.*"

When Quinn finished talking, the room was silent, except for the tinny pitter-patter of the moth flying up against the metal lid of the jar. People turned in the pews to look at Faron, who sat with Alva, both of them smiling widely.

Myron Sprague broke the silence, standing up to speak. "Now, that was just about the strangest sermon I ever heard, Father Gage, and I'm not sure what to make of it. But I think you must be trying to tell the boy something—not the rest of us, because we already know he's is special. He's special in good ways, and strange ways . . . always was.

"And now he's gone and married someone who is as crazy about birds as he is about bugs—some sort of environmentalist, I think she is, judging from all the feeders in her yard, and the way she's always telling people not to dump their junk in the marshes . . . and, well . . . I'm not sure where I'm going with this, but I think that's kind of a miracle . . . I mean, that the two of them found each other, because . . ."

"Hey, Myron! Sit down and be quiet!" Jarry Gallager shouted from the back.

"Yeah, shut your cake hole!" someone else called out.

Everyone erupted in laughter, and that was the end of Sunday service.

When they gathered in the annex for refreshments, Quinn passed around the jar and a picture of the letter nun, so folks could compare it to the mark on the moth's wing.

When it came his turn, Alden Paisley put down the apple fritter he was enjoying and held the picture up to the jar. "Well, I'll be damned. It's exactly like you said, Father."

"Yes, it is, Alden, and if you made it to church more often you might find that other things are exactly as I say, too."

CHAPTER 58

At seven o'clock on an unusually warm September morning, Alva stood at thc stove making suet cakes. Faron had left for the harbor hours earlier. He'd be at the far edge of their inshore fishing grounds by now, stuffing bait bags to the rhythm of the swells.

Alva was stirring peanut butter and oatmeal into melted sheep fat and thinking about nuthatches and woodpeckers, when her water broke. A high-pitched yelp of surprise was her first reaction, after which she calmly stepped out of the puddle at her feet and carried the hot suet over to the table. No point in wasting ingredients, she thought. She'd just finish this and then call Betsy to take her to the hospital. It was a plan they'd had in place for weeks, in case she went into labor when the men weren't around.

Last night she cut the tops off a half dozen empty orange juice cartons, to use as molds. Now, she poured the warm suet into them. She was filling the last one when a contraction hit. It didn't hurt much, except it came on suddenly and she nearly dropped the hot saucepan.

The spasm passed quickly and she scraped the remainder of the suet into a mold and put the sticky pot in the sink. After she wiped up the floor she dialed the phone. "Betsy? It's time."

Betsy's dented green station wagon skidded to a stop in the driveway. She got out of the car ranting and raving about being stuck behind the only school bus on the island, then ran up the porch steps into Alva's kitchen.

Alva had changed into dry clothes, but just as Betsy opened the door she felt another warm gush between her legs. "Goldarn. How many times does water break?"

Betsy clutched her friend's overnight bag and grabbed her by the arm. "Damned if I can remember, but let's get going before it happens again."

She drove way over the speed limit and didn't slow down until they crossed the bridge over Puddle Cove and neared town. Although the hospital in Willisport was supposed to be top-notch, Betsy had convinced Alva to give birth on Menhaden.

"You aren't one of us unless you're born here," Betsy reminded her friend. "Do your kids a favor and let Doc Batch deliver them."

Just about every person born on the island had slipped from the womb into Owen's hands, or his father's, before him.

"I don't know why I have to go to the hospital now," Alva complained on the ride over. "I'm fine."

"Doc knows his stuff," Betsy reminded her, "and he wants you there early because it's your first pregnancy—and on top of that you're having twins. Stop griping."

After Betsy helped Alva settle into a room, she called the harbormaster and told him to radio Emmett and let him know what was going on. "Hodie, you tell him I don't care how many lobsters he thinks he needs to catch . . . just get back here."

"And call my parents," Alva reminded Betsy. "They're at Quinn's."

Walter and Lydia had driven up last week in anticipation of the birth. They were already awake and at the breakfast table when the phone rang, so it didn't take long for them to get to the hospital.

"How's that for timing?" Walter asked his daughter when he and Lydia got there, pleased with his arithmetic regarding the due date.

Emmett turned the *B. Paisley* around as soon as he got Hodie's call. He opened up the throttle and made good time back to the harbor. Faron went straight to the hospital from the boat, still in his work clothes and jittery as all get-out.

Alva fanned herself with the corner of a sheet. Faron's jumpiness was contagious. "You're making me a wreck. Why don't you go sit outside with the men?"

He hesitated.

"Go on. Betsy and Mom will stay with me. I'll give a yell if I need you."

The first ten hours of labor were easy. The infrequent contractions were mild, but Alva grew more impatient with each one. She sucked down gelatin, wondering aloud why she couldn't go back home.

Around six, when no one could stand listening to her anymore, they left her with a glass of ice chips and went to Scuppers for a quick bite to eat. Afterwards, the women went back to Alva's room and the men retreated to the cramped waiting area.

Emmett, Faron, and Walter sat shoulder to shoulder on a small couch, staring at the television.

After nightfall, Quinn showed up, carrying a cigar box. "I thought you might like this." He handed the box to Faron and sat in a chair across from the others.

Faron was surprised when he took the box and felt it quivering. "Where did you get them?"

Quinn was pleased with himself. "I sat on my porch with the light on. They're easy to catch."

Emmett and Walter looked at each other, both thinking the same thing. *You've got to be kidding*. But, then, out of curiosity, Emmett leaned closer to the box to see if he could hear anything. "Hey, Walter," he said, "turn down the television." They sat in silence. "Sounds like rain on the wheelhouse," Emmett whispered. "I like it."

The men were mesmerized by the gentle thumping, until Betsy came out and reported that Alva's contractions were closer together, and sidesplitting.

"We could do a caesarean section," Doc Batch suggested after a couple more hours passed. "I know how dead-set you are against it, but it is an option."

"No." Alva winced and cursed the pain. "Let's give it more time."

"Okay. We'll wait a little longer, but it'll be my call from here on. Agreed?"

"Whatever you say."

Less than an hour later it was time to push. Hodie Ebel's spinster sister, Roxanne, was the nurse on duty. She wheeled Alva into the delivery room, with Faron bringing up the rear. Doc Batch was already there, gloves snapped on and ready to go.

Alva strained and forced the first kid out in a stream of amniotic fluid. The glistening infant passed easily into the doctor's hands. A boy. Seven pounds, two ounces. Twenty inches long.

"He's smiling!" Roxanne exclaimed. "Beautiful, too, not a blemish on him. And would you look at that dark hair and long, slim fingers?"

He took his first breath and let out a healthy scream while they clamped and cut the umbilical cord. Roxanne wiped him dry and covered him with a warm towel.

The second boy didn't come as easily and when all five pounds of the newborn finally popped out, the excitement in the room ebbed like the outgoing tide.

Alva sensed it. "What's wrong?"

"Nothing to worry about." Doc Batch suctioned fluid from the baby's nose. "He's just a tad smaller than his brother."

Alva lifted her head and pulled the sheet off her thighs, trying to peer down the gully between her spread knees to see what was going on. She was relieved when she heard the baby cry.

Roxanne wrapped him in a soft blanket and showed him to Alva. He was tiny, with a sparse patch of hair and pale skin. Roxanne touched Alva's hand. "Don't worry. He'll be fine."

Alva was exhausted the next morning when she woke. There was a breakfast tray cooling by the side of her bed and her parents and Faron were scattered around the room reading newspapers.

"How are you feeling?" Doctor Batch asked when he walked in.

"Great. Where are my babies?"

"Roxanne's on her way in with the big guy. You can get him started on the breast, if you like."

"What about his brother?"

Doc sat on the edge of the bed. "He's being monitored. It's standard procedure for a baby that small."

Alva sensed there was more. "Is that all?"

"No. There are other complications."

"What?"

"He has something called a patent ductus arteriosus. It's an opening in the blood vessel between the pulmonary artery and the aorta. It's normal in a fetus, but after a baby is born, it's supposed to close up on its own, usually within a few hours or days. If it doesn't, it can put a strain on the heart.

In your son's case, because he was having breathing difficulty this morning, we did an echocardiogram and found that the opening is unusually wide. He's not in immediate danger, but my recommendation is surgical repair."

No one said anything for a moment and Doc Batch felt fear fill the room.

Alva spoke first. "And if there's no surgery?"

"We could give medication and wait to see if the opening narrows, but I don't suggest that for your baby. He's already symptomatic. If he were my son, I'd choose the surgery."

"How dangerous is it?" Faron asked.

"It's very safe. The surgeon will make a small incision between the ribs on the left side and tie off the ductus arteriosus. Of course, we'll send the baby to Portland for the procedure. The fellow I have in mind has done it hundreds of times. He's the best." Doc Batch looked at Faron. "Alva will have to stay here with the other baby, but you can go to Portland with your son. The hospital will have a place for you to stay."

"Go ahead and make the arrangements," Alva said.

Faron didn't bother saying anything, but he silently agreed. In spite of the misgivings he'd felt about becoming a father, he was already feeling very protective of the two newborns.

After Doc Batch left Alva pulled the covers up to her chin and tearfully blamed herself for the baby's condition. "Maybe I drank too much."

"Don't be silly, dear," Lydia consoled her daughter, trying to hide her own concern. "You don't drink to excess and you didn't drink at all during the pregnancy. It's no one's fault." She tactfully changed the subject. "Have you decided on names?"

The entire family had spent the last few months making lists of their favorites. The only thing Faron and Alva agreed on was, since they were having twins, they'd each get to name one.

"I'm not sure yet, but Walter will be the middle name for one of them, after Dad." Alva rolled over on her side and looked around the room. "Where's Faron?"

Lydia lifted her shoulders. "I don't know."

CHAPTER 59

FARON PEEKED THROUGH the nursery window at his son while several nurses were getting him ready to be transported to the hospital in Portland. The teensy infant lay with arms against his sides, as motionless as a butterfly on a cool, cloudy day. Faron couldn't believe how beautiful he was—and he had the perfect name picked out.

When he returned to Alva's room, she was sitting up in bed holding the other baby, taking her first crack at breastfeeding.

Nurse Roxanne was showing her the ropes and telling her what a great job she was doing. "You're a natural," Roxanne complimented as she deftly repositioned the baby's mouth on Alva's nipple.

Walter left the room, unable to face the sight of his daughter's areola. Lydia stayed.

"I've chosen a name," Alva announced, gazing adoringly at the boy on her breast. "Brant Walter Goss."

"That's lovely," Lydia said. "What do you think, Faron?"

Faron couldn't take his eyes off his wife's chest. He had never seen a baby breastfed before, although it felt strangely familiar. He licked his lips.

"Faron?" Alva snapped him out of his trance.

He gave a start. "What?"

"Mom asked what you think about the name—Brant Walter Goss."

"I like it. Isn't Brant the name of the bird over the bar in Scuppers?"

"Yes!" Alva exclaimed, amazed that Faron remembered that. "Well, it's a goose, actually. My favorite. At one time there were less than ten thousand Atlantic brant in the entire country, but now the population's recovered."

She kept chattering, never taking her eyes off her hungry son. "They're small, but loyal—they mate for life.

"They sleep at sea during the night, and they don't fly in a V-formation like other geese." She stopped talking for a moment and kissed the top of Brant's soft head. "His dark hair is what made me think of the name. Black as a brant's head."

"Just like his father's." Quinn caught the tail end of the conversation as he entered the room holding a bouquet of wildflowers for Alva. "It's a wonderful name," he said, leaning over to kiss the new mother.

Faron stood behind him. "You think he looks like me?"

"He sure does. I wasn't there when you were born, but you had the same head of hair when I did see you for the first time."

Walter also came into the room during Alva's explanation about the Atlantic brant. He kept his eyes averted, careful not to look at his daughter's exposed bosom, and sat next to his wife, not quite sure what to make of the name his daughter had chosen.

"Oh boy," he wisecracked under his breath, fiddling with a stack of magazines near the window, "she named him after a goose."

Everyone heard him, including Alva. "Yes, Dad. I named him after a goose, and you. His middle name's Walter."

Walter held a hand over his eyes, peeking squeamishly through his fingers at his daughter. "Really? My name for the middle? Maybe you could switch it around. I think . . ."

Lydia jabbed him with her elbow. "Just be grateful and leave it at that."

"What about you?" Alva asked Faron. "Have you thought of a name for Brant's brother?"

Faron's eyes twinkled with delight. "Karner Blue."

Walter looked up from tying his shoelace. "Karner who? What kind of name is that?"

"It's a butterfly." Faron stood his ground.

"What'll we call him for short, Karner or Blue?" Walter asked.

"Oh, Walter. Really," Lydia chided.

"What? Are we supposed to call him the whole thing?"

"Mom. Dad. I don't want my son named after an insect," Alva interjected, taken aback by her husband's assertiveness. When she agreed to let him name one of the boys she honestly thought he'd end up letting her choose for both.

"But after a goose is okay?" Faron asked her.

The Dodges and Quinn, not wanting to be in the middle of the argument, left the room and walked down the hallway to the visitor's lounge, where Walter and Lydia told Quinn about the smaller twin's heart condition.

Faron and Alva sat in prickly silence while Brant nursed. When he finished, Alva draped a clean towel over her shoulder and rapped lightly on his back until he let out a loud burp. Both she and Faron laughed, staring with pride at their newborn son until he fell asleep in his mother's arms.

Alva's thoughts drifted back to her other boy. "What did you say the name of the butterfly was?" Alva asked Faron in a whisper.

"Karner Blue."

Doc Batch had tried to put their minds at ease about the surgery, but Alva was still scared. "I'm sorry," she said to Faron. "I'm tired, and worried about Brant's brother. I shouldn't have argued with you about the name you chose." Thinking it wasn't any worse than some of the other outlandish names people gave their children, and feeling badly about reneging on their agreement, Alva reversed course. "If it'll make you happy, Karner Blue is okay with me."

The morning Alva and Brant went home there was thunder rumbling in the distance. Fast-moving, dark clouds pressed down on the island. Betsy met them in the hospital lobby and the three of them piled into Emmett's rusted pickup truck.

Halfway to Alva's house it started to rain. Huge drops pounded the windshield and Betsy couldn't see where she was going. She pulled over to wait for it to let up. "Damn. These wipers aren't as good as the ones on my car."

"Where is your car?"

"The old man's working on it." Emmett had taken the rainy morning off and was home in the garage, changing the oil on Betsy's reliable green wagon. Now the two women sat in his unkempt truck on the side of the road, with the newborn between them.

Betsy lit up a cigarette. "God, this tastes good."

Brant yawned and stretched. "Maybe we should open the windows," Alva said to Betsy, worried about the baby breathing in the secondhand smoke.

Betsy coughed on a lungful of smoke, trying not to exhale. "You're right," she gasped, cranking down her window to let the smoke out.

Not too much was moving this morning. A couple of vehicles splashed by in a wet blur—probably fishermen on their way to Scuppers to sit out the downpour in the company of their own kind. None of them would be taking their boats out in this slop. The storm was supposed to build through the day and move out to sea after midnight.

Alva shifted in the seat. It was damn hard finding a comfortable position after delivering twins. She stared dreamily at the rain. "Lydia and Faron won't be home until tomorrow." They were down in Portland with Karner Blue while he was recovering from surgery. Everything had gone well, much to Alva's relief.

Betsy draped a thick wrist over the steering wheel and exhaled smoke through the open window. "I could stay with you tonight," she offered.

"Thanks, but I'll be all right. Dad's there."

Betsy flicked her cigarette out into the rain. "Suit yourself." She rolled up the window and put the truck in gear. "Let's go, or we'll be sitting here all day."

They crept along in third gear the rest of the way, grounded by the rubber tires when lightning struck close by. When they got to Alva's, the storm was still booming and Walter ran outside with a raincoat to hold over their heads. The baby stayed dry but the two women and Walter got soaked.

"Good Lord, Dad," Alva scolded when they got inside and shook off the rain, "why didn't you use that?" She pointed emphatically to an umbrella leaning against the wall in the small entryway between the kitchen and back porch.

Her father's hurt expression made her instantly regret the criticism. Both he and her mother had been such a big help. Lydia scrubbed the house until it sparkled and she stocked the kitchen with food. Walter built matching cradles for the boys and set them up in Alva's bedroom.

Alva put an arm around her father's shoulders and pecked him on the cheek. "I'm sorry, Dad. Guess my hormones haven't leveled off yet."

CHAPTER 60

WALTER ACHED from sleeping on the lumpy bed in Alva's guest room and was glad when Faron and Karner came home so he and Lydia could spend nights in more comfort, at Quinn's.

Weekday mornings they went to their daughter's house after Faron left for work and stayed most of the day helping with whatever needed doing. On weekends Faron gave his in-laws a break.

Alva hadn't realized how exhausting motherhood would be. The hardest part, besides sleep deprivation, was feeding Karner. He could barely drink from a bottle, and the breast was even more difficult. His feedings took twice as long as Brant's.

Roxanne Ebel offered to come over and give her some instruction. "Problem is, he's got a weak suck," she explained. "See?" She demonstrated by gently putting a finger in Karner's mouth.

Faron stood to the side, fascinated with the size of Alva's breasts. She kept them mostly covered up during the pregnancy, but lately it seemed like they were always exposed. He thought they'd shrink by now, but they didn't.

"It's easier with a bottle," Roxanne explained, "but the effort of breastfeeding will help develop his jaw muscles." She kept talking and squeezed Alva's breast against the baby's mouth. "Come on, little guy, it's good for what ails you!"

Betsy stopped by Saturday with freshly baked cinnamon rolls. Alva devoured three of them and immediately felt guilty. She went into the bathroom and hopped on the scale, weighing in at one hundred and sixty pounds.

"That's thirty pounds more than the day I got married," she moaned when she came back into the kitchen. "The worst part is it's more than Faron weighs."

"Nothing unusual about a wife outweighing her husband," Betsy declared in her typically unvarnished way. "Look at me and Emmett—I'm as thick as a fence post and he's like a bean pole."

Faron laughed, which earned him a dirty look from Alva. His shirt was stained with regurgitated milk and cobalt turquoise. He'd gotten up early to work in the studio, but the smell of warm rolls lured him away from his easel.

"Think I'll go over to Beaudry's and get some fish," Alva said to him. "I'll make cod cakes for supper." She eyed Betsy. "Want to come along?"

"Why not," her friend answered, grabbing a cinnamon roll for each of them on the way out the door. "I'll drive."

After they left, Faron put the teakettle on the front burner of the stove and stood there waiting for the water to boil, wondering just how heavy Alva was going to get, not that it really mattered.

Just last week, when a bunch of the guys were down at Scuppers trading stories about overweight wives, Faron told them he liked large women.

"Oh, then you'll love marriage," Jarry Gallager predicted. "They all get bigger after they tie the knot."

Faron chuckled, thinking about the advice and opinions he routinely got from the guys. The funniest part was, a lot of it was turning out to be true.

He leaned against the stove and looked outside. It was a bright blue morning. During the night a cold front from the north blew out a dirty, gray sky that had been hanging over them for days. Now, sunlight streamed into the kitchen.

When the kettle whistled, he made a cup of tea, put on a jacket, and stepped out onto the back porch. The boys were sound asleep and, with any luck, would be for another hour or so.

It was his favorite time of year. Cool, but not cold. He sat on a rocker that had belonged to Alva's grandmother and inhaled deeply. The salt smell in the air was more noticeable now that it wasn't mixed with humidity. Gulls soared low, their shadows crisscrossing the meadow. Butterflies flitted among the purple asters and blue vervain, making their way south.

He was daydreaming about when he was younger, chasing black swallowtails through gardens, when Betsy's car pulled into the driveway. Alva got out with her arms full of groceries and said goodbye to her friend.

Faron put his tea down and went to help Alva. "Need a hand?"

"Thanks."

He lugged the bags inside and was sliding a box of cereal into the kitchen cupboard when Brant woke up, screaming.

"I'll get him," Alva said wearily, opening the refrigerator and plunking down a large slab of codfish.

The day Brant was born he was so happy. Beatific, Quinn had called it. But the last few weeks he was insistent and cranky. Between him and Karner, Alva was worn out. She called Doc Batch for advice but he sloughed it off.

"The first year's tough," he said, "especially with two."

Alva picked Brant up and carried him into the kitchen. He was all arms and legs, kicking and waving to make his point. His face turned red and she thought he was choking, until there was a sharp intake of breath and another shriek.

The whole time Brant cried Karner never batted an eye. He was a sleepy baby who had to be wakened for his feedings. He slept through most of his brother's outbursts, and always woke up calm.

Alva opened her blouse and Brant sucked aggressively. "He almost seems angry."

Faron raised his eyebrows. "Don't know what a newborn has to be mad about."

Alva frowned. "Neither do I. Would you go get Karner?"

When Faron returned they traded babies and he walked in circles with Brant squirming on his shoulder, waiting for the milky burp that always came after a feeding.

Alva struggled to feed Karner, who flopped in her arms like a ragdoll. She pinched her nipple to get the milk flowing, trying to make it easier for him. His mouth dropped open and stayed that way. "Like a baby bird waiting for a worm," she said frustratedly.

She held Karner's head firmly against her breast, just like Roxanne had shown her, and worried aloud, "What if he doesn't get enough to eat?"

Brant spit up warm milk and a thunderous burp on Faron's shoulder. "Why don't you call Doc Batch again?" Faron suggested in a whisper, trying not to disturb Brant, who was already drifting off to sleep.

"It's not unusual for the smaller one to lag behind a bit, especially after a surgery," Doc Batch told Alva when she brought the boys in to be weighed. "Stop being so stubborn and switch to the bottle. It'll be better for everybody. At least until Karner's stronger."

•

"This really helps," Alva said to her father after a few days bottle feeding Karner. "He's definitely eating more, and faster." She tucked a towel under his chin.

"Why don't you let me move the cradles into the kitchen during the day?" Walter proposed. "That way you can nap in your room without being disturbed. Faron can move them back at night."

"That's a great idea, Dad. Thanks."

Faron followed the same routine, moving the cradles and padding back and forth between his studio and the kitchen to check on the twins while Alva slept, except sometimes he was so absorbed in painting he forgot about the boys. When that happened, and their crying woke Alva up, she reprimanded him as though he were a naughty child.

"Shouldn't let her talk to you that way," Walter said to Faron one afternoon when they were having lunch together at Scuppers.

"Shouldn't let who talk to you what way?" Billy Gallager barged in and pulled up a chair next to Walter, eager to get in on the conversation.

"His wife," Walter responded, scooting over to make more room for Billy.

"Oh. I should have known." He looked at Faron. "She's got you going like a bee in clover . . . from errand to errand. Welcome to married life." Billy tilted his chair back on two legs and laughed.

Faron jumped in protectively. "This is her father," he reminded Billy, pointing to Walter. "Careful what you say."

Walter waved a hand as if to indicate no harm done. "It's okay, Faron. I've lived with my Alva for thirty-eight years and no one knows better than me that she's a bit on the bossy side."

Billy nearly gagged on an onion ring he'd snatched off Faron's plate. "What the . . . thirty-eight years? She's practically old enough to be your mothe—" He caught himself. "Sorry, Faron. Didn't mean to mention your mother."

The three of them were quiet for a moment until Walter asked, "Why can't we talk about your mother?"

Billy brought his chair down solidly on all fours and said, "Because when I was just a dumb kid, I used to tease him about her. Now we avoid the subject."

Walter looked at both young men over the tops of his bifocals, wondering how Billy was going to get out of this one. But before anyone could pursue the embarrassing moment any further, Jeannie Ebel whizzed by with a pitcher of water. In the time it took her to fill three glasses the conversation switched to the new set of storage shelves Walter was building in Faron's garage.

Faron enjoyed having Walter around. He was good company and he was a skilled carpenter who could fix just about anything, including his daughter's occasional bad moods.

"Don't know what you'll do when I'm gone," he joked with Faron when they got home from lunch and Alva handed them another To-Do List.

Alva laughed her wonderful laugh. "Don't worry, Dad, I'll go easy on him."

By the time Walter and Lydia boarded the ferry for home, Alva was well rested and thinking about birds again. "How do you feel about helping me make some log feeders?" she asked Faron on a chilly, misty day.

That's one of the things Faron admired about her—she didn't mind doing a bit of outside work on a damp day. He thought that said a lot about a woman. He also knew by the way she phrased the question, it wasn't really a question.

"Now?" Faron had hoped to do some painting, but log feeders shouldn't take too long.

"Yes. If you have time." Alva was already bundling the boys in warm clothes. She pushed Brant's chubby arm through a sleeve. "I thought we could put these guys on the porch where we can keep an eye on them, and you could help me drag some chunks of oak from the woodpile so I can drill holes in them. I've already picked out the ones I want."

He admired her again, this time with his eyes. It wasn't even midday and she already had yeast dough rising on the stove and had made him a hot breakfast while Karner gurgled on her shoulder. Now she wanted to get her hands dirty.

Alva felt his gaze. "Why are you looking at me that way?"

Faron took Brant from her and finished zipping up the wooly outfit she'd jammed him into. "I was just thinking how lucky I am to have you and the boys." He surprised himself. It was the first time he'd felt this way enough to say it.

"Ha! You don't think I know what everyone says about me? That I'm bossy? *Just like Betsy Paisley*, they say. And too old for you." Alva gave a final defiant tug on Karner's zipper. "Are you saying you don't mind the way I am?"

"Yep, I don't mind the way you are."

Faron was not one to express love easily. Alva figured it all had to do with his dead mother, so she laughed and said, "That's good, because I don't mind you either."

CHAPTER 61

There was a strong offshore breeze whipping through the brilliant early morning sunshine. Emmett had forgotten to order fresh bait, so Faron knelt on the slippery dock hacking through a lump of frozen herring.

He was baiting up a little later than usual because Emmett had some errands. He was grateful for the delayed start since he had been up most of the night with crying babies. When they finally slept, he couldn't. Instead, he sat watching their eyelids flutter, wondering what they could possibly be dreaming of.

Gulls careened above the dock, jostling for landing space nearby, pecking at scraps of the icy fish. Water lapped gently against the pilings. It was the end of October and the oak, maple, and birch trees ringing the harbor cast sparse, colorful reflections along the shoreline.

Faron stopped chipping at the herring and stood to stretch his back. His fingers were numb from handling the cold bait. The other fishermen had left the dock hours ago. He tilted his head and listened.

The singing cicadas were gone—their hatchlings burrowed deep underground where some of them would stay until Brant and Karner were nearly grown. There was a dog barking nearby, and the sound of a boat engine starting up, its bilge water streaming overboard. Farther up the pier several retired men sat on a bench, talking quietly.

Faron startled when Emmett came up behind him and grunted a greeting.

"Good morning." Faron blew warm breath on his stinging hands. "Didn't hear you coming."

Emmett chewed on a doughnut, lips coated with powdered sugar. He saw that Faron was just about finished filling the bait box. "You're done already?" He handed his sternman a rumpled brown bag and a paper cup of hot coffee. "What time did you get here? I thought you'd sleep in."

"Thanks." Faron took the cup and warmed his stiff fingers with it, fumbling to open the lid. He took a sip and reached in the bag. "I did . . . until five," he answered, biting into a glazed cruller. He wiped crumbs from his mouth with his sleeve. "The boys had us up since then. No point trying to sleep after that."

"Guess not." Emmett hawked back a wad of mucus and spit into the harbor. He watched the clot of snot float on the water, remembering what it was like when his own daughter was an infant. Up half the night—mother sitting in the lamplight with the kid latched on.

He sat on a spindly chair in front of the bait room, chomping another doughnut. After some silent deliberating he said, "You know, the season's almost over. I can handle the next couple of weeks by myself. Why don't you stay home with the family? Give you a call when we haul the boat. You can help out then. I'll need a hand straightening out the shed, and you can still work your winter hours. In the meanwhile, Alden can give me a little time—Betsy, too, if I get that desperate."

"That's fine with me."

"Besides, from what Betsy says you'll be busy babysitting."

"How's that?" Faron asked, unsure what Emmett meant.

"The Christmas Bird Count."

"Oh, damn. I forgot about that." Alva was running the count this year and had told him to arrange for time off to watch the boys. He didn't mind, but he also needed to start thinking about his upcoming exhibit, not that there was much for him to do. The gallery was taking care of most of the details.

What he really wanted was to spend time in his studio, painting. He'd been thinking about his boys, imagining them in brushstrokes.

Faron shook his head to break his contemplation and turned back to his work. The herring was starting to melt in the warming air. The outer pieces fell away easily. He tossed them into the bait tote, waving his hands at gulls that hopped too close.

"Let's go." Emmett stood up, licking his fingers. He squashed the doughnut bag and dropped it into a trash can. "We'll follow the tide out."

CHAPTER 62

"TIT AS BIG AS A LOBSTER BUOY and he can't seem to find it," Emmett said when he dropped by to bring Alva and Faron some of Betsy's shrimp salad and slaw.

"Easy for you to say." Alva pulled a towel over her breast in a terse show of modesty. She was in no mood for jokes. Since Karner had been doing so well with bottle-feeding, she wanted to give the old-fashioned way another try, but she wasn't having much success.

Emmett had a lot of experience sensing a woman's foul moods. He grimaced at Faron behind Alva's back and headed for the door. "Guess I'm not invited to stay," he teased on his way out.

The smell of dampness was strong in the drafty kitchen—a chilled, earthy scent— just behind the wainscoted walls. Faron wore the same paint-stained trousers from yesterday. Bleary-eyed, he pretended to listen as Alva talked about birds. He opened the refrigerator and took out some eggs, butter, and jam,

Karner made a sucking sound and held on. Progress.

Alva was already planning for spring. "At the end of March I'm counting razorbills on Crenbow Island. Betsy's coming with me." She used both hands to keep her floppy boy from slipping away.

Faron spooned butter into a frying pan and turned on the burner while Alva talked. Cracked two eggs and dropped them into the sizzling grease. *The end of March*—that would be a full year married, he thought. He stared at Alva. He'd been spending a lot more time at home since the *B. Paisley* was hauled for the season and he and Alva had been getting on each other's nerves. The daily routine was wearing on him. He got the sympathetic idea that maybe bickering drudgery is why so many of the guys hightailed it over to Scuppers every chance they got. It sure wasn't because they liked Red's food.

"First year's the hardest," Billy Gallager said when he and Faron compared notes at Scuppers earlier that week. "You'll get used to it."

Now, while the eggs fried, Brant stirred in Walter's handcrafted cradle in a corner of the kitchen, already fed and dozing. When Faron looked at him, he instantly regretted his resentments. Married life wasn't easy, but there was no doubt that he adored his children and wanted to be a good father.

Karner fell asleep mid-suck. Milk dripped onto his forehead.

"Probably have to put in a week, maybe more. That's what I promised." Alva was still on the topic of birds.

The eggs broke when Faron flipped them. Alva kept talking, not waiting for replies from him. When he put a plate in front of her, she wiped the milk off the baby's forehead and handed him to Faron without saying anything. Not even a "thank you."

While his wife ate and his children snuffled softly in their sleep, Faron felt ignored. The guys were right about things changing after marriage. He was getting less sex and doing more of the cooking.

•

"We saw sixteen Carolina wrens!" Alva exclaimed the next day when Faron came home tired and irritable. "That's unusual this far north."

"And three white-winged crossbills," Betsy chimed in.

Both women were sitting at the kitchen table doing tallies for the Christmas Count. Papers were strewn about and Faron thought he smelled something burning. He hoped it wasn't supper, because he was famished.

"Is something on the stove?"

"Supper," Alva answered flatly. "Help yourself."

Betsy chuckled, "Sorry, Faron. We're distracted. Cheer up, at least there's burnt stew. Emmett's got nothing until I get home."

"Always looking on the bright side, aren't you, Betsy?" Faron muttered sarcastically. He scraped some stew out of the pot into a bowl. He was trying to decide where to sit down and eat it when he realized the cradles were empty. "Where're the boys?"

"Quinn's got them . . . seventeen, eighteen . . ." Alva kept counting, ". . . nineteen . . . he's meeting Mom and Dad at the ferry."

Faron had forgotten about that. Walter and Lydia were coming a week before Christmas so they could attend the school pageant. All twenty-eight children on the island were in it, including Brant and Karner Blue, who were both cast in the role of baby Jesus.

Alva scribbled a number on a piece of paper and said out loud: "Thirty-one." She directed a puzzled glance at Betsy. "Isn't that low for pine siskins?"

"Don't know. Never even knew what a pine siskin was until you talked me into doing this."

The two of them had spent the better part of the month furiously counting birds, but it was Faron who was exhausted.

With Alva so busy he had to pick up the slack, and he was still working his winter hours for Emmett.

He was afraid to ask the women to clear a place for him at the table so he leaned against the kitchen counter with his bowl. He was swallowing his first mouthful of charred mush when he heard cars pull into the driveway.

Alva heard it too. "Faron, go give them a hand with the kids, will you?"

CHAPTER 63

MID-JANUARY, Menhaden Island was still strung with Christmas lights and would be until spring, when things warmed up enough to lug ladders from garages and take down the tangle of bulbs and wires, although some folks wouldn't bother.

Faron's show opened in Portland on an overcast afternoon. During the hectic holidays there wasn't much time to worry about the opening reception, but now he tensed at the thought of being the center of attention.

Alva wore the prettiest flowered dress he'd ever seen. She and the boys, Betsy, Emmett, and Alden packed into the Chevy Suburban with him and Quinn for the long ride down coast.

Brant fussed and hollered most of the way, switching alliances between Alva and Betsy, although neither one of them could completely calm him. Karner Blue slept in Faron's arms, as content as a caterpillar on the underside of a milkweed leaf.

"Over there." Faron pointed to the red brick gallery.

Quinn flipped on the turn signal and drove down the narrow side street. "I'll let you guys out and come back after I find a parking space."

Faron nearly panicked inside the gallery. It was overflowing with people. Walter and Lydia were already there, waiting for them in the lobby and getting acclimated to the intimidating crowd.

"Here, let me take Karner," Betsy offered, noticing that Faron seemed dumbstruck.

"Faron!" Del yelled from the crowd. He hurried over to greet them. "It's wonderful to see you." He gave Faron a warm hug and introduced himself to everyone else. "Laric's inside with Holzer and Gaines," he informed them, motioning for them to follow him.

Glimpsing so many of his paintings in one room was unsettling. It must have showed because Quinn came up behind him and asked, "What's wrong?"

"I don't know."

Del noticed too. "Feeling exposed?" he asked.

Faron shrugged. "Maybe." He stared at the paintings. The way the gallery lights lit them made them more beautiful than he remembered, but he felt detached, as if they weren't his.

"You are, you know."

"I'm what?"

"Exposed. When artists hang their work, they may as well be tacking themselves up on the wall. Want to walk around?"

Faron went with Del, and the Menhaden folks made a quick pass through the exhibit on their own, then circled back and hovered close to the food and drink.

Alden overheard a conversation between the gallery owner and a well-dressed man scribbling in a notebook, and now he shared the information with the group. "The show's a huge success. There're sixty paintings and forty-seven of them are already sold—each one in the four figures."

Walter was unbelieving. "Are you sure? How do you know?"

"I told you. I heard the bigshots talking."

Emmett ate cheese and crackers and did the math in his head. "We hear you've struck it rich," he said when Faron rejoined them. "You're not going to quit on me, are you?" Emmett looked more than a little worried. "You're the best sternman I got."

Alden made a face. "What about me? I never heard any complaints."

"You know what I mean. He's steady. I need someone steady."

Faron was only half listening. Being surrounded by his early paintings made it hard to stay in the present, but he reassured Emmett he'd be back on the boat come spring.

Betsy and Emmett shared looks of relief over the rims of their plastic wine glasses. They'd gotten used to having Faron around. Odd as he sometimes was, he was reliable, and they didn't want to lose him.

They were all still standing by the refreshments when the gallery owner barged into their circle and took Faron by the elbow to steer him toward the admiring crowd. "Let's mingle, it's good for business."

The rest of them stayed put, filling up on the free buffet and discussing ways for Faron to spend the proceeds from the show.

"He should save it," Walter stated unequivocally. "For the kids."

Quinn and Lydia agreed.

Alva had another idea. "Save some, but invest some, too." She spoke directly to Emmett. "Maybe he could be a partner. The *B. Paisley*'s getting old and if Faron bought in you could use the money for an overhaul." She handed Brant off to her mother and poured herself a fourth glass of wine, taking several long sips before giving Emmett more advice. "You could join the co-op too. You'd save more money that way."

Emmett wasn't sure how he felt about having a partner, but he was adamant about not joining the co-op, and he hated it when the women brought it up. "No need for that," he said with as much tolerance as possible, keeping in mind that Alva was probably half in the bag and not responsible for what she was saying. "I'm doing just fine on my own, thank you very much."

Predictably, Betsy jumped in. "You know, Emmett, I think Alva's right."

"Ayuh, I bet you do." Emmett looked angry. "Why, I . . ."

"Oh, be quiet," Betsy interrupted. "Being independent isn't all it's cracked up to be. I heard the co-op just got another member. What'll you do when the whole island's in?"

Emmett chugged his wine and rolled the empty glass between his palms until the plastic stem fell off. Tipsy women or not, his patience was gone. "I know all that, Butsy-insky. Don't need you to tell me. Besides," he sneered, "that makes a grand total of four in the co-op. And you know who the fourth member is? Myron's long-lost brother, who doesn't even own a boat and is only back on the island to mooch off his relatives. No need to worry about the whole island being in. I think it'll be a while before I'm a lonesome holdout."

They all knew by the tone of his voice that it was time to drop the subject, although he didn't give them the chance. He turned tail and crossed the room to where Laric was standing alone, nursing a glass of room-temperature wine.

Betsy shrugged off Emmett's abrupt departure. She held Karner Blue with one arm and dug out a baby bottle from a canvas sack. "Alva, I'm going to find a spot to sit and feed him. Okay?"

Alva poured herself more wine, annoyed there was no more ice. "Go ahead. I'll join you in a minute."

CHAPTER 64

The gallery was open until midnight but when a light snow started falling at six o'clock, Quinn suggested it was time to leave.

"I guess you're right," Faron agreed, cuddling Karner Blue on his shoulder, watching delicate flakes fall from the black sky. "Want me to get the car?"

"No. I'll get it. You find the others."

Walter's car was parked out front, across the street.

"Why don't I drive, Walter?" Alden offered when he saw the older man jiggling his keys in his pocket and gazing nervously out the window at the snow. "I've navigated these roads lots of times, in worse weather than this."

"Thanks, Alden. I am a little tired." Walter didn't like handing his car over to anyone, but he wasn't as fearless about driving in snow and ice as he used to be.

All the women opted to ride with them, liking the idea of heading into the snowstorm with a sheriff behind the wheel. Lydia took Brant, who seemed more content with her than anyone else, but when Faron insisted on taking Karner Blue with him in Quinn's car, Alva changed her mind about riding with Alden. "Think I'll go with Quinn. Won't be as cramped."

Quinn held the front passenger door open for her. Faron had already made himself comfortable in the middle seat with Karner. Emmett was sitting behind them. "Why don't you go ahead of me, Alden," Quinn suggested. "You're better driving in this weather than I am. Just take it slow so I can follow."

"I will, but we do need to make the last ferry in Willisport or we'll be stuck there all night.

In spite of the hulking plows that were busy pushing away snow and spreading sand, the roads were nearly impassable. Several times, when Alden looked in the rearview mirror and didn't see Quinn's car, he slowed to a stop until the Suburban's headlights shone behind him again.

They were lucky with the ferry in Willisport—it was making its last run for the night and they got there ten minutes before it was about to depart.

The crossing was rough and the large boat pitched and rolled in the frosty darkness. No one got out of their cars, except Alden. "Need some air," he explained as he hefted himself up and out into the cold. He steeled himself against the wind and found his way to the wheelhouse, where he helped himself to a cup of strong tea and traded stories with the captain—one of the perks of being in law enforcement.

"Wasn't sure you'd go out in this," Alden said, sweetening his tea with too much sugar.

"Eh—this is nothing. Remember the winter we discontinued service?"

Alden had to stop and think for a moment. There'd been a helluva storm a few years back and the ferry didn't run for days.

"Anyway," the captain continued, "no point in going back to the mainland tonight. We'll tie up in Menhaden and me and the crew'll sleep aboard."

"You're welcome to stay in my office. We've got a couple of beds there."

"No need—we'll be fine on the boat."

When the ice-coated ferry reached Menhaden, weather conditions had worsened and they drove off the metal deck into a powerful storm, sliding off the ferry onto the pavement.

"Got your seatbelts on?" Alden asked his sleepy passengers.

They grunted replies. It had been a long day of driving and free wine.

The heater in Walter's car was doing its job and everyone was warm. Lydia dozed while Brant slept contentedly on her chest. Betsy sucked on an unlit cigarette trying to decide if she should light it, and Walter was doing some back-seat driving from the front. "Careful, Alden."

The cautious sheriff slowed to a crawl. Bulky flakes swirled wildly beyond the windshield. He pulled the car over several times so he could get out to knock caked snow and ice off the wipers. "What a mess," he complained, knocking his boots together to shake off the snow, before climbing back in behind the wheel.

"Quinn still behind you?" Walter asked.

Alden glanced in the rearview mirror but didn't see any headlights. "I don't see him. They probably had to stop to clear their windshield." Alden put the car in gear. "No point waiting for them this close to home, I guess."

Walter clutched the door handle as Alden got underway again. He was thinking that maybe they should wait, but Alden didn't seem too concerned so he didn't say anything.

They dropped Betsy off first. The road from the ferry to her place was treacherous. You could see a plow had been through but snow was coming down so fast the road crew couldn't keep up, and what the plow left behind was frozen solid.

Alden struggled to keep the car moving forward without sliding. After he got everyone home, he'd give Keith Cyr a call and make sure Public Works stayed on top of things. If it got any worse, he and Keith would have to pitch in. The thought of spending the rest of the night clearing snow didn't make him any too happy.

Getting up Betsy's long narrow driveway made him even less happy. It was nearly impossible. Coming back down wasn't much better. The brakes were all but useless on the freezing snow and the car skidded most of the way. All he could do was try to find the curves by memory and stay off the brakes as much as he could.

Walter held his breath as they slid back onto the main road. He didn't exhale until the car stopped veering and was safely back on course.

He breathed another sigh of relief when they pulled into Alva's driveway. "Thank God."

"What's the matter," Alden teased as he took the keys out of the ignition and handed them to Walter, "don't trust my driving?"

Walter already had one leg swung out of the car. The blast of cold air from the open door woke Lydia. "Why don't you stay here tonight, Alden?" she offered groggily, yawning as Walter helped her up from the back seat. "We'll have buttermilk pancakes in the morning. I know you like those."

Alden's car was at the church and he planned to drive back there with Quinn to retrieve it. "That's tempting, but I've got the early shift tomorrow. God knows it'll be a mess with all this snow." He looked upward to draw Lydia's attention to the falling flakes, to make his point. "The others should be along soon. I'll just stretch my legs and have a smoke until they get here." He pulled a fresh pack of cigarettes from his pocket and shook one out, shielding it from the wind with his cupped hands while he lit it. He took a deep drag. "Go on . . . don't worry about me." He gave Lydia a gentle shove. "Get inside."

Lydia boosted Brant up higher on her shoulder. "Don't be silly. Come on in." She turned and slogged through the snow to the back door. Walter followed her.

Alden pulled his collar more tightly around his neck. He didn't want to let on that he was worried but he did wonder how Quinn could have fallen so far behind. He started second-guessing himself. Maybe he should have waited for them the last time he stopped. He couldn't even call, since none of them owned a goddamn cellphone except him and Betsy, and she was already home. Stuck in the dark ages, they were.

He looked at the house, briefly comforted by its coziness when the kitchen lights flicked on in the snowy darkness. He stayed outside a few minutes more, squinting through the storm, hoping to see car headlights. When the snow had nearly doused his cigarette he took one last damp pull, then tossed the butt and went inside to wait with the Dodges.

Emmett was stretched across the rear seat in a full snore. Alva was up front sleeping off the wine. Faron was in the middle row holding Karner Blue and trying to stay awake. They'd all had a bit too much to drink, except for Quinn, who was the designated driver.

Quinn yawned behind the wheel. Cracked the window for some air. "Where's your friend Laric staying tonight?" He met Faron's gaze in the rearview mirror.

"In Portland."

Quinn nodded his approval. "Good. Not the best night to be out on the road alone."

The snow whirled through the dark in front of them. They hadn't seen another car since losing sight of Alden. The island was battened down, although it looked like a plow had been through not too long ago.

Quinn had been keeping up with Alden pretty good since they off-loaded the ferry, but the last few miles he had to stop several times to scrape ice and snow off the Suburban's windows. The first two times he could still see the red taillights of Walter's car in the distance but the third time he stopped he wasn't able to catch up to them again.

"The defroster in Walter's car must be better than mine," he said to Faron, assuming Alden was far ahead of them, maybe even back at Alva's already.

"Could be," Faron mumbled sleepily.

"Yup. Alden's got to be worried about you driving in this," Emmett announced from the back seat, suddenly fully awake. He sat up to get a better look out the window, eyeing the storm like a fisherman checking out the morning sky.

"You know how Alden is," Emmett said. He sat further forward in his seat but lowered his voice when he realized Alva was sleeping. "He's worse than an old lady."

A strong wind blew the snow into drifts all around them. Quinn could barely see the road. He kept his eyes aimed straight ahead and answered Emmett. "I know. I'm surprised he didn't pull over and wait for us to catch up." Quinn reached to wipe condensation off the inside of the window. "Can you believe this weather? I can't see a thing."

CHAPTER 65

"WANT ME TO DRIVE?" Faron asked half-heartedly, his energy dulled by the storm and alcohol.

Quinn shook his head. "No, thanks. We're nearly to the bridge." He was thinking they should have stayed in Willisport, or at the rectory, rather than driving everyone back to their own homes. Too late now. He took a swipe at the fogged-up windshield but still couldn't see much. "Darn. I'm going to have to stop again and clean off the wipers and windows."

He put his flashers on and stopped in the middle of the road, not wanting to risk getting stuck in deep snow on the shoulder. He grabbed an ice scraper from the dashboard and got out, then walked around the car, clearing all the windows. When he climbed into the front seat again, fresh snow already covered the glass. He flipped on the wipers and slowly got underway. "These are blizzard conditions. What do you think, Emmett—when was the last time we had a storm like this?"

Emmett thought a moment. "I don't know—a few years, maybe four. It was the last year Remmy Hodgdon set traps right through December. Remember? Damn fool went out in light snow but when he got back there was nearly three feet on the ground. He practically froze to death. The harbor-master was just about to notify the Coast Guard when that numbskull came limping in."

Quinn chuckled good-naturedly, vividly recalling the icicles hanging off Remmy's beard. "Yeah, but he came back with a full livewell, didn't he?"

"Ayuh. He come back with lobsters, all right." Emmett's pride was still hurt. He considered himself the most skilled and the heartiest lobsterman on Menhaden, except for the Cutter brothers. But the facts don't lie. Hodgdon had been around a long time and he was tough competition. "Well, I'd still go out in December, too, if it weren't for the wife. That Betsy, she . . . well, you know." His voice trailed off.

Quinn chuckled. Everyone knew how Betsy was. She let Emmett think he was the boss in public, but behind the scenes it was Betsy who decided how things would go.

They drove on in silence, nearly hypnotized by the white snow blowing against the blackness on the road ahead. The storm muted everything, even the sound of the car, giving the quiet sensation of being motionless while the night moved toward them. They were still staring at the inaudible blizzard when Quinn hit the brakes. The car was at a right angle to the Puddle Cove Bridge, heading for the riprap that sloped down to the cove.

None of them even saw the bridge until it was too late. It loomed out of the blustery blackness with jaw-dropping surprise. Once Quinn's foot was on the brake pedal all four tires lost traction. The heavy Chevy Suburban spun in a full circle and the left rear quarter panel smashed into the metal guard rail, sending the car over the railing, headlong into the drink.

It happened fast, but to the three men it seemed like slow motion. They were still gawking at the length of the bridge trying to figure out what happened when the car was airborne—they were disoriented—spatially tricked out of the awareness of falling.

As they tumbled into Puddle Cove, the windows on the passenger's side smashed against the rocks, dousing them with a torrent of frigid water. The car quickly leveled off and floated, sinking only up to the bumpers. Quinn knew that was in their favor, and except for hitting his head on the steering wheel and being jarred by the icy crash, he seemed to be all right.

He heard someone groan, and the baby crying, then Emmett say, '*Jesus Christ, Quinn. What the hell happened*?' Then there was a terrible, loud gurgling noise and the Suburban settled deeper in the water.

Quinn knew there wasn't much time to get everyone out before more water gushed in and engulfed them. "Faron?" There was no answer, just Karner crying. The headlights were still on, but it was dark inside the car.

The ice-cold impact startled Alva awake, but unconsciousness came quickly after that. She was aware just long enough to feel her chest tighten with a swift, searing pain at the first shock of freezing seawater. Now she lay gasping alongside Quinn.

Quinn struggled to unclasp her seatbelt, overwhelmed with despair at the thought of leaving her behind. He nearly panicked when the car's front end tipped downward.

When the windows shattered a piece of glass sliced a long gash in the side of Faron's head. A large stone broke loose from the rubble that lined the shoreline and smacked him in the lower jaw, splitting his lip and knocking out some teeth. He gagged on blood and salt water, then blacked out, losing his grip on Karner. The infant floated like a seedpod to the rear of the car. Emmett was there to catch him.

Emmett Paisley thought quickly in fifteen feet of water. He'd spent his entire life at sea, in all kinds of weather, and he was damned if he'd endure the humiliation of drowning in a car.

The electrical system hadn't shorted yet and the headlights lit the cove like a hotel swimming pool. The tail end of the car was sticking out of the brine and there was just enough murky light for him to see that Faron had passed out, his bloody head still above water. Emmett let go of the screaming baby and reached for Faron but when he did the car lurched and began sinking deeper.

As the water rose, Emmett knew there was no time to help anyone except Karner. He grabbed the bundle of boy that bobbed near his chin, sucked in a mouthful of air, and swam through a broken window. Out of the corner of his eye he thought he saw someone following him.

CHAPTER 66

ALDEN WAS STIRRING three spoonfuls of sugar into a strong cup of coffee when worry got the best of him. He pushed himself away from the table after just one sip. "Lydia, call Keith Cyr and tell him I'm driving between Alva's place and the ferry, and he should come find me. I've tried him several times but can't get through." He scrawled on a scrap of paper. "Here's his number. Keep trying until you get him. Tell him to call Owen Batch and find out if he's at his home office or the hospital. Whichever it is, have Keith tell him to stay put."

Lydia and Walter looked at one another.

"You're scaring us," Walter said.

"Don't worry," Alden reassured them. "It's only a precaution. Probably just Quinn's slow driving—you know how he is—as slow as sap without a freeze. At worst, they're stuck in a drift, and if that's the case I can help unstick them and keep them warm while doing it." He went down the hallway and returned with an armload of blankets. "Go ahead, make that phone call."

The snow wasn't letting up.

Alden rummaged through the garage for a shovel and a long rope, threw them and the blankets into the back seat of

Walter's car and retraced his snow-covered tire tracks along Sheepscot Road. Just as he approached the bridge he saw Quinn's car fly over the guardrail. It bounced off the rocky seawall and landed in the water, glowing like an apparition, taillights shimmering red above the surface, headlights glinting off the icy cove.

Alden crossed the bridge and turned his car toward the wreck, leaving the high beams on and the engine running. He grabbed the rope, tied one end off to the guardrail, and lowered himself down to the edge of the water, pelted by the freezing mix still falling from the sky. His eyes scanned the water.

When Emmett's head broke the surface Alden was balancing on the slippery embankment, fighting his growing panic. He could see Emmett struggling to hold on to Karner Blue. He needed to get them out of the water, and fast. He tied a loop in the end of the rope and tossed it into the cove. "Grab it!" he yelled to his brother.

His first throw didn't reach. He quickly recoiled the rope and tried again. This time Emmett was able to get his frozen fingers around the loop and hang on. As Alden worked the rope hand over hand, straining to pull his brother and Karner Blue towards shore, the lights on the partially submerged car flickered and went dark.

Just before the lights quit Faron regained consciousness and lifted his head. He was nauseous and dizzy and for a moment, unsure where he was. But, suddenly, everything became clear—and he saw her. He was certain of it.

After worrying every trap the *B. Paisley* raised, here she was, trying to make her way to him. Her slender arms stretched in his direction. Her flowered cotton dress was cheerful in the darkness and her long hair floated around her beautiful face.

There was no bloated terror as he'd so often vividly imagined, only a serene smile and an unmistakable loving gaze. Faron sucked in the last of the air. Black water filled his ears, muting whatever sound was left, and he went to her.

Emmett shivered uncontrollably in the wintry air. Waterlogged and clumsy, he held on to the stiff line with the determined grip of a lobsterman and clawed his way up the embankment, holding tightly to Karner Blue.

Alden grabbed his brother's arm and helped him over the railing onto the road. He took the baby and opened the car door to the backseat. "Get in, Emmett." He'd left the heater blasting. "Hurry up, take off those wet clothes and wrap yourself in a blanket." He slid in behind the wheel and took off his jacket, short of breath. "Emmett, give me your knife," he huffed.

Emmett unclipped a lanyard from his soggy pants, pulled his fishing knife out of a pocket, and handed it to his brother.

Alden cut carefully through Karner's soaked layers of clothes and removed them. He tilted the baby's head to the side, then back again, and put his ear close to the child's face to see if he was breathing. He couldn't tell, so he put his lips over Karner's tiny mouth and blew into it until the squishy boy spit up saltwater.

Despite the freezing temperature Alden was drenched in sweat. He turned Karner on his side again and stuck a finger in the baby's mouth to scoop out any vomit. When the boy was breathing normally Alden felt his own body relax, then tremble. He wrapped Karner in a blanket and held him close, amazed he was still alive.

Emmett huddled in the back seat with his brother's coat and a blanket pulled tightly around him. He handed another blanket to Alden. "How's the k-k-k-kid?" Emmett asked, with chattering teeth.

Alden looked at Emmett's reflection in the rearview mirror. "He's okay. Breathing. But I'll feel better when Doc Batch has a look at him—you too."

"Nah. I'm fine."

Alden gazed toward the water.

His brother read his mind. "Don't even think about it," Emmett cautioned. "Quinn and Alva were up front . . . probably didn't have a ch-ch-chance, and Faron . . . I don't know. On the way up I thought I saw someone moving . . . but I guess I was wrong . . . it was dark. There wasn't time for me to help anyone else. No point in you being a hero, either." There was sorrowful regret in his voice. He put a hand on Alden's shoulder. "Don't you think?"

"I guess so." The words stuck in Alden's throat. "I hate leaving them here like this." He kissed the top of Karner's fuzzy head. "But at least we got him. Let's get going."

Alden was about to put the car in gear when Deputy Cyr's vehicle pulled in behind them. He got out and hurried over to Alden. He took one look and ran back to his patrol car for some emergency blankets. He handed one to Emmett and the other to Alden. It didn't take much thinking on his part to figure out what happened. "I called the Doc. He's at his place." The deputy's eyes followed the beam of Alden's car headlights and he saw the rope dangling off the guardrail. He motioned toward the water. "Anyone else in the car?"

"Yup. Three. Faron and Quinn. And Alva." Emmett answered before Alden could.

"Damn."

Alden tried to stay focused. "Keith, get a hold of Doc again and tell him we're on our way over."

"Okay. Phones are spotty, but I'll try. What about them?" Keith asked, gesturing toward the cove.

"You stay here and keep an eye on things. Start making calls to get some men out here with a tow truck first thing in the morning, we'll bring them up then. And tell everyone to keep their yaps shut. Not a word. I don't want this making the loop until the families are notified." He glanced again at the water. "And don't . . ." Alden stopped midsentence. "What the hell?"

Quinn's head was still above water and he was able to roll his window down far enough to pull himself through and swim to the surface. At the top he gulped oxygen and dove back down for Alva. He swam to the broken window to pull her out, but Faron was already there, pushing her through the jagged glass. The two of them paddled upward, away from the car, with Alva between them. At the surface they gulped air and held Alva's head above water while they kicked the short distance to shore, legs cramping, faces stinging in the snowy night.

"Get out of the way!" Alden shouted to his deputy, who was leaning against the car door. Alden shoved the door open and ran to where Quinn and Faron had fallen in a crumpled, frozen heap on the embankment, slightly out of range of the cruiser's high beams. They had Alva in their arms and were trying to boost her up the rocks.

Alden grabbed her arms and tugged as hard as he could.

"I'm all right," Quinn gasped, when they were all safely up on the road. "Take care of them."

Keith knelt beside Alva, doing chest compressions. Emmett lifted her chin and tilted her head back to give mouth-to-mouth, his bare rear end sticking out from under the blanket. They kept at it until she coughed and dribbled saliva.

"Put her in the cruiser," Alden shouted. "I'll follow you to Batch's place." He flinched at the sight of his brother's buttocks. "Jesus, Emmett, get in the car. You're going to freeze your ass off out here."

•

Blood gushed from the deep cut on Faron's head and he mumbled incoherently. His lower lip was split in two. The gash went through the gum and midway down his chin. Alden and Quinn helped him to his feet and shoved him into the back of Walter's car. Quinn wadded up the end of a blanket and held it against Faron's head.

Alden got in and stepped on the gas, driving as fast as he could through the storm, warming baby Karner on his lap.

CHAPTER 67

Owen Batch answered his front door on the first knock, alerted by the deputy's call and well accustomed to middle-of-the night emergencies. Emmett and Deputy Cyr carried Alva through the doorway. Behind them, Alden steadied Faron on the doorstep and Quinn cradled Karner in his arms.

"Put everyone in there, for now," Owen said, pointing to his living room. He'd already stoked a roaring fire, had heating pads plugged in, and a stack of clean woolen blankets on a table. Hot water on the stove.

He took one look at Faron's injuries and did what he could to staunch the bleeding. Faron was still conscious, but groggy. He handed him a towel. "Hold this over your face and apply pressure," he told Faron. "I need to check on the others."

Relief passed across the doctor's face as he put his stethoscope to Karner's chest. "Seems like the kid's holding his own," he said. He grabbed a large pillow, covered it with a heating pad and blanket, and lay Karner down on it. He put another blanket on top of the boy and turned his attention to Alva, whose skin was bluer than a heron.

He held her wrist to check the pulse. "Go into the kitchen and make some tea," he instructed the deputy "Water's already boiling. We need to get some hot liquid in everyone.

Put plenty of honey in it. I keep some infant formula in the closet in my office. Get some and warm it up for Karner. The baby bottles are in there too.

"Quinn . . . Faron . . . take off those wet clothes. Emmett, can you walk?"

Emmett stood up from the chair he'd flopped in, still shivering and gripping a blanket around his waist. "A little shaky, but yes."

"Good. Go upstairs and poke around my bedroom. Find some shirts and pants for everyone—socks. Anything will do." He still had hold of Alva's arm. "Alden, let's get her into the other room."

They laid Alva on the examining table and switched on the overhead lamp. She looked even worse under the harsh light, and was in and out of consciousness. Owen took her temperature and felt for broken bones. "She needs to go to the mainland but there's no way the chopper can transport her tonight. Not in this storm—already made some calls and confirmed that before you got here. Supposed to clear by morning, for now, let's get everyone to the hospital in town. Can you get us there, Alden?"

Alden nodded in the affirmative. "I'll get the road crew over here and we can follow their plow—if the phones are working." He went into Doc's office and made the call. After several attempts, he got a static-filled connection.

Karner mewled softly in his hospital crib while Doc Batch bent over him. The baby's temperature had risen and the heart sounded normal, but given his history, there was cause to worry. It wasn't clear how long the boy had been unconscious. Alden said he did mouth-to-mouth and the baby spit up and started breathing, but he also said he wasn't really sure if the kid had actually stopped breathing, or for how long. There was no gurgling in the infant's lungs, so maybe he'd just swallowed a small bit of seawater. Maybe he'd been breathing all along and Alden just didn't detect it. He'd have to be closely watched. They could do more extensive tests on the mainland. For now, he was warm and stable.

Karner fidgeted and cried when the doctor covered him with a blanket.

Nurse Roxanne came running. "Everything all right?"

"I think so. Probably hungry." Doc Batch rubbed his eyes. "I'm beat."

Roxanne took the baby in her arms. "Try to get some rest. I'll take care of him."

Faron's head throbbed when he woke. His vision was so blurred he could barely make out Quinn lying in the next bed. There was a baby crying in the background. The wailing tugged at his every instinct, but he couldn't move. The pain in his head and jaw was blinding and his chest hurt, but he remembered what he saw. "It was her," he slurred.

Doc Batch walked in and found Quinn standing alongside Faron trying to make out what he was saying. "I can't understand him," Quinn said.

"The knock on his head's garbled things. He may not remember everything that happened. I've given him a good dose of painkiller too." Owen Batch took Quinn by the arm. "But right now I'd like to have another look at you. Get back in bed."

"I'm fine," Quinn insisted.

Quinn had good color and appeared alert and Owen wasn't overly concerned, but he did want to monitor his vital signs for a while longer. He took Quinn's blood pressure and pulse.

"Heart been racing?"

"Nope."

"Confusion? Difficulty moving?"

"No."

He listened to the preacher's lungs. "You're lucky to be alive. You all are."

Quinn didn't always understand why things happened the way they did, but being a man of God, he didn't believe that luck had anything to do with it.

"Ninety seven point nine," Owen said, taking a thermometer out of Quinn's mouth. "Perfect. By the way, did anyone call Betsy or the Dodges?"

"I did," Quinn said. He knew from hard learned experience that bad news is best delivered in the light of day, so he'd fibbed when he called them earlier. "I told them my car skidded off the road, but everyone was all right. I said Alden slipped and twisted his ankle so we were all going over to your house and to spend the night. Hope that's okay with you."

Owen stood up, knees cracking. "Fine with me. They couldn't have gotten here anyway. Spared everyone a few hours worry. I'll call them now and fill them in." He nearly bumped into the nurse on his way out the door. She was loaded down with a tray of hot soup.

"Here you go," Roxanne said, handing a steaming cup to Quinn.

Faron needed help eating. He couldn't drink from a cup and could barely sip the hot broth through a straw. "Try some," Roxanne coaxed. "I know it hurts, but you'll feel better." He wasn't shivering anymore but Roxanne had seen enough hypothermia to know that sometimes things got worse after the shaking stopped. "Come on, just a sip."

Faron pushed the cup away and closed his eyes. Owen had cleaned his wounds and closed them up with neat rows of stitches, but the pain was still there. The craggy slashes in his head and face pulsated with an ache that was nearly unbearable.

Roxanne checked her watch. Time for another dose of painkillers. She popped a pill onto Faron's tongue and told him to swallow.

Within minutes his face relaxed. As the intense pain subsided, it was replaced with the image of his mother's watery grace and the unmistakable sense of knowing that whatever he feared might rise from the depths of Puddle Cove, never would.

At six in the morning Alden and his crew were already at the crash site raising the sunken Suburban. A light snow sprinkled the men as they worked, but there was a hint of blue in the early morning sky.

Owen Batch phoned the Dodges and told Lydia there'd been an accident, omitting the part about the car going off the road into the water. "We didn't feel right about not telling you last night, but considering the roads were impassable and you couldn't have gotten here, we didn't see the point in worrying you."

He was upbeat about Karner and downplayed Alva's and Faron's injuries—told them LifeFlight transported Alva and the baby to a trauma center on the mainland, just to be on the safe side. "They're better equipped than we are," he reassured them. "They'll be fine. Later today, when the ferry's running, you can go see them."

He phoned Betsy next. "No, don't bother," he said when she wanted to come see Emmett. "He's sound asleep. Better if you check on Walter and Lydia. They're pretty upset, and they haven't even heard the worst of it."

Quinn slept fitfully. He felt responsible for the accident and kept wondering what he could have done differently. Remorse had taken hold.

In the bed next to him, Faron woke up, unsure where he was. The room spun when he struggled to sit up.

"You should be resting," Owen scolded when he saw Faron dangling his feet over the side of the bed.

Faron's jaw ground with pain when he tried speaking. The only word Owen could make out was 'her,' so he made assumptions. "What's that? Alva? Yeah. You and Quinn pulled her out of the car. Remember? Saved her life." He fluffed Faron's pillow. "She's pretty beaten up. Got a bad head injury and a fractured sternum. Busted her ankles. Had to transport her to the mainland. She'll get good care there." He was blunt but there was no way to conceal the fact that Alva wasn't here. He made a sweeping motion with his hands, gesturing that Faron should swing his feet up onto the bed and lie down. "You'll be joining her there tomorrow. Your jaw's broken and you need surgery. Left wrist is fractured, too, but I've already put that in a cast."

Quinn said something about it being the 'painting hand,' but Faron's latest dose of painkiller kicked in and he'd already drifted off to sleep.

CHAPTER 68

FARON SAT with Walter Dodge in the front pew of Good Shepherd by the Sea. Brant and Karner fidgeted between them. Faron's wrist was still in a cast and his jaw was wired, but the plastic surgeon who worked on his face had done a good job. There was only a thin, jagged scar stretching down one side of his head, through his bottom lip and chin. Later on, when the wire was removed, he'd have his teeth fixed.

Occasionally there was a strange sensation in his ears, a sound like rushing water. It made it hard to listen to Quinn's sermon and he only heard part of what was said—something about Alva flying with birds to a speedy recovery.

The blow to her head caused a severe concussion with some memory loss, complicated by nearly drowning. Both ankles were broken when they jammed up against the Suburban's floorboard. But it was a fractured sternum and ribs that caused most of her problems. The broken breastbone pressed against her heart, and the ribs punctured both lungs. It was going to be a long, slow recovery.

Alva had been moved to New York to be closer to her parents during her convalescence and Faron hadn't seen her since right after the accident, when they were both in the same hospital on the mainland. They did speak on the phone, but her pain and his wired jaw kept their conversations brief.

Given his injuries, Quinn hadn't expected Faron to go with him when he took the boys to see Alva the first time, but the next time he drove to New York and Faron declined to come along, Quinn was annoyed. Faron brushed him off with the excuse that he didn't feel up to the drive, but Quinn suspected it was more than that.

After the church service, there was potluck in the annex. Red Sedgwick donated cases of beer and soda to wash it all down and raised his own glass in a toast to Faron's and Alva's continuing recovery. "Here's to God—who looks after children and drunks!"

That particular sentiment didn't go over too well with Quinn, though, deep down, he supposed there might be an ounce of truth to it.

Walter was glad to be there with his grandsons. His wife was right when she suggested it would do him good to get away for a while and visit Brant and Karner. He and Alva had been getting on each other's nerves lately, now that she was better enough to complain.

Walter sat in the warmth of a cast iron woodstove in the church annex, shaking everyone's hands when they came over to ask about his daughter. Someone gave him a large plate with a little bit of everything on it. He balanced it on his knees, taking bites between conversations. It took him over an hour to finish the meal and by then he was ready to leave.

He put on his coat and walked gingerly down the salt-melted ice on the church steps. Quinn and Faron stood with him in the brittle sunshine. "You sure you won't change your mind and stay another night?" Quinn asked.

"No, that's all right," Walter replied. "I'll be fine. I'll stay in a motel at the halfway point. I'll call you when I get there." He was worn out from the weeks of worry about his daughter. The visit to the island was refreshing, but he wasn't looking forward to the drive home to New York.

Faron slung an arm around Walter's stooped shoulders. "Glad you came," he said through his wired jaw.

Walter gave him a hug. He had hoped he could persuade his son-in-law to drive back with him, but when he'd asked him earlier, Faron said he didn't feel up to it. He tried one more time. "Sure you won't come along? Alva would love to see you."

Faron shook his head 'no,' avoiding Walter's eyes. "Maybe next time," he said, turning to hurry back inside.

"I'm sorry," Quinn said, sensing Walter's disappointment. "I don't understand what's going on with him. But he'll come soon, I promise."

"Thanks, Quinn. It would mean a lot to Alva."

Quinn watched until Walter's car disappeared around the first curve toward the ferry, and reminded himself to speak with Faron again about going to see Alva, maybe after they removed the wiring from his mouth.

In the church annex Faron paced back and forth with Brant in his arms, trying to calm him. The boy was inconsolable, crying and holding his breath until he turned purple.

"Maybe you should give him one of your bug boxes," Hodie Ebel suggested to Faron, only half joking. "Worked for you."

Brant was developing a tendency for angry outbursts, behavior that worsened in his mother's absence.

Faron bristled at the suggestion. "I never had tantrums."

"Still—might be worth a try."

Across the room Karner drooled and giggled while everyone marveled at his survival.

"It's a miracle he lived," they all agreed.

"Not really," Jarry Gallager said. "The mammalian diving reflex is what saved him." Jarry wasn't a tall man and you could barely see his the top of his head among the rest of the towering crowd, but his voice carried and people were fascinated by what he had to say.

"That's why the kid lived," Jarry explained. "When you're face down in freezing water, nature takes over." He stopped talking and took a fistful of appetizers from a tray that Nanny Doyle was passing around. "As I was saying," he continued, popping a bacon-wrapped midget hotdog into his mouth and spitting crumbs while he ate and talked, "a drowning victim's heart slows down and there's a restriction of blood flow to the extremities."

"How's that?" Minna Beaudry asked, shoving her way into the group.

"The blood flows to the most important parts—the organs. Mainly the heart and brain, so they get more oxygen and the person has a better chance of surviving."

"You don't say?" Minna was genuinely interested.

Emmett stood next to her, holding Karner Blue. "Well, that's good," Minna said, turning to Karner to wipe drool from his chin with a knobby finger, "because the last thing this little fellow needs is a restriction of blood flow to the brain, if you get my drift."

"You can say that again," someone at the edge of the crowd remarked.

Owen Batch stood off to the side, drinking beer from a bottle and listening to the conversation. He'd heard the talk. *That kid's not quite right*, and, *He's so much smaller than the other one*. Frankly, he doubted that Karner's time underwater would make much difference in his development one way or the other. In fact, he was pleased with the way Karner had progressed since his birth. He hadn't caught up to his brother's size, and his motor skills were slightly lagging, but all things considered, Owen thought Karner would be just fine. Hell, after surviving a dip in Puddle Cove in the middle of winter, anything was possible.

CHAPTER 69

BRANT TOOK his first tentative steps on the sun-softened ground the same week that trillium and grape iris pushed their way through the rain-soaked soil. Karner crawled behind him.

"Where's Faron?" Betsy asked when she arrived at his house and saw Quinn in the yard with the boys. She'd been spending a lot of time there, helping with the children and making meals. This morning she was hurried, and just stopping by to deliver some cold chicken and rolls, leftover from last night's supper.

"He's inside." Quinn sounded tired. The stress of caring for the twins had taken a toll, and he was worried about the fact that Faron still hadn't been to see Alva.

The last time he'd broached the subject, Faron mumbled some gibberish about pulling his mother out of Puddle Cove, not Alva, and refused to say any more about it.

Quinn held Brant's tiny fingers as the boy toddled over to Betsy. Karner brought up the rear, knees and hands caked with mud. "Would you take over, Betsy? I need to speak with Faron."

Betsy was already squatting to pull Karner out of the slime. "About what? Him getting Alva confused with Alison?"

"You know about that?"

"No offense, Quinn, but sometimes you've got your nose stuck so far in the Good Book that you can't see what's right in front of your face."

Quinn was dumbfounded. "What's that supposed to mean?" Betsy had been a godsend the last few months, but right now he was not happy with her. He tried counting to ten, reminding himself that it was just Betsy being outspoken and cranky, like always. Nothing personal.

He was on number eight when Betsy said, "Forget it. Hurry up and go have your talk. I'm just not feeling all that accommodating this morning."

Betsy picked up both boys and carried them to a less muddy part of the yard. Weeks ago, Emmett told her that Faron said it was his mother he wanted to rescue the night of the accident, not Alva. "Says he saw her plain as day," Emmett had said. "Looking just like when he was a kid, he says. Now he's all mixed up."

In her opinion, Quinn should've insisted Faron visit Alva long before now. But, as Emmett reminded her, it was none of her business. Now she just hoped Quinn would do more than throw Bible verses around, and set Faron straight.

Quinn sat next to Faron. It was eleven in the morning and the disheveled young father was quilt-bound on the sofa, holding the hummingbird frame Alva made for him. Since she was unable to give it to him herself, she asked Quinn to. She couldn't remember where she put it and Quinn had searched all over the house until he found it in a closet, gaily wrapped in birthday paper, hidden under some towels. He'd hoped it would lift Faron's spirits, but it seemed to do the opposite.

"You know," Quinn said, struggling for patience, "whatever's wrong, you can tell me."

"I told you. I saw her underwater."

"Who?"

"My mother." The wire had been removed from Faron's jaw but he still couldn't move his mouth very well and his words were garbled.

"You mean Alva?" Quinn asked.

"No. My mother. She was wearing a flowered dress."

"Alva was wearing a dress. Maybe, you . . ."

"You don't get it," Faron interrupted angrily. "*That night* I thought it was my mother, and I felt relieved."

"Why?"

"Because it wasn't the way I imagined. She looked beautiful. Peaceful." Faron stood up and shook off the quilt, peeking out the window at his children.

"So, what's wrong with that?'

"Nothing. It's just that . . . it felt like I was rescuing my mother."

Quinn got it then. "And not Alva?"

Faron nodded. "That's right."

Quinn knew as well as anyone that guilt is a powerful emotion. He also knew how disorienting it was in the water that night, not to mention that Alison Goss had drowned in the same cove. He could only imagine what went through Faron's mind. "I believe you did see your mother, but that doesn't diminish your relationship with Alva. It's okay to love them both. There's no reason to feel guilty.

"One of your greatest qualities is your capacity to forgive. I've seen the way you let people into your life, in spite of having been hurt. Sooner or later you'll have to forgive yourself."

Quinn got up from the couch to go back outside. "One more thing—take a closer look at your children—you'll see your wife *and* your mother in them."

"What's that supposed to mean?"

"It means they're both a part of you and always will be. And I know if you'd just go see Alva and explain, you'd feel better. She'll understand. No matter who you thought you were pulling from the water that night, Alva—and everyone else—knows you saved her life.

"If you'd just talk about it instead of sulking around here . . . who knows . . . you might put a lot of old feelings to rest."

CHAPTER 70

THEY LAUNCHED the *B. Paisley* even later than usual, and in spite of the customary ribbing from the gang, Emmett didn't seem to mind.

It was a magnificent day, one of those first deep-felt warm ones of the year, the kind that nudges even the grumpiest old salts into good moods. When Emmett and Faron motored into the harbor at the end of a long day setting traps, Betsy was standing on the dock waiting for them with Brant and Karner.

Faron hadn't given much thought to who'd take care of the children when he went back to work, until Betsy offered.

"Ayuh. It's a good arrangement," Emmett said to Faron when they saw Betsy and the boys waving at them from a chunk of sunshine. "She loves them like her own."

Emmett dropped Faron at the dock. "Go on. Get the kids home. Butsy'll help me snag the mooring."

Betsy swore to Emmett she'd keep her nose out of things and not say anything to Faron about the vision of his mother on the night of the accident, but that was a promise she couldn't keep. Faron was finally going to visit Alva and the last thing she needed was hearing some nonsense about Alison Goss.

So when Faron asked her to join him on a count for the Maine Butterfly Survey, Betsy jumped at the chance. She didn't much care for traipsing around outdoors at the height of black fly season, but it was the perfect opportunity to tell him what she thought.

As they wandered amongst leatherleaf and laurel, sidestepping deer-haired sedge, Betsy mulled the best way to say what was on her mind. She was about to speak when Faron spotted a dreamy duskywing resting on a sprig.

"Shhh," he said. "Look at that."

And then he told her about seeing his mother in Puddle Cove.

Betsy held her tongue and focused on the butterfly while he spoke, pretending it was the first time she heard the story. At the end of his halting confession, the duskywing gave a start and flew.

Betsy pursed her lips, then said, "Know what your problem is?"

"What?"

"You think too much, and a lot of that thinking is barse-ackwards." She sat down on a log and took a crumpled pack of cigarettes out her pocket and fired one up, preparing to tell Faron what a dunderhead he was, but as it turned out, she didn't have to.

Faron watched her blow out the match and realized that, for the first time, the smell of cigarettes didn't remind him of his mother. "Maybe Quinn was right," he sniveled.

"How's that?"

Faron wiped his eyes. "Never mind."

Betsy took in a lungful of smoke, not quite sure what to make of Faron's sudden enlightenment, but happy to take credit for it. "Well," she said, exhaling loudly, "I'm glad we got that sorted out."

The rural town of Millbrook was charming. The Dodge's house had a distant view of the Catskill Mountains and was surrounded by woodlands and fields that were populated by foxes, rabbits, wild turkey, and deer. And birds.

The moment Faron walked into the sunroom and saw Alva stretched out on the couch, looking at robins through a pair of binoculars, his worries disappeared. He grinned, then chuckled aloud, reminded of the time he saw her in Mr. Brady's store, flat on her back in a cascade of buckets.

Alva didn't mind Faron's amusement. She guessed she was quite a sight, with both her legs in casts from the ankles to the knees. When she saw Faron's reaction, she put down the binoculars and laughed her wonderful laugh, which caused Karner and Brant to break out in a squealing clamor. Lydia, usually more reserved, joined in, wiping tears from her eyes, complaining that her belly hurt from laughing so hard.

"What the hell is so funny?" Walter asked when he came home with the daily newspapers and found his entire family in a gleeful uproar.

"Everything!" Alva said, raising her voice to be heard over the joyful din. She knew about Faron's reluctance to visit and she had her own misgivings about not being able to forgive him for staying away, but right now none of that mattered. "It's good to see you," she said to him when he leaned in for a kiss.

"You too." Faron sat on the edge of the couch trying to keep the boys from pouncing on Alva. He couldn't remember when he'd seen them this excited. "I'm sorry it took me this long to get here."

"That's all right, you haven't missed much. I haven't been very good company. Just ask my father."

Walter agreed. "You can say that again. As soon as she started feeling better she got grumpy."

"Don't worry, Dad, you'll be rid of me soon . . . when these come off." Alva raised her plaster-encased legs and wiggled her toes.

Faron watched the boys settle down and cuddle with their mother. He felt good ever since leaving the island, and even better now. He turned down Quinn's offer to ride along, looking forward to making the drive alone with his sons. It was the first time he'd traveled any distance on his own, and it was exhilarating.

All during the trip from Menhaden he wondered what he would say to Alva, but it turned out to be needless worry. Their conversation came easily and the three days he was in Millbrook passed quickly. When he and the boys pulled out of the Dodge's driveway to head back home, Faron was already looking forward to his next visit.

After supper the day they returned to the island, the boys followed Faron into his studio. He hadn't done any painting since the accident, but he felt tethered by the familiar routine of building stretchers and preparing canvas, which he'd been able to do since the cast was removed from his wrist.

He turned on the fan and relaxed to its low, soothing rumble while he primed a canvas with thick white gesso. Brant and Karner amused themselves on the floor, playing with sable hair brushes and puckered tubes of oil paint.

There was a dry canvas on the easel. Faron stopped what he was doing and stared at the stark white surface. He flexed the fingers of his left hand. They were stiff. He bent down and reached between Brant and Karner for a tube of paynes gray. He poked through a jar of brushes and chose a double-thick filbert. If he was ready to work the *B. Paisley's* stern, he was ready to paint. And he did.

CHAPTER 71

ON THE BACK PORCH, where there was better light, Quinn admired the finished painting of Alva.

"It's amazing. Your best, I think." He wondered if Faron had been inspired by his recent visits to Alva, which, much to his relief, seemed to go very well.

Faron agreed it was a good painting. Technically, it surpassed any of his previous work.

"It's more than that," Quinn said at the mention of technique. "There's tremendous emotion." He stepped off to the side for a different view. "And I like the birds in the background."

They talked in hushed voices, pausing their conversation periodically to listen for any sounds from the bedroom, where Karner and Brant were napping.

Quinn sat on the porch railing. "What'll you do with it?"

"I'm sending it to the Dodges."

Quinn approved with a slow bob of his head. "That will mean a lot to them."

When the cumbersome package arrived in upstate New York and the Dodges saw Faron's return address, they guessed correctly that it was a painting, and perhaps some recent photographs of the children, which he'd been so good about sending them—but they were surprised to tears when they saw the heartfelt likeness of their daughter.

The letter Lydia wrote that very same day, and which Faron opened not long after—sitting in the glow of a luminous sunset at Keeps Pond with Brant and Karner—made all the difference to him.

Dearest Faron,

We've received the painting you sent and are overwhelmed by its beauty. You have portrayed Alva as she truly is, and in doing so you have honored her.

We are aware, from our conversations with Quinn, that through these difficult months you have questioned your commitment to our daughter. We want you to know that we have never doubted your devotion to her, and when we look at the portrait we are reminded of it.

Faron, if you cannot bring yourself to believe the reassurances of others, then trust in your art. A good painting can never hide the truth.

We thank you for the cherished gift,
Lydia and Walter

Faron folded the letter and tucked it into his pocket. Alva would be home soon, and he was glad. The sky's rosy brilliance shone on his sons' faces, and a feeling of pure contentment swept over him. He delighted in the evening air and the pungent smell of pine boughs and wondered if the scent would be one of his children's earliest memories when they were old enough to mine their lives for nuggets of meaning.

CHAPTER 72

When Alva came home, she had a shorter haircut and was ten pounds lighter than her wedding day. Although her broken ankles were mending well, she still used a cane to steady herself on uneven ground. But Faron thought she never looked more beautiful, and he told her so.

Her parents rented a cottage on Preble Point so Lydia could help Alva reacclimate to her household routines. Walter, relieved that everything was almost back to normal, spent the better part of most mornings sitting at a sunny table in Scuppers, downing cups of black coffee with fellow members of Veterans of Foreign Wars.

When their rental agreement was up, the Dodges decided to buy a small summer house of their own on the island. Walter put up a stink when Lydia first suggested it, but it was he who called Evie Belden and said, "Find us something—not too expensive."

Karner Blue surprised everyone when he started talking at the age of fifteen months, although his words were as choppy as a sea in a gale and no one could understand him except Alva. Her small, quiet boy was thriving. He squealed with delight bouncing from knee to knee at church suppers, and his smile was as bright as the glare twinkling off Menhaden Harbor.

He was easy to please. Content to sit sifting flour through his pudgy fingers in the doughy warmth of his grandparents' kitchen, or turning pages of picture books in the flickering light of a log fire, where it was plain to see how his eyes resembled Alva's.

His brother was very different. Brant preferred waddling along the tidal flats, preferably with Walter. He loved scouring the beach at low tide, no matter the weather, picking baby crabs from the seaweed along the wrack line, and digging for clams, or looking for periwinkle snails on barnacle-covered rocks in tepid tide pools. He was as happy in the saltwater environment as the goose he was named after—although not always as sociable as the Atlantic brant, who preens in gaggles at sea.

The only photograph of Faron's great-grandfather was a faded, grainy class picture in a high school yearbook, but the old-timers on the island vouched for the fact that Brant was a dead ringer for Zed Goss.

As different as they were, both boys took comfort in the gentle motion of a lobster boat motoring through a becalmed sea, which pleased Emmett and Faron.

One lazy morning, after the fog lifted, the entire family hitched a ride on the *B. Paisley* to look for surf scoters on an outlying island.

Brant insisted on coming aboard with an armful of his father's tattered cigar boxes. He and Karner sat quietly in the stern, on the cockpit sole with Alva and Faron, stacking and restacking the boxes as if they were miniature lobster pots.

Quinn leaned on the gunwale, taking in the familiar scene.

Betsy stood forward of the livewell with the Dodges, where she could smoke a cigarette out of the wind.

Lydia nudged Walter and eyed their grandsons, wringing worry out of her hands. "Those are Faron's bug boxes."

"I know," Walter answered.

Emmett let out a loud laugh and, with his knack for paring things down, shouted over the engine noise, "Ayuh! Life's a loop . . . like Sheepscot Road!"

Acknowledgments

Thank you to the early readers of the manuscript—Susan Powers, Diane Uhle, Christine Zikas, and Cathy Grossi—for their time, suggestions, and encouragement; to my aunt, Linda Cauley, for reading several drafts, cheering me on, and always being there to listen; to CWO Chuck Chavtur, USCG, for graciously answering my questions about all things nautical when I showed up unannounced at his office in Boothbay Harbor, Maine; and Capt. Ethan Maass for his advice; and to Pat Hammond, friend and poet, who read the first draft and urged me not to change too much. My thanks go also to publisher Dede Cummings at Green Writers Press, and editor Sarah Ellis, for their fine work and for loving the book as much as they do, and to my supportive agent, Meredith Bernstein, who didn't give up on me.

Most of all my love and gratitude go to my husband, Douglas Maass, for making it possible for me to stay home and write, for sharing his vast knowledge of sailing, for reading and proofreading many revisions of *Faron Goss*, and for his enduring belief that it would be published.

And I am forever grateful for the love and support of my late parents, George and Dolores Lechleitner. How I wish they could hold my book in their hands.

About the Author

Diane Lechleitner's poems and short stories have appeared in numerous literary magazines. *Faron Goss* is her first novel. In addition to writing fiction, Diane has exhibited her visual art, received an Exxon Award for Printmaking, was a recipient of several artist residencies, and worked in ateliers printing etchings for artists, including Peter Max and Salvador Dali. She now writes full-time and lives along the Hudson River in Sleepy Hollow, New York, with her husband Douglas Maass, their beloved dog, Bracken, and Flynnbean the cat.